Brenda's
MOTEL

Barbara Trombley

Brenda's Motel

Copyright © 2019 Barbara Trombley

Some Scripture quotations are taken from The Message.
Copyright © 1993, 1994, 1995, 1996, 2000, 2001, 2002.
Used by permission of NavPress Publishing Group.

Some Scripture quotations are taken from The Holy Bible,
English Standard Version® (ESV®)
Copyright © 2001 by Crossway,
a publishing ministry of Good News Publishers.

Author photo by Missy Talmadge

Book layout and design by
Cathy Wimmer
COPYpro
Chisago City, MN 55013

The Spirit of the Lord God is upon me,
    because the Lord has anointed me
to bring good news to the poor;
    he has sent me to bind up the brokenhearted,
to proclaim liberty to the captives,
    and the opening of the prison to those who are bound;
 to proclaim the year of the Lord's favor,
    and the day of vengeance of our God;
    to comfort all who mourn;
 to grant to those who mourn in Zion—
    to give them a beautiful headdress instead of ashes,
the oil of gladness instead of mourning,
    the garment of praise instead of a faint spirit;
that they may be called oaks of righteousness,
    the planting of the Lord, that he may be glorified.
They shall build up the ancient ruins;
    they shall raise up the former devastations;
they shall repair the ruined cities,
    the devastations of many generations.

                         –Isaiah 61:1-4

CHAPTER ONE

The official-looking envelope postmarked Miskomin, Wisconsin, caused Brenda Miller to imagine all manner of the worst things. Who had died? Was someone suing her? Did she owe money for some long ago bill?

Brenda was sandwiching a stop at the post office between working a shift at the nursing home and picking up her granddaughter, Ellie, at school. Because she was running late, she needed to make it a quick stop, but this curious letter had her confused and afraid.

She held it, studied the authoritative "Schneider Law Firm" embossed in the left-hand corner, stuck a fingernail under the flap, stopped. "Deal with it at home," she told herself, and threw the mail–circulars, bills, and unexpected letter–into the back seat of her elderly Ford sedan before driving as quickly as she dared to Ellie's school.

Flustered and apologetic, Brenda bustled into the building, her soiled yellow pea coat unbuttoned, gray-blonde hair wind-blown. Ten-year-old Ellie, waiting in the lobby, came toward her at once, a smile on her thin freckled face.

"I couldn't clock out until my relief came," Brenda told the school aide who was waiting with Ellie. "She was late. I am so sorry, Carla."

"There's an overtime charge," Carla said, annoyance tightening her tone. Her back was ramrod straight, her odor sour.

"I'm so sorry." Brenda fumbled for her purse. Payment dealt with, she focused her attention on Ellie and smiled. "What do you say we head on home, Ellie? I have something special in the crockpot for supper."

"What is it, Granda?" Ellie grabbed a strap of her faded pink backpack. As a baby, Ellie had tried to say "Grandma Brenda" but could only manage a "Granda." The name endured.

"Chicken spaghetti. You can make a salad, and I'll toast some bread. We can put garlic butter on it. Sound good?"

"Sounds perfect." They went out together into the gloom of a blustery early April evening. Spring came late to the prairies of central Illinois, and the wind was especially harsh as it whipped across the school parking lot. Brenda shivered and put an arm around Ellie, sheltering her.

A savory aroma greeted them even before Brenda unlocked the scarred door of their second-story apartment. Brenda hung her key on the nail she had pounded into the paneling eight years ago for that very purpose but did not remove her coat before ripping open the mysterious envelope. She took out a single sheet of heavy, cream-colored paper, started to read, sat down abruptly. The worn wooden chair creaked under her weight.

"Oh my," she said, spaghetti forgotten. She read the letter carefully, once, twice. "I can't believe it."

Ellie, standing in front of the Formica countertop tearing dark green lettuce leaves into bite-size pieces, dipped her chin toward the toaster. "Believe what? I thought you were going to make us

2

garlic toast."

"I was," Brenda said. "I will. It's just, we..." She paused, trying to absorb the truth of what she had just read. "Do you remember that motel I told you about? The one my aunt and uncle owned?"

Ellie looked blank.

Brenda tried again. "The one up in Wisconsin I got to help out at?"

"Back when you were a kid?" Ellie left her salad-making to peer at the letter. "Yeah, I remember. Do we get to go see it?"

"Child." Brenda dropped the letter and it fluttered to the floor. Reality was sinking in. She grabbed her granddaughter's hands and squeezed, too excited to continue. Taking a deep breath, she started afresh. "It's ours!"

"Huh?" Ellie wrinkled her nose.

"We inherited us that motel, child."

Working together, they finished meal preparations and sat down at their tiny table. Surrounded by the pungent smell of garlic, Brenda stemmed the flow of Ellie's questions. "We'll talk after we eat, sweet thing."

Ellie nodded and scooped up a generous portion of chicken spaghetti. Delicious as it was, Brenda only managed a couple of bites, chewing instead on the surprise inheritance. Instead of containing bad news, the envelope held an opportunity that could mean a whole new life for her and Ellie.

In her mind's eye she could visualize the pristine white motel with its row of doors, each with an individual stoop. She particularly remembered sitting on the step in front of her unit, gazing into the oak tree across the street, thinking about what it would be like to have a motel of her own.

"When I grow up," she had vowed, "this is what I will do. Run a motel."

She confided her wish to Uncle Ed, and he let her sit behind his big desk and check in a guest. It had been glorious. And now that motel was hers!

Incredible. Terrifying. Perfect!

Ellie cleared away the supper dishes while Brenda changed out of her work scrubs, opting to spend the evening in gray sweatpants and a Chicago Cubs T-shirt. Then they sat face-to-face at the table, the letter and a yellow legal pad in front of Brenda.

"What does it mean to 'herit?'" Ellie wanted to know. She blinked rapidly.

"IN-herit," Brenda corrected. "It means to get something when someone dies. Uncle Ed and Aunt Ruth put in their will, that after they both passed away, I would be the owner of their motel."

"How are they related to us? And, Granda, what's a will?" Ellie's face was scrunched in bewilderment, and Brenda knew she had a lot of explaining to do.

"Uncle Ed was my mother's brother. He's the one who owned the motel. He died, oh…must be about five years ago now. Yes. When you were in kindergarten."

Brenda picked up the letter and scanned it again. "And Aunt Ruth passed away just a couple weeks ago. I feel so bad I lost touch."

"What's a will?" Ellie impatiently repeated her question.

"It is a paper that explains what should be done with your stuff after you die."

Ellie nodded, blinking. "How far away is that motel? Can we go there?"

"It's a ways away." Brenda pushed aside the unease she felt in having to take such a long drive. "But we certainly will go. And Ellie! There is a house we can live in."

"A house! And will I…" Ellie's eyes were enormous, yet she

4

hesitated. "And will I…"

"Ellie, come out with it," encouraged Brenda.

"At the new place, will I have my own room?"

"Yes. Yes, you will have your own room." Right now, they shared a bedroom, crowded with two single beds, affording very little privacy.

"And I can get a dog." Ellie bounced in her chair, causing it to chitter. "I'll have my very own room, and we can get a dog."

"Yes. We will need a dog." Brenda stroked the letter from the lawyer. She glanced around the shabby apartment with its pressboard laminate paneling, mauve shag carpet, and dim corners. Despite her best efforts, she had not eliminated the bleak air that permeated it. "There's nothing holding us here." Her eyes flickered over the thrift-store items that furnished the place. "We'll only take what we can fit in the car. The rest, well, let's have a yard sale shall we? And start fresh in the new place. We don't want this old stuff there."

"This old stuff," echoed Ellie. She blinked twice, rapidly. "But what about my art supplies? My new sweatshirt? Schmoe?" She cast a glance at the much-loved purple stuffed dog.

"We'll have room in the trunk and in the backseat of the car for your treasures," assured Brenda. "We won't leave behind anything you love." She rose and hunted through a stack of magazines until she unearthed an atlas. "See? This is where we live." She flipped from the Illinois page to the Wisconsin page. "And this is Miskomin." Using a torn off edge of a page as a guide, she calculated the distance. "It's about four hundred miles away." Again, dread at tackling such a long trip assailed her, but resolutely she pushed it aside. "Let's stay overnight at a motel on the way. We can call it research."

"Really? Stay overnight in a motel?"

"Yes, we'll stay overnight in a small motel. And we can take notes of everything: How they treat us at the front desk, what the rooms are like, if they serve us breakfast, how they do it. Everything. So pay attention, Ellie, won't you?"

"Oh, I will! When are we leaving? Will I finish school?"

Brenda took a deep breath, expelled it with a huff. Hope and anticipation, both long dormant, rose inside of her chest. "I'll see if they'll accept two weeks' notice at the nursing home. Two weeks, and we'll be gone. This is our chance, Ellie, to start a new life. And no, you won't finish out the school year here. I hope you're okay with that."

Ellie's finger traced a looping groove embedded in the tabletop as she rocked back and forth slightly. Brenda could only imagine what was passing through her head. School was difficult for Ellie, and she didn't have many–if any–friends. Still, it was a familiar place, the only school she had ever known. After a long moment Ellie's finger stilled and she raised her chin.

"Let's get packing!" she cried.

They set to at once. While Ellie sorted through her stuffed animal collection, Brenda attacked a box marked "Historical Documents." Many she tossed, but a few she set aside to bring along: her 1984 high school diploma in its faux leather binder, immunization records, a certificate of divorce from 1997. Near the bottom of the box Brenda discovered a yellowed catalog from Stout State University. It fell open to a dog-eared section highlighting a Hotel, Restaurant and Tourism Management program.

That wish she'd expressed while at the motel as a twelve-year-old had stayed with her, and as a high school junior she had checked into career training. But between her father discouraging her from furthering her education and Dale pressing her to marry, the dream had dwindled. Until now. She read through the list of

6

courses associated with the degree and bit her lip. There was a lot to this. Would she be able to run a motel with no training?

Ellie interrupted her musings, squatting down beside her, eyes filled with woe.

"What about Mom? When she comes back, how will she find us?"

Mom. Brenda caught her breath and set the catalog aside. It had been months since Ellie had spoken of her mother, the mother who had abandoned her when she was eighteen months old. She touched the back of the child's hand.

"Have you been thinking about your mom lately, sweet thing?"

"Kind of." After a beat the little girl added, "Some of the girls at school think it's funny I live with you."

Brenda's protective radar rose. "Are they teasing you?"

Ellie pressed her lips together.

"I can give Dottie at work our forwarding address," Brenda said. "If–when–your mom comes back, I'm sure she'd check with them at the nursing home for where to find us."

"Can you leave your cell phone number, too?" Ellie glanced up, her face clearing. At Brenda's decisive nod, she scrambled to her feet. "Let's get back to work."

With renewed determination, Brenda reached for her legal pad. It was bad enough that she herself felt scorned, but if the past was affecting Ellie now, too, the stakes were considerably raised.

"Number One," she wrote. "Give notice at work. Number Two…"

CHAPTER TWO

Brenda lifted a cramped hand from the steering wheel and massaged the side of her neck. It was mid-afternoon of the second day of travel and between concentrating on driving defensively and second-guessing her decision to move, the tension was taking a toll. The long hours on the road were providing too much time for thinking. Was she doing the right thing in taking Ellie, the little grandbaby she cherished, to an uncertain future in an unknown place?

But it's not unknown, she reminded herself, thinking back to that road trip with her parents, and the two nights they had stayed at the motel.

"Perhaps we shall go all the way to the Black Hills of South Dakota," her father had said with an unusual degree of enthusiasm.

But it was not to be. They only made it to their first destination: Miskomin, Wisconsin, and Uncle Ed and Aunt Ruth's Neat as a Pin Motel. There, Father developed a stomach ailment and spent most of the second night in the cramped bathroom. In the morning, without discussion, they headed southeast, toward home.

It had been the first and last road trip of her childhood.

But the time in the motel was wonderful! Brenda roamed about freely, peeking into closets, exploring the shed behind the motel where she discovered cardboard boxes filled with cute little bars of soap, and stacks and stacks of clean white sheets, all smelling mountain fresh.

Brenda's mother and Aunt Ruth had had a great time visiting together. Brenda had even heard her mother laugh.

Yes. Operating a motel was a long-standing dream. She would figure it out. She and Ellie would be happy.

"Are we almost there?" Ellie's voice broke into the pep talk she was giving herself. The little girl, wedged in the back seat between boxes, canvas bags, and oddly shaped bundles, was becoming increasingly fidgety. Brenda's eyes met Ellie's in the rear view mirror. She mustered up an encouraging smile.

"Real soon, honey. We'll be there – Look!" Brenda slowed the car considerably and pointed to a green sign with wide white letters.

MISKOMIN

Population 3,250

"We're here!" Ellie bounced once. They passed a couple of well-kept houses, a gas station, an office building. Just beyond a car dealership, complete with fluttering pennants and shiny cars, Brenda gasped, hit the brakes, and turned wildly into a crumbling parking lot.

She came to a stop next to a signpost with a rusty eight-foot straight pin extending perpendicularly from the top. A wooden sign with "Neat As a Pin Motel" inscribed in faded blue paint dangled from the tip.

Brenda sat, eyes wide, clutching the steering wheel. Try as she might, she was unable to align the desolate, weather-beaten structure before her with the immaculate motel that had floated in her mind's eye.

"This is the motel?" Ellie's voice was incredulous. "Is it, Granda?"

Brenda could not answer. Vaguely, she was aware of Ellie fumbling with her seat belt, the slamming of the car door. As if watching a video, she regarded Ellie, her light brown hair caught in two ponytails bobbing against her shoulders, picking her way across the trash-filled parking lot, heading for the motel.

The motel! Two of the windows in the long, low building were boarded over. The once-white siding was cracked and covered with dark blotches. Mold? Mildew? Tall, brittle weeds left over from last summer filled sidewalk cracks. And all ten of the unit doors were dingy and screaming for fresh paint.

She swallowed her rising panic and continued to watch as Ellie turned the knob on the door marked with a 4. After a bit of tugging, the little girl managed to open the door. She glanced back at her grandmother, her nose wrinkled. She beckoned.

Brenda propelled her unwilling body out of the car and crossed the lot to join her. Together, they stepped into the gloomy room, brushing aside cobwebs that crisscrossed the doorway. Rank, stale air assailed them. The bed was unmade, and a broken chair lay on its side. She flipped the light switch uselessly. A mouse scurried across the floor, and Ellie squeaked. Her hazel eyes, wide and shocked, mirrored Brenda's reaction.

Back outside, Brenda savored the fresh, clean air. A brown two-storied house tucked slightly behind the motel caught her eye. It appeared clean and inviting, a balm to Brenda's horrified soul. She gave Ellie a tiny push.

"Meet me over by that house, sweet thing. I'll bring the car."

Ellie nodded and skipped toward it.

"The house looks pretty much the same as I remember." Brenda rejoined her granddaughter and regarded the welcoming building thoughtfully. "But the motel....after Uncle Ed died, Ruth must have let it go to pot. But we're here; we'll see this through. Right?" Brenda tightened her lips and took Ellie's hand.

"Why does it say 'OFF'?" Ellie pointed to the neon sign beside the front door as they mounted the steps of the porch together.

"It's supposed to say OFFICE. The ICE is burned out."

"Yikes."

The wide porch needed sweeping, and there was a box overflowing with aluminum cans on one end, but the sign on the door said "Enter," so the two went inside. They were blocked from further explorations by a six-foot long reception desk with a dead philodendron and a dusty service call bell on it.

"Do you want me to ring that?" Ellie asked.

"I guess that's the procedure."

Ellie tapped the bell two times.

After a long minute, they heard slow and heavy footsteps on the stairs. A barrel-shaped woman wearing a wrinkled blue and white muumuu came into view. One side of her face had a red mark imprinted, and her gray hair was matted down as if she had been laying on it. She rested her hands on the top of the reception desk and regarded Brenda without expression.

"Yes?" she barked.

"I'm Brenda Miller."

"And?"

"I'm Ed Cornell's niece. I inherited this motel."

The older lady perked up. "Ohhh. Nice to meetchu. I'm Mrs. Canfield." She opened her mouth in a semblance of a smile, revealing a gap between her two front teeth. "Didn't know you'd be coming quite yet, could ya mebbe stay in the motel tonight? I'd like a little time to pack up my things." She sighed heavily before leaning forward to confide, "I'm so glad to be done with this stint. This is not my line of work. At all."

"Are guests really staying here?" Brenda did not think so. "It seems–abandoned."

"Oh, ever so often, someone checks in." Mrs. Canfield scratched her chin. "Say, don'chu wanna go down to the Schneider Law Office? And introduce yourself to Kevin? Schneider. He's the one handlin' Ruth's affairs, may she rest in peace."

"I didn't expect the motel to be so–" Brenda began, but Mrs. Canfield was already turning away, selecting a key and setting it on the desk.

"I'll put you in the top-end unit. Unit One. Has a kitchenette." The gappy smile made a brief reappearance.

Brenda picked up the brass key and put it in the front pocket of her blue jeans, curious to discover how the "top-end" unit compared with Unit Four.

"Let's go to the lawyer's office, Ellie, and make this official." She tucked her hair behind her ears and straightened her shoulders.

Ellie rose on her tiptoes and strained to peer beyond Mrs. Canfield. "I want to see the house," she said. "I want to look around, I–"

"Ellie." Brenda's tone held a warning.

Ellie subsided.

***

Brenda directed Ellie toward a black wooden chair near the edge of the room and gave her a colorful magazine to page through before she settled herself in front of the lawyer's desk.

Kevin Schneider, who was young, restless, and smelled of baby powder and chocolate, produced a thick manila folder. He spread its contents in front of Brenda, who stared, trying to make sense of the legal jargon.

Kevin pushed the papers aside abruptly. "We were sure you would sell. There's even a buyer for the property. He wants to bulldoze that old eyesore…we were sure you would sell." He named a figure, and Brenda's eyes widened.

Brenda's hands had been clasped in her lap. Now one drifted up to her neck. Her gaze shifted away from Kevin. Her heart pounded. "No," she said. "I want to run the motel."

"Do you have any idea what that will take? With all due respect, you seem to be rushing into something you know nothing about. There is only a small, very small, amount of cash included in this inheritance."

Brenda looked squarely at the young lawyer. She had not had anything to dream about in a long time, and she was not going to be denied this chance. "I realize it'll take work, but I want to fix it up and run it. Uncle Ed used to have a nice place there, and I intend to restore it to its…its former glory."

"If you're sure." Kevin Schneider, regarding her with skepticism, tapped the bottom of a document. Brenda nodded firmly, took a deep breath, and signed.

CHAPTER THREE

Brenda sat in Unit One's only chair, listening to Ellie's steady breathing, feeling alone and lonely. She had slipped into her usual nightclothes, a frayed T-shirt which, in its heyday, had belonged to her then-husband Dale and had been bright red. Now it was a brownish maroon, but so soft and worn that it was a comforting garment. And tonight Brenda needed comfort.

What had she gotten them into? She glanced at the double bed, made out the lump that was Ellie. Her heart swelled with love for the child.

Why hadn't she looked before she leaped? This impulsive act of quitting her job and leaving town was so unlike her usual behavior. After the demise of her unfortunate marriage, Brenda had schooled herself to learn from her mistake. And so she trundled safely and steadily through a dull, careful life, providing for first Janna and then Ellie the best she could. Until now.

Brenda closed her eyes, shook her head. Oh why, why hadn't she made a trip up here, scouted out the place, made sure it would be a good move before uprooting Ellie? Her hands were shaking, and she clasped them together tightly. And although she had not attended church in years, prayed in years, she found herself whispering, "God, help us. Help us, please."

If God heard her, He was silent, but Brenda did feel herself grow calmer. What was done, was done. Just do the next thing, she told herself. And that next thing was to get the motel in shape.

Not wishing to risk rousing Ellie, Brenda positioned the chair under the window, so as to take advantage of a streetlight. She opened her legal pad to a fresh page. "To Do," she wrote at the top. "#1. Pest Control."

Brenda scribbled rapidly: fix windows; paint doors; do something (What?) with the siding; replace, or at least clean, the carpets; inspect each room and list individual needs...

She'd start with this room, the one Mrs. Canfield had referred to as the "top-end unit." Brenda surveyed it, taking stock. The "kitchenette" consisted of a filthy mini-frig, a microwave sitting on a chipped counter, and a wooden box fastened on the wall. The box, serving as an open cupboard, held a few pieces of mismatched crockery and a dishpan. Water would have to be fetched from the tiny sink in the bathroom.

As for the furniture, the dresser was a bit scuffed, but adequate. Furniture polish would add a bit of shine. The bed? Would the smell of urine dissipate if she lugged the mattress outside and aired it out for a day? The only other furniture in the room was a wobbly round table and the chair she was sitting on, and they would not be out of place in a landfill. Could she find some nice but reasonably priced things to replace them?

The motel they'd visited on the way to Miskomin had a little coffee pot right in the room, and the television was a flatscreen, not a clunky old-style television like the dusty one perched on the dresser in this room.

Overwhelmed, Brenda abandoned her list and tried to think

of a positive. The roof. Comforted by the fact that as far as she could tell, the roof was in great shape, she went to bed.

The next morning, after Mrs. Canfield wedged herself behind the wheel of her Toyota hatchback and puttered out of the parking lot, Brenda nodded a "Let's go!" to Ellie. Ellie ran ahead across the parking lot, but waited on the porch of the house. Brenda stopped at the car for the box of foodstuff, final remnants from their apartment. They went in together, squeezed past the reception desk in the hallway, and on through to the rest of the house.

The kitchen was bright and sunny. Brenda set the box on the counter and peeked inside the refrigerator. It was empty but would need cleaning. Ellie swung open the dark wood cupboard doors to reveal matching sets of dishes, pots and pans, and small kitchen appliances. The rag rugs on the floor and the green-and-white checked curtains created a general pleasant air about the room.

"I like this kitchen," said Ellie. "It seems like a happy place, don't you think?"

"I do," agreed Brenda. "I really do. Let's go on, sweet thing." She was equally pleased with the dining room, appreciating the solid table and buffet. The living room, while a bit stuffy and in need of a good dusting, was definitely an improvement from their old apartment. In addition to an almost-new flowered couch and matching armchairs, the large picture window framed a secluded back yard.

After a quick inspection of the laundry room, they went upstairs. Brenda noticed that Ellie had crossed the fingers of her left hand, and she joined the little girl in hoping for a bedroom just right for a ten-year-old.

Four doors, all closed, lined the perimeter of a little hallway. Ellie opened the first door, the one at the top of the stairs. This was the room Mrs. Canfield had been using, and was probably the master bedroom. It was large, bright, and airy. Despite the jumble of blankets and sheets the older woman left behind, Brenda smiled with delight. What a haven this room could be!

They went on down the hall, and peeked into the next room, a bathroom. It showed evidences of Mrs. Canfield's recent use, but the tub was large and included a showerhead and the tiled surfaces were unstained.

The third room had been transformed into a sewing room.

"I didn't realize," said Brenda, "that Aunt Ruth was such a seamstress. Look at all of that fabric!" The two of them stood for a moment, impressed by the colorful bolts of material piled haphazardly on built-in wooden shelves. A fancy sewing machine was positioned under a window overlooking the parking lot. As Brenda stared down at the faded "Neat As a Pin" sign, she realized it was Ruth's love of sewing that probably inspired the name of the motel. She squinted her eyes, focusing on the three capitalized letters before resting her hands on Ellie's shoulders, and giving them a slight squeeze.

"What does N-A-P spell, Ellie?"

"Nap." Ellie looked up at her grandmother for approval, then followed her gaze and made the connection with the oversized letters on the sign. "I guess that's a good thing to do at a motel, huh?"

"The best. And now, let's check out the room across the hall."

It was the final door. Ellie held her crossed fingers high.

It was another bedroom, smaller, with a single bed in it. Together, they admired the walls, softly pink, the built-in shelves, the big window that opened right into a budding tree in the back yard. Smile matched smile.

Brenda walked over to the window and after a considerable tussle, managed to open it. She breathed in the fresh air. It smelled of springtime and new beginnings.

Ellie, joining her, pressed her nose against the screen.

"I sure like this house," she bubbled. "I thought it might be disgusting like our motel room, but it's not at all. And this bedroom is perfect."

When was the last time Brenda had seen such a sparkle in those hazel eyes?

"I like it, too. I really like it. It feels like a home, doesn't it?"

"Yes." Ellie nodded. "This is what a home should feel like." Leaving the window to sit on the bed, she gave Brenda a smile of pure contentment.

Brenda smiled back before she closed the window, becoming brisk, business-like. "Now let's give the motel a once-over, shall we? Even though you were able to get into that one room yesterday, I would hope the other units are locked. Didn't Mrs. Canfield say there was a master key behind that desk?"

They clattered down the stairs, studied the board of keys behind the desk. Ellie reached for the one marked "Master." Key in hand, they went through the kitchen and out the back door into the yard.

It was almost May, and the day was warm. The two detoured through the yard on their way to the motel; they'd never had a yard before. In addition to the budding tree and shrubbery, there was a green wooden picnic table with a tumbled-down fire ring beside it. The ground rose and then flattened in front of the dense hedge of cedar bushes that separated the back yard from the alley behind it. Framed by the cedars and the backside of the motel, the yard stretched on in a narrow rectangle until it was closed off at the far end by a couple of side-by-side garden sheds. It was a pleasant, private space.

"I like it out here, too," Ellie said. "Plenty of room for the dog

we're going to get. I thought maybe I could name him Charley."
She snapped her fingers experimentally. "Here, Charley."

"Let's check out the motel." Brenda was abrupt, not following
up on Ellie's comments about the dog. She was beginning to get
a notion, and it was not a particularly appealing one. The walk
through the motel solidified this notion. All ten of the rooms
were in varying states of disrepair, from Unit Three, which was
filled with an assortment of furniture, to Unit Ten, fairly habitable
except for the fact it smelled distinctly of skunk.

"Eww." Ellie backed out, holding her nose. "Ewww."

Brenda checked the time. "Ellie, I hate to break it to you so
abruptly, but I want to take you over to school this morning yet to
register. Find your new sweatshirt and comb your hair, will you?
And we'll go on down to the school."

"Granda, you just want to get away from here for awhile."

"You are a very smart little girl. Now get ready, please."

Ellie skipped away, and Brenda pulled the door to Unit Ten
shut and sat down on its front step. She surveyed the litter and dirt
next to the stoop and tried to imagine flowers instead. But flowers
would not eliminate the smell of skunk. How was she going to
manage that? A cluster of buzzing insects circling her head had
her checking overhead before rapidly moving away from the building. The next order of business would be to deal with that large
paper wasp's nest in the eaves above Unit Nine. How? Spray? A
broom?

"I'm ready." Ellie interrupted Brenda's thoughts. She had her
new pink sweatshirt on and had combed out her ponytails, leaving
her brown hair hanging limply on her shoulders. Her eyes were
wide and anxious.

Brenda smiled at her. "You look ready. Let's go."

***

After Brenda answered questions in the front office, the secretary brought them to the fourth grade hallway to meet the teacher.

"This is Ellie Miller," the secretary said to the thin bird-like woman who came to the door. The classroom was full of students, all staring in their direction.

"A new student? For me?" The teacher clapped her hands. "Hello, I'm Ms. Winthrop."

"Ellie, you're in good hands with Ms. Winthrop," the secretary said before heading back to her office.

"Are you staying?" The teacher sounded eager, like a child. "Can't you stay?"

"We were planning on her starting tomorrow," said Brenda. "I thought we would just be registering today."

The kids in the room starting to chant, "Stay, stay, stay, stay..." Ellie threw a silent appeal to her grandmother.

"Well..." Brenda hesitated. "There's no reason why she can't... but don't you need time to get things prepared for a new student?"

Ms. Winthrop flapped a hand. "We can get organized together. And if she needs anything, we'll help her. Right, class?"

"Right!" they chorused.

Ms. Winthrop smiled at Brenda. "Why don't you come back here after school? The final bell rings at three-fifteen. Then you and I can chat about Ellie's first day. That is, of course, if she decides to hang out with us today."

The students were grinning at Ellie and nodding. A couple of girls were even beckoning extravagantly. Ellie flushed and took a step toward the door. Brenda squeezed her shoulder and whispered, "See you after school."

CHAPTER FOUR

A heavy-set man in a neon green shirt was standing in the parking lot when Brenda got back to the motel. Hands on hips, he was surveying the run-down property with a proprietary air.

Much as she would have preferred ignoring him and ducking into Unit One, Brenda knew she must act like a responsible business owner. She slammed her car door and joined him. "How can I help you?"

The man's smile revealed a mouthful of startlingly white teeth, so square they looked like tiny slices of bread. He stuck out a beefy hand.

"You must be Brenda. I'm Carl Levy. I own the car dealership next door. Nice weather we're having, isn't it? Good to meet you."

Brenda touched her fingertips to his. "Hello," she said, wondering how he knew who she was.

"Kevin Schneider, he called," Carl informed her. "He told me you were not interested in selling. Big disappointment. We were looking forward to getting rid of this eyesore. It's no sight for sore eyes, you must admit!" His laugh invited her to join in the joke. But she did not. He quieted, made direct eye contact, then continued in a sincere tone, "I'm looking to extend my used car lot, and this space would be just the ticket. Sooo if you change your mind, decide this is just too much for a pretty young lady like yourself, give me a call, won't you?"

Carl Levy thrust his hand partway into his pants pocket, tussling against his ample girth, eventually retrieving a neon green business card. He handed it to Brenda, adding, "I'd be more than happy to help you out and take this property off your hands."

"I'll let you know." Holding the card between her thumb and first finger, Brenda returned to Unit One where she tossed it on the table and sat down. She scrunched up her face and released it, running her hands through her hair before she dug her checkbook out of her purse and stared at the balance. She tried to marshal her thoughts into columns as clear as the diminishing ones in front of her. Even with the addition of the funds from the inheritance, her finances would be extremely tight.

"So," she said out loud; then stopped and with a glimmer of a smile, mimicked Carl Levy. "Soooo," she tried again, "I am going to have to a.) sell this 'eyesore' to Mr. Levy and get me a job, or, b.) start renting out the units as they are or, c.) rent out the house and live in the motel while I'm fixing it up to be real nice."

What would be her best recourse? Absently, she fanned herself with the checkbook. She had worked as a certified nursing assistant for two decades, but was more than ready for a change. Anyway, she would have to be re-certified to work in Wisconsin, and that would most certainly involve jumping through more than one hoop.

And having a motel of her very own, despite the setbacks, continued to resonate. But if she was going to run a motel, she wanted it to be a nice motel, the way she remembered it. Better. If she could rent out the house, that money could be earmarked for living expenses for her and Ellie. Then she could use the inheritance funds towards renovating the motel.

Brenda snapped her checkbook shut, her mind made up. She would find someone to rent the house, and she and Ellie would live in one of the units of the motel while fixing up the others. Once the motel was paying its own way, then they could move into the house. Carl Levy would just have to find himself some other property. She was not selling.

Decision made, Brenda was eager to get moving on her plan. While the house was rented out she'd use Unit One, the so-called top-end unit, as her home base since it had a kitchenette. She found an elderly vacuum cleaner in the hallway closet of the house and lugged it over to the motel. After she pushed it back and forth, removing a layer of dust and insects from the threadbare beige carpet, she finished unloading the car, lining their possessions against the wall in useful groups. Kitchen tools, crockpot, coffeepot. Books. A pink toolbox. Clothes. Toiletries. Ellie's toys. A couple of photograph albums. CDs. Her round green-and-silver tin.

As she worked, Brenda separated out items that she wanted to keep but were not necessary for daily living. Those items she would store elsewhere.

Brenda came to a good stopping place and took measure of the room that would be their home, sweet temporary home. It was crowded, but it would do. She'd finish cleaning and organizing later. Right now, she had other business to attend to.

After detouring into the house to snag an apple from the bag on the counter, Brenda drove to the public library. Soon she was sitting at a computer, navigating on Craigslist. Eventually she figured out how to post an ad: *FOR RENT. Two bedroom house. Furnished. Large yard. Utilities not included.*

She also did a search on the best way to remove a wasp nest. Spraying the nest and swatting it down with a broom once the wasps had died seemed to be her best option.

Brenda stopped for a few groceries and wasp spray before she went on to Ellie's school. She so hoped the child had a good day. That would make it a bit easier to break the news that the house that Ellie had taken such a shine to—that they both had fallen in love with—would not be their home right away.

When Brenda arrived at the school, the neat and colorful classroom was empty except for a smiling Ellie who was stacking books in a box. "Ms. Winthrop took the class down to the buses," she told Brenda. "She said I should wait here. She'll be right back, she said to tell you."

"How'd it go?" Brenda handed Ellie a book.

"Granda, this is the best school. And I'm in the best class. Everyone was so so nice. And the work wasn't too hard for me." Wordless acknowledgement of how hard the work had been for Ellie at her old school passed between the two of them before Ellie said, "I better get busy. Ms. Winthrop asked me to get all these books packed up." Her tone was laced with self-importance.

Ms. Winthrop tripped into the room. "Hello, Brenda," she said. "Sorry to keep you waiting. I'm sure you're anxious to hear how Ellie's first day with us went."

"Yes, I am." Brenda stepped forward. "She's never switched schools before this."

Ms. Winthrop watched the little girl intent on arranging the books just so, and smiled. "You are such a blessed woman. Ellie is a wonderful child. But I expect you already know that." She lowered her voice. "I already realize she'll need a bit of extra help to get her reading up to grade level. Perhaps the new setting will be the best thing for her. We'll keep in touch."

"Good," said Brenda. "I've been concerned about her reading. Let me know what we can do at home. Ellie is very pleased with how her first day here went. Thank you."

"Thank you for sharing her with me," Ms. Winthrop replied, her brown eyes warm and direct.

***

Ellie and Brenda stood side by side in the kitchen of the house preparing chef salads for dinner. Ellie peeled a carrot and handed it to Brenda who chopped it up and tossed the pieces into bowls filled with lettuce, tomatoes, and ribbons of ham. After Ellie's exposition of the wonders of her new class had wound down, Brenda took a deep breath. Oh, but she hated to tell Ellie that she'd have to wait for a dog and a bedroom of her own.

"Honey," she said in as cheerful a tone as she could muster. "We will be staying in the motel for a while and renting out this house. Just until we get on our feet," she added hastily as Ellie's mouth formed an "O" of dismay. "I am not renting out the units of the motel the way they are, and we'll need money coming in." Her voice trailed off as she realized Ellie had put the peeler down and was studying her feet.

"Does that mean we can't get a dog, either?" Ellie's tone was so resigned and sad, it twisted Brenda's heart.

"Not right now, sweet thing."

"And you said I would have my own room," Ellie reminded Brenda. She paused to glare at her grandmother. "So do I get my own motel room?"

Brenda hesitated. "I won't say no," she said cautiously. "All I will say for now is, let's wait and see. We'll walk on over to the motel after we finish our supper and you can see if you really want to be in a room all by your lonesome. I got ranch dressing for you."

They ate their chef salads in silence, and then went out into the back yard. The spring evening was pleasant, and by common consent the two of them moved over to sit down at the picnic table.

"Hello, neighbors!" A small brown-haired lady dressed in hot-pink scrubs stood at the edge of the yard next to an opening in the cedar hedge. "Welcome to the neighborhood. Mind if I join you?"

"Please do," Brenda answered. "Come sit."

"I'm Teak Anderson." The woman walked down the knoll and settled herself at the picnic table. She smiled, exposing a single dimple.

"Teak?" Brenda repeated dumbly.

"My name is Tammy Kathleen but Teak is my nickname. Crazy, I know. My sister Julie coined it years ago, and it stuck." She shook her head, grimacing, and Brenda found herself smiling back.

"I'm Brenda Miller and this is my granddaughter, Ellie."

"It's just me and Granda," piped up Ellie. "Mom's been gone since I was a baby."

"Yes, my Janna," Brenda confirmed. "But Ellie's been a great comfort." Ellie leaned her head against her grandmother's side.

Teak's smile was sympathetic. "It's hard to lose loved ones. I don't know what I'd do if anything happened to my Hailey. It's just the two of us, too."

Brenda realized her vagueness was leading Teak to draw the wrong conclusion, but did nothing to correct it. She did not want to talk about Janna.

"Is Hailey your kid? How old is she?" asked Ellie, her head popping up at the prospect of a playmate nearby.

"Hailey is my daughter," Teak confirmed. "She's twelve. We live in that duplex across the alley." Teak waved a hand in the general direction of the red brick building partially visible above the cedar hedge.

"It's nice to meet you," Brenda said. She fumbled to make conversation. "Have you lived here long?"

"About ten years. I'm a nurse at the clinic here in town." Teak pinched and released the top of her bright scrubs. "And just home from work. What are your plans for the motel?"

"We were planning on running it." Brenda's voice rose. "But we were not expecting it to be in such terrible shape!"

A door slammed and they looked toward the cedars. Teak stood up and waved a hand, and a younger version of Teak slipped through the cedar bushes and joined them at the picnic table. After introductions were made, Hailey directed her smile at Ellie.

"I have a cat," she said. "Smokey. Do you want to meet her?"

Ellie raised her eyebrows at Brenda, who nodded her consent to the visit. The two girls set off toward the duplex while Brenda and Teak resumed chatting.

"Ed was my uncle," Brenda explained. "I visited this motel when I was a kid. But I remember it as being neat and clean."

"When we first moved here it was neat and clean," Teak confirmed. "And very busy. Filled up almost every night. But then Ed got cancer and couldn't keep up with the work. And Ruth, well. Sweet lady, but it was too much for her." Teak smiled reassuringly. "There's a lot of potential here. It's the only motel in town, after all. I'm sure you two have what it takes to get it back to what it once was."

Brenda hoped she was right. Encouraged by Teak's friendliness, she shared her plan for renting out the house, finishing with, "But Ellie is not at all happy about having to live in the motel."

"She'll adjust," said Teak. "She has you, and having someone you love is more important than where you rest your head."

CHAPTER FIVE

Brenda removed the OFFice and Enter signs from the porch of the house and propped them on the side of the building next to the door of Unit One. Even though the evening was growing chilly, she pried open the window. The unit was screaming for a good airing out. She was sweeping the patch of worn linoleum in front of the "kitchen" area when Ellie came in.

"Hailey's cat is cute. Her name is Smokey. She's gray, with white paws. And fat!" She paused to glance about the room. "It is so... plain in here," Ellie complained, waving her arm to encompass the beige walls, beige carpet, beige curtains. "It would be better if it were colorful. Hailey has a very colorful bedroom." She went on to describe Hailey's quilt and curtains, her bright blue walls.

"You and color." Brenda shook her head. She swept her little pile of dirt onto a piece of cardboard and threw it into the trash. "Did you want to check out Unit Two, next door?" she asked, gesturing in its general direction. "See if you really want to stay there alone?"

"Sure." Ellie lifted her chin. "I'd love to."

Unit Two was dim. A couple of essential light bulbs had

burned out. It was dirty and did not meet Ellie's color require-
ments. But the bathroom was functional, and the old-fashioned
rotary dial telephone on the bedside table worked.

"I could call you if I needed you," said Ellie.

"You really want to stay here by yourself?"

"You're right on the other side of that wall. You did say I
could have my own room."

"I guess it's no different than having your own bedroom in
a house. Except you'll have to step outside to get to me." Brenda
thought about how Unit One would also serve as kitchen, living
room and temporary office as well as her sleeping quarters. "If
you're willing to try it, having you next door would expand our
living space a bit. And remember, this is just for a few months
while we get the other units spruced up."

"And you're sure we can't live in the house right now?"

"Honey, we need a few dimes to rub together, and renting the
house seems to be the easiest way to get them." Brenda stifled a
few pangs of her own regret. "I'll work on cleaning in here while
you're at school tomorrow. Sound like a plan?"

Ellie heaved a sigh. "Okay, Granda. It's a plan."

"I'm going to spray the wasp nest now," Brenda said. "You
might want to stay in here while I do. In case I rile up the wasps."

Ellie evidently did not want to get stung, and kept her distance
while Brenda retrieved the can of wasp spray from the car. She
shook the can well before she, with cautious generosity, coated the
nest and the surrounding doorframe. Then she wandered on, past
Unit Ten, to the sheds behind the far end of the motel. Deterred
by rusty padlocks, Brenda spoke aloud to the empty air.

"I'll have to figure out how to saw a padlock off, I guess."

A plastic bag bobbling across the parking lot caught her eye.
Since she couldn't explore the contents of the sheds, she decided

to rope Ellie into helping her pick up trash.

Ellie wrinkled her nose. "That's disgusting."

"I'll find you some gloves," Brenda promised. "It will be nice to be doing something outside anyway. Look on the sunny side." She found a couple of cast-off plastic bags and handed one to Ellie. "If we each get busy, we can make a real difference."

They were only five minutes into their trash-picking up task when Hailey came across the alley with a couple of black trash bags and another pair of gloves. Without a word, she joined them.

"Hailey, this is real nice of you," said Brenda.

"Oh, I didn't have any homework tonight." Hailey brushed off the thanks.

Ellie looked up, stricken. "I forgot! I have math to do. And I am supposed to read for twenty minutes. Mrs. Winthrop said to."

"And I forgot to ask you if you had any homework," Brenda berated herself aloud. "Do you have something to read, sweet thing?"

"I can read anything, she said, just so I'm READING. Maybe I could read the trash labels." Ellie picked up a potato chip bag. "Crunchy, with just the right amount of salt." She crumpled the bag and shoved it into the trash before reaching for a deserted soda can. "Mountain Dew. Do the Dew. Prod-product Questions? 1-800-blah, blah, blah."

Hailey asked, "What are you doing in math?"

"Multiplying fractions. I don't get it."

"Do you want help?"

"Sure!" Ellie abandoned the trash with alacrity.

Brenda worked alone for almost a half hour, finding pleasure in the cool spring air and undemanding task. She had one bag full and a second bag nearly so before Ellie and Hailey returned from the brown house and the homework. The girls stuffed their hands back into their cotton gloves and helped Brenda get the second bag filled and firmly tied. They lugged the bags over to the sheds and shoved them into the narrow space between the buildings.

"I'll figure out where this garbage belongs tomorrow." Brenda's fingers itched for her legal pad and its ever-growing list. "Hailey, you were a lifesaver. Can I give you something for helping?"

Hailey grinned and shook her head. "Glad to help. See you guys." She waved and headed homeward.

The parking lot, while still pock-marked with potholes, was trash-free. Ellie and Brenda stood for a moment longer, admiring the results of their labors.

It was growing dark. Brenda figured all the wasps would be dead by now. She sent Ellie back to their motel unit for a broom. She'd swat the nest down and add it to the trash.

Gingerly, Brenda poked at the nest with the broom, but it remained fastened. Feeling as if she was batting a piñata, Brenda took a genuine whack. The nest broke away from the doorframe and fell with a soft thump onto the top step of Unit Nine. Three or four wasps circled about in a dazed fashion. Brenda took pains to avoid them while she swept away the remnant still clinging to the doorframe. Mission accomplished.

"Ouch!"

Ellie, who had lingered after delivering the broom, had her hand clamped over her mouth and tears in her eyes.

"You got stung, didn't you? Let me see." Brenda pried the hand away and immediately saw the telltale welt with a tiny red center right above Ellie's upper lip. "Oh, sweet thing, I am so sorry." She took the girl by the shoulder and ushered her toward their unit. "Let's see if we can round up some ice, take that pain away."

Ellie was wailing now, tears flowing, but her feet moved

toward their room, and soon she was sitting on the bed, holding a washcloth containing an ice cube against her lip.

Brenda, ever mindful of the possibility of a serious reaction, watched the little girl steadily for the next hour. Ellie eventually fell asleep, still in her clothes, and Brenda let her be, even though her lip was swelling grotesquely as she slumbered. Should she go buy some antihistamine or something? She agonized, but did not want to either wake or leave the child, so in the end, continued to hold ice against her granddaughter's little mouth until she herself fell asleep.

The next morning Brenda was brushing her teeth in the bathroom when Ellie screamed a garbled "come quick." Brenda spat in the general direction of the sink and rushed to join Ellie at the window. She was horrified to see garbage strewn all over the parking lot. The bags, ripped and empty, were tumbling amid the trash. Brenda grabbed a pair of sweatpants and clogs and shoved her legs and feet into them. She raced outside and snatched the bags before they blew onto the road. Wadding up the ruined bags, her eyes roamed over the mess. How did that happen?

She heard a chuckle and whirled. Carl Levy, a can of Mountain Dew in his hand, stood on the edge of his car lot, surveying the scene.

"Raccoons," he said laconically. "Can't leave garbage sitting out like that." He shook his head. "Lady, you have a lot to learn." He took a slow sip and smiled at her. "Soooo, I gave you my business card, didn't I?"

Brenda, aggrieved and furious, said nothing. If she hadn't learned anything else during her years with Dale, she had learned silence could be a powerful weapon.

Ellie, whose lip was still swollen, didn't want to go to school. Brenda agreed it was best for her to stay home and made a quick trip to the grocery store for more trash bags, popsicles, and pudding. After she had Ellie, disfigured but mollified, propped up in bed watching TV and sucking on a red popsicle, she worked for a couple of hours cleaning up her parking lot again. Some of the trash did not seem familiar; there were coffee grounds and other food scraps she hadn't noticed previously. This time, the bags got wedged into the back seat of her car when she finished. Brenda planned to drop the trash off at the waste management depot, out of the reach of any raccoon.

Brenda couldn't help but wonder if the raccoon's name was Carl.

CHAPTER SIX

Ellie's swelling was down a bit by lunchtime, and she told Brenda she would like to try school for the afternoon. After she dropped her off, Brenda made a detour on the way home to dispose of the bags of trash—and the wasp's nest—at the proper site.

Once back to the motel, Brenda turned her attention to Ellie's new sleeping quarters in Unit Two. She worked steadily: mopping, vacuuming, and scrubbing. She discovered a hole in the back wall. Had someone's fist gone through it? Brenda rummaged through a box until she found the atlas. She tore out the Wisconsin page and pinned it on the wall, covering up the hole. It would be good for the child to get familiar with the state she now called home.

It was almost time to pick up Ellie when Brenda, inspired, ran over to the house and raided Ruth's fabric stash, unearthing a bolt of cotton fabric, pink with tiny yellow dots. Perhaps she could drape some of it over the bed. Ellie, with her love of bright colors, was sure to appreciate it.

Brenda ran a comb through her hair and brushed the dust from the front of her T-shirt before driving over to the school where she waited, engine idling, in the pick-up line. Soon Ellie, smiling a lopsided smile, came out of the building, flanked by two girls. Both girls hugged Ellie before they headed for their own rides. Ellie spotted Brenda and ran to the car.

"Hi, Granda, those are two of my new friends." Her voice was filled with the wonder of it. "Gabby and Meg. They are so nice. We played horses today at recess. With Lilly and Maureen."

As Brenda drove back to the motel, Ellie talked steadily while Brenda smiled, pleased the child was finding friends so quickly at this new school. When there was a break, she said, "Your lip is almost back to normal. That's a relief. Do you have any homework?"

"Yes. I have to do some social studies I missed from this morning and I'm supposed to practice multiplication facts. I have flashcards. Will you help me?"

"Of course." Brenda parked in front of the house. "Right after supper, okay? I thought we could walk through the house now and put aside anything we don't want the renters to have access to. And I need to clean that bathroom and wipe out the frig, too. We want to have everything all set for the renters...when we get some." As if on cue, her phone buzzed, and soon Brenda had an appointment to meet with a potential renter at ten-thirty the following morning.

Brenda set Ellie to stacking the dozen or so cans of the food Ruth had left in the cupboards in a cardboard box while she riffled through the rest of the kitchen. She put a can opener, three well-worn cookbooks, and a few pretty dishes in a cast iron frying pan and lugged it out to the car. In a drawer filled with random items she found a key to the sewing room. She decided rather than over-burdening her temporary housing in the motel with too much stuff, she'd store some of the nonessentials there.

Brenda gathered up her Aunt Ruth's best dishes and other personal items. These she carted upstairs and also placed into the room to be locked away. Ellie contributed a few items as well before she retreated to the bedroom she had hoped to call her own while Brenda freshened up the bathroom.

Brenda studied the key board screwed to the wall behind the service desk. She'd come back with a Phillips screwdriver from the toolkit she'd brought from Illinois and get that out of the house, too.

"Come on, sweet thing," Brenda called, taking one long look around the pleasant house. "Let's go back over to the motel. I want you to see what I accomplished in Unit Two before I rustle up something for supper."

"Okay, Granda. Good-bye, dear bedroom." Ellie was not moving very fast, but she was heading in the general direction of the motel. She walked across the lot behind Brenda who drove the car filled with the items they were taking from the brown house.

Brenda held open the door to Unit Two and beckoned to Ellie. Ellie stood in the doorway silently, and Brenda tried to see the room through the child's eyes. It was far from elegant. But one of the two single beds had been freshly made up, the second pushed against the wall serving as a wide couch, and the shabby beige carpet vacuumed.

Brenda spread a length of the pink fabric over the bed to show Ellie how nice it would be. Did Ellie approve? Ellie's smile was answer enough. The door to the two units stood open while clothes, books, toiletries, Ellie's art supplies, a handful of CDs and a battered-but-functional player, card games, and a few stuffed animals–including Schmoe—were hauled into Unit Two.

While they were working, Teak pulled into the parking lot in her little blue Kia and rolled down her window.

"I picked up a rotisserie chicken," she said. "Would you ladies like to join us for a little supper tonight? Nothing fancy," she warned, "but Hailey and I would love to have your company."

The kindness warmed Brenda's heart. "Thank you. That would be real nice."

***

At six o'clock, Brenda, with Ellie dancing beside her, walked across the alley to the Anderson's home. A trio of wooden crates, each housing a sassy ceramic bird was stacked beside their shiny yellow door. Teak welcomed them with a friendly, "Come on in and make yourself at home," and they were immediately engulfed in a homey kitchen with white cabinetry, spunky touches of colorful crockery, and a tantalizing aroma. Teak, tossing a salad, gestured with her chin toward the sitting area beyond the kitchen. Brenda, Ellie pressing shyly against her side, stepped deeper into the airy, open space.

The large wall decal centered over a plump, buttery couch caught Brenda's eye immediately. Ellie, too, was looking at it, mouthing the words while she sounded them out.

Christ is the center of our home
a guest at every meal
a silent listener to every conversation.

Brenda watched Ellie attempt, then abandon, the final word. She felt a pang and worried her bottom lip between her teeth, reminded that she needed to spend more time in the evenings helping Ellie with her reading.

"Who is Christ?" Ellie's clear voice rang out in the quiet room.

"We don't go to church much," Brenda said, embarrassed that a child in her care did not recognize the name of the Lord.

Teak's smile did not dim. "Christ is Jesus Christ, the Son of God," she told Ellie. She left the salad to join them. "He is an invisible presence in our home."

Brenda felt uncomfortable, for spiritual discussions were unfamiliar to her. She did not know where to look or what else to say and was glad that Ellie let the matter drop when Smokey padded into the room. The little girl immediately fell to her knees in front of the fluffy feline, inundating her with murmurs and pats. Hailey emerged from her bedroom where she had been, she explained, practicing a speech for school. She joined Ellie and Smokey on the floor.

Brenda turned to Teak and asked, "How can I help you?" Soon she was pouring milk for Hailey and Ellie. She set their glasses on the table, which was covered with a vinyl tablecloth, a swirl of pinks and greens and yellows, perfect for springtime.

It was not long before the four were gathered around the table. Brenda was about to take a bite of her salad when she noticed that Teak and Hailey both had their heads bent and their hands folded. She followed suit, nudging Ellie to do the same.

"Lord bless these dear friends and help them in their new endeavors," Teak prayed in her sweet voice. "And bless our conversation and time together and this food to our bodies. In Jesus' name, Amen."

"Amen," said Hailey, and Brenda and Ellie both made sounds that could be taken for Amens. It was a simple meal of salad, brown beans, and shredded chicken on buns; simple, but filled with friendliness and warmth. Afterwards, Hailey invited Ellie to hang out in her bedroom. Teak urged Brenda over to the couch.

"I'm so glad you could come over," she told Brenda. "It's going to be fun to have you for neighbors. Is there anything we can do to help you right now?"

"Well." Brenda, perched on the couch next to Teak, hesitated. She thought about telling Teak about the trash that had re-littered the lot and her suspicions that Carl had something to do with it, but didn't want to appear to be either whiney or a tattletale.

"Do you have any ideas for curtains?" she asked instead. "I want to figure out something for Ellie's unit. Ruth left a stash of fabric, and I found some pink cotton that would be perfect."

"I could whip you up a set of curtains," Teak said. "I love to sew and it would be my pleasure." She leaned over and lit a wide, squat candle resting on the coffee table in front of them. Soon the scent of lilacs filled the air.

Brenda, finding the fragrance cloying, breathed shallowly. She and Ellie were strangers. Why was Teak being so nice?

Sarah came to mind, and an alarm began to clang inside Brenda's head. Sarah, a co-worker at the nursing home, had urged Brenda to stop over for doughnuts and coffee one Saturday a couple years back. She had listened to Brenda talk, laughing at her feeble attempts at jokes, encouraging her. Brenda felt appreciated, emboldened, relaxed; her heart warmed and her guard came down. Then Sarah left the room and returned holding a glossy folder filled with information about an "opportunity" in a pyramid program. Brenda was not interested, and the pastries and pleasantries ceased with the pitch.

Was Teak trying to disarm her, in order to take advantage of Brenda in some way? It simply did not feel right to Brenda, and she rose to her feet.

"I don't want to bother you," Brenda said. "I'll figure something out." She raised her voice. "Ellie, we should go."

"Whoa." Teak stood too. She reached out, touched Brenda's arm. "Brenda, if I'm being too pushy, please say so. Actually, you did a good job of letting me know I was too pushy. I'm sorry." She cocked her head to one side and smiled uncertainly.

Brenda, ashamed of her brusqueness, tried to explain.

"We never met folks like you and Hailey, picking up trash, inviting us for supper, offering to make curtains…"

"You inherited a lot of headaches along with a home. If we can do a thing or two to help out, it is our pleasure. And really, a little measuring and a quick seam or two, I could have a set of curtains made for Ellie in no time."

Hailey and Ellie were standing in the hallway, listening to the exchange. Brenda heard Ellie's quick intake of breath. She wanted those curtains.

"We would appreciate it." Pride stiffened Brenda's voice.

Teak didn't appear to notice. Her dimple flashed.

"Great. When should I come over to pick up the material and measure the window?"

"How about now?" blurted Ellie. "Could you come now?"

So it was decided, and they all walked to the motel together. After cutting off enough fabric to serve as a bedspread for Ellie's bed, Teak and Hailey spirited away the rest of the bolt, and Ellie bent her head over her homework.

It was growing dark when Brenda suggested, "Dial my number right now so I can see if it goes through. I want to make sure you can get ahold of me." Ellie carefully dialed the number of Brenda's cell phone. It buzzed, and they smiled at each other.

"Are you sure you want to sleep in here, sweet thing?"

Ellie was positive.

Brenda hugged and kissed the child, and was hugged and kissed in return. Brenda went out the door, shutting it carefully. Unit One seemed empty without Ellie underfoot, but Brenda was worn out from her busy day. Soon she was asleep.

***

Promptly at ten-thirty the following morning Violet Baxter presented herself to Brenda. A small, faded woman, her short, graying hair was combed back severely and held in place with several bobby pins of varying shades. "It was me that called about the rental for me and my boy," she informed Brenda.

Since Violet appeared to be solidly in her sixties, Brenda wondered how old her boy was, but didn't ask. Violet looked the house over appraisingly and appeared flabbergasted when Brenda told her that the sewing room would be kept locked and unavailable for her use. She hemmed and hawed before deciding to take it.

Brenda knew from her own renting experience that she could ask for a deposit, and so she did.

"And an extra month's rent in advance," she added firmly.

Violet recoiled. "I never hear of such a thing. Don't you trust me? I am a good reputable person. I'll pay for each month as it comes up. That is the way we do things here. Maybe it's different from where you come from. But that's the way we do things here."

Brenda swallowed. She was dubious, but didn't want to go against the culture of the place, didn't want to anger Violet.

"Fine," she said.

***

Violet and a skinny man in his early twenties with shaggy brown hair and a half-hearted goatee were already unloading household items from the back of a rusty truck when Brenda returned from picking up Ellie from school that same afternoon. Ellie opted to go into her unit, but Brenda walked over to the truck where she learned that the young man was Violet's son, Buddy. She enlisted his help in moving the service desk from the front hallway of the house, down the porch stairs, and, after a stop midway across the parking lot to rest and flex cramped fingers, into Unit Three, an apparent catchall. Then they walked back toward the house together.

"What kind of work do you do?" Brenda thought it might be prudent to get to know her renters a bit.

Violet was hovering nearby.

"He graduated high school." Her tone was proud. "Three-four years ago. Considering his options now." She paid the first month's rent with a bundle of twenty-dollar bills. "It's all there. You don't need to count it."

"I'm sorry, it's a habit," Brenda apologized, and counted the money in front of Violet. It was forty dollars short.

Violet's chin jerked.

"Can I pay that last little bit on Monday?" she asked. "I need to buy eggs and milk. I'll get my check on Monday."

Today was Thursday. After a moment, Brenda nodded. A knot was forming in the pit of her stomach. She hoped that renting to Violet and Buddy was not going to end up being a huge miscalculation.

CHAPTER SEVEN

B renda returned to Unit One and cut an apple into wedges. She added a dollop of peanut butter to the plate before carrying it over to Unit Two where she set it in front of Ellie. Ellie, sitting at the round, rickety table sketching dogs and cats on the back of her notebook, put her pencil down and reached for a piece of apple.

"I'll be down by the sheds," Brenda said. "You okay here?" Ellie nodded, her attention plainly on her snack, and Brenda headed for the far end of the motel, a tiny hacksaw from her toolkit in hand. She stopped to open up the door to Unit Ten, hoping the fresh air would hasten the departure of the skunk smell.

Brenda continued around the end of the motel, following the worn path leading to the sheds. She appraised the two buildings. If her memory served her right, motel supplies were kept inside one of them. The nearest shed had a window covered with dust. Peering in, Brenda spotted a riding lawn mower, a workbench with a collection of tools, a wheelbarrow, and various other odds and ends. Ed's workshop. The second, larger shed had no windows. She was eager to see what all was inside, and so it was with determination that she attacked an arm of the door's padlock with the hacksaw. Again and again she jabbed at the lock, but only managed to rough up the surface. Concentrating on her task, she barely heard a motorcycle drive into the lot.

"Breaking in?" asked a gravelly voice in need of a good throat-clearing. Brenda, startled, looked up and into the kind but sad eyes of a man with curly gray hair in need of a trim and an oil stain the size of a saucer on his tan vest. Brenda drew the saw away from the padlock.

"No, this is my shed," she said. "I-I lost the key. I mean, I don't know where it is." Stop babbling, she chided herself.

"May I?" He reached out a hand. "You're going about it wrong. Gotta make back and forth motions, don't just peck at it."

She hesitated, and he held up his hand as if taking a vow. "Just want to help. Scout's honor." Soon he was sawing away, describing his technique as he did so. When the lock broke free, he made no move to enter the shed. Instead he handed her the saw, bowing slightly.

"Thank you," said Brenda. She was itching to see what was inside, but felt the stranger deserved a bit of courtesy.

"I appreciate your help. What brought you here?"

"Looking for a place to bed down," he responded. "I came through this way five, six years ago, and I had recollection of a cheap—pardon me, ma'am, inexpensive–motel in your fair city." His eyes flicked over the obvious downtrodden appearance of the motel, but he said no more.

"Take a look, if you like," Brenda offered. "I'm the new owner, just starting to freshen the place up. You can see if there's anything here that suits you." She led him back to the front of the motel. "I'm airing out this end unit here best as I can but–"

He peeked into the open door. "This room is fine."

"It smells like skunk!" Brenda exclaimed.

"Oh, keep airing it out. Like you are, ma'am, keeping the windows and doors open. And ma'am. Check the filter on the air conditioner. I reckon some of the smell might-could be clinging to that." He took a deep breath. "…I don't like bringin' it up, but I took a bad spill couple-three years ago. Got me a concussion. After that I lost my sense of smell."

"Oh, I'm sorry! And you really can't smell the skunk stink?"

He stepped inside the room and inhaled deeply, shook his head. "Not a bit. Happened on my fiftieth birthday. Not a very nice present." He reached out and pushed on the mattress. "Seems firm enough. I'll take the room."

My first guest! Brenda rejoiced within, but managed to keep her countenance neutral.

"Come down to Unit One, that's the office for now, and I'll register you. If you're sure about the room being okay."

He nodded and stuck out a hand.

"Jimmie," he said. "Jimmie Stephens."

"Brenda Miller."

After registration was complete, Jimmie took off on his motorcycle, and Brenda went back to the shed accompanied by Ellie, who had finished her apple and was wearing a smear of peanut butter on her cheek. Brenda was pleased to find the shed was organized and efficiently laid out. She located plastic totes filled with pillows, sheets, blankets, and towels. Ellie plopped down on a dark green Adirondack chair to examine the contents of a wheeled cart filled with cleaning supplies.

"Granda, this is going to be so much fun!" she enthused.

"We'll take that chair down to our unit," Brenda mentioned. "We need another chair there, don't you think?"

While Ellie lugged the plastic chair down to Unit One, Brenda carefully opened a dusty tote and selected a set of sheets and some towels and headed for Unit Ten. Ellie came in while she was making the bed and busied herself arranging the towels on the rack in the bathroom.

"Tomorrow I'll help you clean." The little girl was plainly caught up in the novelty of their new endeavor. "Wait for me to come home from school, okay?"

Later, Ellie and Brenda sat at the little table in Unit One, eating bologna sandwiches and potato chips. Brenda was ashamed of the scanty meal, but the day had gotten away from her. After she helped Ellie with a spot of homework, the two went for a walk down the main street of town, swinging linked hands, enjoying the spring evening with its lengthening daylight. Together, they checked the store windows, expanding their knowledge of their new hometown. The two newcomers eventually reached the end of the business section and turned onto a tree-lined street.

"Second Avenue," noticed Ellie. "Say! Mrs. Winthrop told us she lives on Second Avenue. Let's see if we can find her house. She said she has a birdbath in her front yard."

Brenda murmured her assent, and considered that she, herself, had never had a birdbath. Growing up in her parents' somber, stifling house, she had not come into contact with any even vaguely frivolous yard ornamentation. As an adult, she had always lived in apartments, and had been too intent on self-preservation to consider the needs and pleasures of the birds.

Her daughter Janna had been a difficult, strong-willed child, and still only a child when she became a mother herself. Janna! The thought of her was a wound, a pain that Brenda tamped down. Now there was Ellie to think of, sweet Ellie, who hummed as she skipped along, searching hopefully for a house with a birdbath in the yard. Ellie, Janna's daughter, who deserved a nice home and a chance to grow up without the past to haunt her.

"Granda, cute! Look at that toad." Ellie squatted to observe the unexpected amphibian.

"You've always loved toads, sweet thing."

***

The first time Ellie had ever noticed a toad was in Prairie City, when she was a little bit of a thing. It had been a sunny spring day, Brenda remembered, rather like this one: green and lush and sweet-smelling after a particularly long, dull winter.

Brenda had been pushing Ellie in a stroller through the town park that consisted primarily of a rusty swing set and teeter–totter, a walking path, trees, and bushes. Brenda sank down on a convenient bench and released the little girl from her stroller. She soaked up the warm sunshine and the fragrance of the lilacs as Ellie toddled about, wandering behind a nearby bush. When the little girl didn't instantly reappear, Brenda, investigating, found her transfixed by a fat, motionless toad. He hopped once, suddenly, and Ellie shrieked in delighted terror.

Sheltered by the bush, Brenda settled in the grass and gathered her granddaughter's solid little body in her lap. Ellie was breathing hard in her excitement. The toad blinked, and Baby Ellie gasped.

"Look at that pathetic piece of junk."

Instinctively, Brenda's hands covered the baby's ears, protecting her from the criticism. Her own cheeks burned.

"I think I've seen Brenda Miller using it to push Janna's brat around." A second voice, higher-pitched.

"Figures. I haven't seen Janna in a while."

"Didn't you hear she took off?"

The speakers were drifting out of earshot, but their final comments were audible.

"No…but that's not a surprise. She always did get around."

"Like her old man."

And the giggles.

Brenda remembered the giggles.

Brenda's thoughts drifted from the past to the near future. For Ellie's sake and her own, she must make a success of her motel!

"I'll prep a pot of coffee when we get back," she told Ellie as the toad hopped away. "Then it will be all set to brew in the morning. I want to be able to offer our guest a cup."

"Okay." Ellie was still intent on finding Mrs. Winthrop's house. It wasn't until they had walked two entire blocks that she spotted a concrete birdbath, surrounded by blooming red tulips, in front of a small white house.

As they watched a robin getting in a quick bath, Brenda decided that someday, after the motel was back on its feet and they were settled in the brown house, she would put a birdbath in their yard. They retraced their steps back to the motel, pausing to size up the car dealership next door with its rows of cars, flapping neon pennants and oversized signs.

LEVY'S LOT!

BEST SELECTION/BEST VALUE!

Brenda could see that the cars were crammed together, and how expansion would be beneficial. There was no sign of Carl, and for that she was grateful. His over-the-top jovial air grated on her nerves.

Across the street from the motel an old oak tree sheltered a brick building housing an insurance agency and a barbershop. They would be unobtrusive neighbors, Brenda thought as she shepherded the little girl back to the motel. Ellie cast her eyes at the house but refrained from comment. Violet was sitting on the porch in a transplanted kitchen chair but didn't appear to hear Brenda's called greeting.

Jimmie's motorcycle buzzed into the lot as they reached the

steps of Unit One. He parked in front of Unit Ten and approached them. "This your little girl?" he called out, indicating Ellie.

"Granddaughter," Brenda replied, and Ellie offered a quick, shy wave.

"I might-could be staying on for a week or longer," he said. "I agreed to help a navy buddy in town here with a little building project."

"You're welcome to stay as long as you care to." Brenda was glad for the prospect of steady room rent coming in, and Jimmie seemed like a nice enough guy.

It was high time for Ellie to get to bed. Brenda walked over to Unit Two with her, sat on the bed, and waited while Ellie brushed her teeth and performed the rest of her nightly ritual. After a goodnight hug and kiss, Brenda left the unit. She was reaching for her own doorknob when she heard a scream. She swiveled and raced back.

Ellie was kneeling on her bed, face red.

"A mouse! A mouse ran under there!" She pointed to the ratty chest of drawers. "Can I sleep with you? I don't want to stay here with a mouse."

"Oh, child."

"Granda, please." Ellie began to bat her eyes.

Brenda, relenting, nodded.

"Carry me," Ellie begged. "I don't want it to run over my foot."

"I think it is as frightened of you as you are of it," Brenda said. "It will stay hidden now. You can walk, Ellie. Think of it as a furry toad."

The remark brought a smile to Ellie's face, and Brenda handed her her shoes. Still perched on the bed, Ellie stuck her feet into them, grabbed her grandmother's hand, and hurried into the relative safety of Unit One.

Brenda paged back through her legal pad to where she had written "Pest Control." She drew three large stars in front of the words. They simply could not have guests encountering mice.

It was growing dark when Brenda walked across the parking lot to the motel sign. She studied it for a moment, then reached up and flipped over the wooden square to the left of the word VACANCY, revealing a red NO. She would not be opening any more rooms in the motel until it was acceptable.

The next morning, Brenda remembered to put the coffee on, and when Jimmie came in she was cheery but subdued, as Ellie was still sleeping soundly.

"Good morning. Do you want some coffee?"

"Morning, ma'am. Cuppa joe'd hit the spot."

"Did you sleep well, Jimmie?"

"That bed had a spring stickin' out of the mattress, kept me awake half the night. So I'm only gonna pay you half." He laid some bills on the table with an air of finality.

Brenda, thankful to have a guest, didn't argue.

"I'm sorry about the poor night sleep."

"I'll try it again tonight. But turn that mattress over, will ya? Then I'll pay what you're asking. I'll be gone most a the day, save me my room." Jimmie waved his hand and went out, clutching a white Styrofoam cup of coffee.

"I might need you to help me turn his mattress," she mentioned to Ellie, who was sitting up in bed rubbing her eyes.

"Okay," Ellie answered. They listened as Jimmie rumbled away. His front tire dipped into a pothole and made a clunking sound.

"I'm going to have to get those holes filled, too, won't I?" Without waiting for a response, Brenda added, "You better hustle if you're going to get to school on time."

Ellie gobbled down a bowl of corn flakes adorned with sliced banana and was ready in record time.

"I'll be outside," she called to Brenda. The door slammed. Brenda splashed some water on her face and scowled at her reflection in the bathroom mirror. She grabbed her keys and went out.

Ellie was standing on top of a little mound of gravel near the edge of the parking lot, talking to Carl Levy. When she saw Brenda, she jumped from her perch and ran over to join her grandmother at the car. Carl saluted her with a can of Mountain Dew.

"He's a nice man," Ellie said. She got into the back seat, and began to fumble with her seat belt until it clicked. "I told him we had mice. He was real interested. He felt bad for me, he said."

"You told him we had mice?" Brenda was horrified. What was Carl going to do with that information?

CHAPTER EIGHT

That evening, while Brenda was coaching Ellie in spelling, someone knocked on the door. Ellie stopped mid-word to bound over and fling it open. Teak, smiling, displayed a set of newly made curtains. They were all eager to see how they would look, so they went into Unit Two at once.

"Can I borrow Smokey, just for a couple nights?" Ellie was leery about sleeping in the room where she had the mouse encounter. "She'd protect me from the mice, wouldn't she?"

"Rodent trouble?" asked Teak, threading a section of the new curtains through the rod. The discarded beige curtains formed a soft heap on the floor.

"One mouse. We saw one mouse." Brenda was on the defensive.

"Can't Smokey please stay?" Ellie persisted.

"Okay by me," said Teak. She picked up the second piece, efficiently threaded it onto the rod. "Okay by you, Brenda?"

Brenda sighed.

"I bought some spring traps, and I am trying to find the entry points into this room. But if you are willing to share the cat for the night, it would give Ellie peace of mind."

Teak and Brenda popped the rod into place over the window, stepped back and surveyed the room. The new curtains added a grand air.

"If we painted the walls light, light pink, this could be the pink room," Ellie said. "You could find a picture for the wall that is mostly pink instead of that ugly one." She flicked a finger disdainfully at the nondescript landscape, so faded it appeared blobby. "And," Ellie went on with enthusiasm, "we could put pink flowers in a vase, and maybe pink towels in the bathroom and buy a pink carpet for the floor, and make it all pink in here."

"Oh honey," Brenda said, "that would be too pink."

"I would love it," Ellie assured her.

"But remember, this is only temporarily your room. We have to decorate it to please all our guests, not just one ten-year-old girl."

"A lot of people like pink." Ellie was not giving up.

Teak listened to the exchange with a hint of a smile. "A few pink touches would tie this room together. You could check the thrift store in town. I bet you could find a painting there that would suit the room better than that one does." She wrinkled her nose in the general direction of the tired landscape.

"Thank you very much for making the curtains," said Brenda.

"My pleasure," Teak said. Her dimple flashed. "And I'll send Hailey over with the cat. Good night, ladies." Teak tugged the door open and shut it quietly behind herself.

"Back to the spelling," Brenda directed. "And then I want to hear you read a few pages of your book."

"Granda, we've done enough."

"I love you too much to let you sluff off, sweet thing. Now let's get back at it so we'll be done before Smokey gets here."

Ellie made a face but bent over her word list once again.

When Hailey, the gray cat draped over her shoulder, tapped on the door of Unit One, Ellie hastily stacked her schoolwork and led the way to Unit Two. The older girl gave Ellie some tips on settling the feline down for the night. Ellie promised she'd bring Smokey back to Hailey in the morning.

"But not too early," Hailey begged. "Saturday's my only chance to sleep in."

"It's really nice of you to share your cat," said Brenda from the doorway. She was glad to see the cat was already calmly settling in. "Thank you for bringing her over."

"I wanted to invite Ellie to something going on at our church anyway," said Hailey. She gave Smokey a pat and smiled at Ellie. "We have Kids' Club tomorrow night."

"What do you do there?" Ellie asked.

"Oh, play games, have a Bible lesson, eat pizza, hang out. I think you'd like it."

"Can I, Granda?" Ellie was eager.

Brenda hesitated.

"We don't go to church," she told Hailey. "I don't know if she'd feel comfortable."

"Whatever you decide," said Hailey. "No pressure." She gave Ellie a high-five. "See you."

"See you," Ellie echoed.

As soon as the older girl was gone, Ellie pleaded, "Please can I go with her?"

Although Brenda could see little value in it herself, she didn't think any harm would come from Ellie going to church. She gave Ellie permission and helped her and Smokey bed down for the night before she returned to her own room.

Brenda curled under the flimsy gray blanket and reviewed her day. Taking advantage of Jimmie's absence, she had spent a great deal of time in Unit Ten, vacuuming and scrubbing and restocking the bathroom. She had managed to flip the mattress by herself and brought in a chair from those stored in Unit Three, but the room still seemed Spartan. Mulling over decorating options, Brenda nodded off.

A piercing scream jolted her out of a deep sleep. Within seconds, she was fumbling with the knob on Ellie's door. Ellie cowered on her bed, wailing and moaning. Smokey, with evident enjoyment, was batting a limp mouse between her paws in the center of the room.

"Something woke me and I turned on my light to look!" Ellie shuddered, and Brenda kicked herself for not thinking through the ramifications of having a mouser spending the night with her sensitive granddaughter.

"I'll put them out." Brenda opened the door wide and with her bare foot encouraged Smokey and her prize to pass through it.

Ellie sank onto the bed, sighed in relief.

"That was so gross."

"Try to go back to sleep now," Brenda encouraged. She patted Ellie's pillow.

But Ellie's face was a mask of worry.

"What if Smokey runs off?"

Brenda squeezed her eyes shut and tried to will away a threatening headache. Taking a slow, measured breath, she surveyed the empty parking lot. "

Here, kitty, kitty," she coaxed. "Here, kitty, kitty."

There was no sign of the cat. Brenda did not want to have to tell the Andersons that she and Ellie had lost their pet. She had left the door to Unit One wide open in her haste, and now peered inside, hoping to see Smokey. No such luck. Brenda thrust her feet into her clogs, pulled a sweatshirt over her head, and clomped outside. She sighed. Two-thirty a.m. was not an optimal time to be tracking down a gray animal.

Eventually Brenda located Smokey sitting on the front steps of her own house, washing herself. Thankfully, there was no sign of the mouse. Brenda scooped up the cat and brought her back to the motel. Ellie, calmer now, was almost asleep. Smokey jumped up to curl beside the little girl. After Brenda assured Ellie that all other area mice had definitely been scared off, she returned to her own bed.

The night passed without further incident, but Brenda's sleep was fitful.

***

Saturday dawned gray and wet, and it was almost lunchtime before Ellie brought Smokey back to the Andersons. After that, she opted to hang out in her own unit while Brenda placed mouse traps in all of the rooms, looked over motel records and regulations, and did a bit of scrubbing. Mid-afternoon, Ellie barged into Unit One.

"You have to wipe your feet," cried Brenda. "Look at all that mud you tracked in. Ellie, wipe your feet. Please." She could hear her own voice, sounding more agitated than the situation warranted. Even after only a week, the close confines of the motel room, exacerbated by today's rain, were affecting her, and not in a pleasant way.

Serving as kitchen, sleeping, and living quarters as well as office was a lot to ask of a room. Brenda was doing her best to keep everything tidy and in order, but it was a constant struggle. She felt her frustrations mounting, clamoring to be expressed in a torrent of words, but she clamped them down. She grabbed a dishtowel draped over the back of her chair, the plastic Adirondack that had so caught her fancy but was now another indication of the cheapness of the furnishings, and threw it with more force than necessary in Ellie's general direction.

Ellie stood, stricken, halfway into the room, a muddy trail marring the freshly-scrubbed linoleum. She caught the towel and held it a moment before she bent over and dabbed at the mud, smearing it.

"I was just checking to see if you wanted to play Old Maid or something." Ellie sat down on the floor and took off her shoes. "I'm sorry I made a mess, Granda." Her smile was apologetic, hopeful.

Brenda weighed the list on her legal pad against how long this rainy Saturday must seem to Ellie.

"All right," she said. "If you can clean up that dirt you tracked in, I'll deal us out some cards."

Old Maid was a game that required at least three people to create any sense of suspense, but Ellie enjoyed making pairs, and hooted when Brenda was left holding the Old Maid. Brenda, feeling as if it were an appropriate but unnecessary reminder of her status, gathered up the cards. Through the window, the rain continued its steady downpour, churning up a fresh layer of mud. Brenda swallowed hard. "This, too, shall pass," she reminded herself.

***

Sunday morning, the rain had abated and Ellie was still charged up about the previous evening.

"Kids' Club was fun. They have it the first Saturday of every month. Can I go next month? Did you ever go to church when you were a kid, Granda? How come you never brung me?"

Brenda, sitting at the table peeling potatoes, didn't know what to tell her.

"When I was a kid, my parents did take me to church. Once in a while." Fumbling, she continued, "I never saw much sense in it. A lot of sitting. And we had to shake hands with everybody around us and I didn't like that part."

"Kids' Club was so NOT like that," Ellie declared. "We played games and Pastor Don had a ping-pong ball and a hair dryer and when he turned on the hair dryer, the ping-pong ball stayed up, but when he turned it off, the ping-pong ball fell down and rolled away. He said the hot air of the hair dryer is like the power of the Holy Spirit. What's the Holy Spirit, Granda?"

Brenda was not up for a theological discussion. She stood, gathering up her potato peelings.

"Why don't you ask Hailey the next time you see her?" A sharp rap on the door effectively ended their conversation. Ellie bounded over to open the door while Brenda disposed of the peelings.

"Brenda Miller?" A deliveryman held out a vase with a single red rose. "Happy Mother's Day." Brenda wiped her hands on the front of her jeans, took the vase, murmured thanks.

"Oh, I forgot!" cried Ellie. "I made you a card at school. I'll go get it." She followed the deliveryman down the step, heading for her backpack stashed in Unit Two.

Brenda stood holding the vase, breathing in the perfume. Every Mother's Day for years a rose from an unidentified source had been delivered to her. Even here, in Miskomin, Wisconsin, miles and miles from her old home, someone was keeping track of her whereabouts, paying tribute to her on this day. She set the vase in the middle of the table, blinking back tears as memories and questions resurfaced.

CHAPTER NINE

On Monday Brenda waited until after lunchtime before she picked her way across the parking lot and knocked on the door of the brown house. She was appalled to see that someone—she guessed Buddy—had affixed a Green Bay Packer bumper sticker to the door. It looked tacky. She waited; knocked again. Eventually, Buddy came to the door, hair tousled, eyes heavy with sleep.

"Yeah?"

"Is your mother home?"

"What do you want her for?"

His tone was surly, and Brenda's hackles rose.

"I came to collect the rest of the rent. She said she'd pay up today."

"Are you going to be this anal every month?" he asked, and before she could respond, he closed the door. Brenda could not believe the rudeness. Not knowing what else to do, she walked off the porch, thinking that she'd watch for Violet and accost her in the parking lot if she had to. Forty dollars was forty dollars, and Violet wasn't the only person who needed to buy milk and eggs.

Brenda checked on the mousetraps and was relieved to find them all empty. She'd keep a vigilant eye out, and if she spotted any more signs of rodents, she'd hire an exterminator.

After consulting the list on her legal pad, she decided to work on the bathroom in Unit Nine. Her anger at her new renters fueled her elbow grease. Before she went to pick up Ellie at three, the Unit Nine bathroom shone...except for rust rimming the drains, and she wasn't sure what to do to get rid of those stains. Another item for her list.

"Today we started a club," Ellie told Brenda, settling into the back seat and fastening her seatbelt. "We call it the Wild Horses Club. All of us are wild horses, except Gabby. She's our master. Tomorrow we're going to have a race. I bet I'll win."

Via the rearview mirror Brenda's eyes met Ellie's, so full of fresh young optimism, excited and involved with her classmates. She smiled.

"Sounds like fun." Ellie reminded Brenda of the happy girl she herself once had been, back when she thought winning a race would make a difference and she'd count for something. She did not want young Ellie to be disillusioned as she had been. She wanted better for her. She would do whatever she could to see that it happened.

The next morning, after Jimmie, fortified with coffee, had zipped away on his motorcycle, Brenda headed for Unit Nine with a container of baking soda in hand. She was determined to tackle the rust in the sink. She paused to watch a car pull into the driveway, bump over the potholes and rattle to a stop in front of the brown house. An older couple got out and made their way to the porch. Brenda was right behind them. She was determined to get her forty dollars from Violet, and this might be her chance.

When Violet opened the door for her visitors, Brenda, still

holding the baking soda, walked in too, glancing around the front hallway. Piles of clothes and empty food containers took the place of the wide service desk. The dead philodendron lay on the floor, its pot tipped over. Brenda hated seeing her aunt's immaculate home degenerate into such squalor. Her heart sank, even as her resolve stiffened.

Violet was busy greeting the couple and did not seem to notice Brenda. Finally Brenda spoke up. "I thought I'd come over and get the rest of the rent money, Violet, and save you the trouble of bringing it over to me."

Violet's eyes filled with venom.

"I was planning on paying you tomorrow."

Brenda's heart was pounding.

"You said Monday," she reminded her. "That was yesterday."

One of the visitors, a younger version of Violet, spoke up.

"Hello, I'm Violet's sister Rose, and this is my husband, Harold. We've come to see Vi's new place." She smiled widely, revealing a gap between her two front teeth.

Brenda murmured a hello. Harold, a gray, mousy man, ducked his head in an almost-greeting.

Rose went on. "She tells us she helped you out, moving in mid-month and all. I should think that forty dollars would be a nice gesture of thank you. For being willing to occupy mid-month."

"She moved in during the first week of the month, and—" Brenda began.

"Let's not be splitting hairs, shall we." Rose's tone was smooth, and all three regarded Brenda with disdain.

"Fine," said Brenda, backpedaling. "But next month's rent is due in full the first of June." She left the porch, berating herself for being such an easy mark. To vent her frustration, she poured herself into scrubbing every surface that could possibly be scrubbed in Unit Nine. Before she left to pick up Ellie from school, the entire unit was as clean as it could possibly be.

Ellie had another good day at school and was eager to inspect Brenda's work. Unit Nine was sparsely furnished, but clean and fresh. A hint of lemon furniture polish was in the air. Besides the credenza which sported a hole on one end, the furnishings were tolerable.

"Green," said Ellie at once. "Let's make this a green room. There already is a green bedspread. You can paint the walls green and it will be beautiful." She hugged her grandmother exuberantly before continuing, "And we should go to the thrift store. The one Teak told us about. And find decorations. Pink for my room. Green for this one." Her eyes shone. "This is fun!"

Eventually Ellie called it a night, and Brenda was planning on following suit. She removed her stained T-shirt and bra and, leaving her jeans on for the time being, slipped her nightshirt over her head. Feeling untethered but comfortable, she decided to relax by paging through one of the cookbooks she had brought over from her Aunt Ruth's kitchen.

She padded barefoot to the books she had added to her back wall pile of possessions and picked up the top one. A recipe for Overnight Oats caught her fancy. It wouldn't be much of a problem to whip up a batch for breakfast. It could cook in the crockpot and provide Ellie with a warm and filling breakfast.

Her stash against the wall included a carousel of spices and a round container of oats. Raisins were handy, as was a bag of brown sugar. Soon she had the ingredients in the crockpot. She put the lid on, plugged in the ancient appliance, and turned the knob to "low."

"Low" or no, there was a surge and a flash. The electricity in the unit went out, leaving Brenda in darkness.

Ellie yelped from the next room. Had she lost power, too?

Feeling her way, Brenda left her unit, closing the door behind her. The streetlights provided her with enough light to see her way to the next door. Ellie's window was dark. Brenda rapped on the door and she could hear her granddaughter scrambling, fumbling for the lock, letting her in.

"Granda!" Ellie grabbed her grandmother's waist. "How'd it get so dark?"

"We blew a fuse. I think. How come you weren't sleeping?"

"I was drawing. What are you going to do, Granda? Can you fix it?"

"I'll have to find the fuse box, reset the circuit. At least I think that's what I have to do...You don't have a flashlight in here, do you?"

"Isn't there one in the car?"

"You're right. I'll get the car keys. Hold on." Brenda returned to Unit One where she found to her horror that the door was locked. She rattled the knob in disbelief. It must have locked when she shut it. And the keys were on the counter: the room key, the master key, the car keys, everything.

Including her phone and her wallet.

"Leave your door open!" she yelled to Ellie who was still standing on the threshold.

Ellie looked startled as her barefooted grandmother lunged toward her and held on to the door as if it were a lifeline.

"Go on in, sweet thing. We'll both be staying in here tonight."

Brenda curled up on top of the second single bed in Ellie's room, still wearing her jeans. Her eyes were open in the darkness. Tomorrow, she planned, she'd get up, get Ellie off to school– but she was locked out of her car. How would she get Ellie to school?

She must have spoken her question aloud because Ellie's

voice, heavy with sleep, carried to her through the darkness.

"Teak'll bring me."

CHAPTER TEN

After a fitful night, Brenda rose early. She felt grubby and rumpled, with nasty breath and tangled hair. She fumbled through Ellie's shoe collection, settling on a pair of flip-flops. She wedged her toes through the toe piece and then, most of her foot protected by the thin foam sole, except for her heels which dragged on the ground, she minced her way across the yard to the Anderson's home, leaving Ellie sleeping soundly. It was a cool morning, barely daylight and drizzling. Brenda shivered. Light spilled from Teak's back door, brightening her spirits.

Teak opened the door before Brenda knocked and warbled a cheerful, "Good morning!" while upbeat music swirled between them.

Brenda stepped inside and wiped her feet awkwardly on the welcome mat. "I'm sorry to bother you, but I got locked out of my unit. And I don't have access to my car keys. I was wondering if you could–possibly–drive Ellie to school this morning?"

"Oh dear, I'm sorry! Of course I can. Send her over. She can get ready here and I'll feed her breakfast, too." Teak adjusted the volume of the radio.

"Hope she likes hard boiled eggs and toast," said Hailey, her words muffled by the Miskomin Hawks sweatshirt she was pulling over her head.

"I don't think she's ever had hard boiled eggs," Brenda said. The smell of the eggs made her feel uncomfortable, and she wanted to leave as quickly as she could. "She might like them."

"Or I can fix her a bowl of cereal," Teak said. "Send her over, Brenda. Would you like an egg?"

"No thanks," she said, needing to escape. "But I'd appreciate it if you fed Ellie."

***

Ellie was thrilled with the novelty of eating breakfast at the Anderson's, and she chattered continually while she slipped into her clothes.

"Meg had a hard-boiled egg in her lunch once. I don't think I ever even seen one before. How come we never have them, Granda?"

Brenda stared vaguely in Ellie's general direction through the open door of the bathroom where she was cleaning up after her granddaughter's morning ablutions.

"Granda?"

"Oh, I don't know." Brenda pushed the corners of her mouth up. "I am not sure why I never boiled you an egg, sweet thing. Not sure at all. Now go on, scoot, run on over to the Anderson's. And tell them thank you!"

She knew full well why she had never boiled an egg for Ellie. She herself hadn't fixed or eaten hard-boiled eggs since June 1982.

***

"These potatoes are mushy," Dale had said. "Can't you even cook potatoes?" He gave the bowl a rude little shove. "And where's the meat?"

"I–didn't have enough money for any meat," Brenda said, faltering. "And–sometimes at home we had egg gravy. I thought you might like it." With a hopeful smile, she set a bowl of creamed hard-boiled eggs on the table.

He cursed. "It stinks," he said. He got up from the table, grabbed his cap.

"Where are you going?" she asked.

"Out. Out to find something decent to eat." The door slammed.

Brenda looked at the table she had set so carefully: two placemats, the blue flowers in a small vase, pickles in a cut glass bowl, the potatoes and the eggs. She had sprinkled a bit of paprika on top of them, and thought the egg gravy looked elegant. Plainly, Dale did not agree. One tear fell, and she caressed her enormous stomach, tracing the outline of a tiny foot, thinking about the gift she had spent too much of the grocery money on: a red Western style shirt for Dale. It was gaily wrapped and hidden under the bed with a handmade card: Happy Birthday, Daddy!

***

With an effort, Brenda pulled her thoughts out of the morass. She studied her empty fingers, resting motionlessly in the bathroom sink. The water was cold. She sighed, pulled the plug, and watched as the water swirled and disappeared.

Someone was knocking. Brenda wiped her hands on the front of her jeans and went to the door.

"See you swapped rooms!" Jimmie's tone was hearty. He peered into the gloomy interior of Ellie's unit. "No coffee this morning?"

"Oh, I'm sorry." His coffee was the least of her difficulties. "I got locked out of my unit last night. I blew a fuse, and–" It all seemed like too much: past, present, future troubles engulfed her.

Tears filled her eyes, and she turned away, feeling embarrassed and exposed.

"Whoa, Nellie," Jimmie said. "None of that. You don't need to feel so kicked in the teeth, ma'am. You just settle down. I'll get your door opened and your power restored. Scout's honor."

Jimmie retreated to his motorcycle, dug around in his saddle-bag for a bit, and returned with a canvas wrapped parcel. Brenda sat dully in Unit Two in the rickety chair with the uneven legs that rocked when she leaned forward. She could hear Jimmie talking to himself, trying his own key in the lock, poking and prying with various wires and who knew what all.

An hour went by; Brenda continued to sit. Finally Jimmie came to the door. There was a streak of oil on one cheek, his gray curls were rumpled and his hands dirty, but he was smiling.

"I mastered that lock," he crowed. He didn't wait for a response before searching out the fuse box and restoring power to Units One and Two.

Brenda went into her own unit and grimaced when she caught sight of her reflection in the mirror. Braless, sloppy nightshirt, wild hair, tear-stained face. No wonder Jimmie was alarmed. Remorseful, she took the time to prepare a special brew of coffee, adding cinnamon, nutmeg, and ginger to the grounds before heading for the shower.

She was freshened up and calmer by the time Jimmie returned. They sat and sipped their coffee in two mismatched mugs while Jimmie delivered bad news: He had poked around a bit and discovered that mice had been chewing through the coating on some of the wires. Also, he added apologetically, he believed the wiring was outdated and wouldn't meet code.

"You'll have to get an electrician over here, check it over, give you an estimate." He took a sip of coffee, held up the mug in a salute. "This is good stuff, ma'am. Thank you."

"You deserve it." Brenda didn't know what she would have done without Jimmie.

"Are you all right?" Jimmie's blue eyes were gentle.

"I'm fine." Realizing she sounded short, she offered a bit of explanation. "It's just that, on top of this trouble now, I got to thinking about something in the past…It wasn't a good time for me. I don't want to talk about it."

"I know what it is like to not want to talk about something." Jimmie finished his coffee in three great gulps, stood. He pushed a hand through his curls, adding to their disorder.

"Well, ma'am, I'm off. You got plans for today, keep your mind off of things?"

"I'll be fine," she said again, grateful that he didn't press. "And I do have a lot to think about. Today I'm going to figure out where I can buy some hotel furniture. I'll need to replace at least a couple of the bed frames, and most of the dressers. And new mattresses would be nice, but they might be out of my price range right now."

"You might-could think about getting some memory foam, top the mattress with. Could get by with that for now. And you might want to look at TVs too," Jimmie said. "People expect TV with good reception when they're stayin' at a motel."

Brenda heard what he didn't say: that the TV in his room was sub-par. She reached for her legal pad, made a note to rectify that situation as soon as she could.

Soon Brenda was seated at one of the public computers in the library, gathering names and information about area electricians and researching places that resold hotel furniture. Miskomin wasn't too far from Minneapolis and St. Paul. Surely there would be a store there that handled motel furnishings.

She scoured the sites avidly and jotted items and prices on her legal pad. She'd have to rent a truck, Brenda realized. She tapped her bottom lip absently as she thought. That could be a challenge. Could she possibly ask Jimmie to go with her, or was that presuming too much?

And Ellie. She wouldn't want to take her out of school if she could help it. Could she go over to Teak's after school, and stay with Hailey, or was that presuming too much, too? Brenda sighed and logged off the computer. So many details to work out. But she knew the sooner the motel was fixed up, the sooner she'd have money coming in, and she could send Violet and Buddy Baxter on their merry way.

Brenda's thoughts tumbled and churned as she drove to Ellie's school. She was not paying attention to her driving, and almost rear-ended the car in front of her at an unexpected stop sign. Shaking her head, she focused on her driving. Paying for car damage or a ticket was not in her budget. Her eyes narrowed as she realized Carl Levy was in the car in front of her. Was he going to add "inattentive driving" to her list of sins?

She found out soon enough.

Bright and early the next morning, even before Jimmie had stopped in for his morning beverage, there was a lively rat-a-tat-tat on her door and Carl stuck his head in, teeth first.

"Noticed you were distracted yesterday, driving," he said, recomposing his features into a mask of concern. "Soooo dangerous. Is this overwhelming you?" He gestured with his can of Mountain Dew to indicate the general surroundings.

"Because you remember," he went on without giving her a chance to respond, "I am willing to take this whole lot off of your hands."

Brenda, who had been disposing of the coffee grounds, wiped her hands on a paper towel before wondering aloud, "Why is it so important to you?"

"I've had my eye on this property for years," Carl said, his tone wistful. "My dad started this dealership twenty-five years ago and encouraged me to expand it to a whole new level. I'd been in talks with Ed before he passed." He took a sip of his Mountain Dew.

"We could help each other out," he went on. "You would get rid of the headache. I'd get the space I need to build up a place my wife and daughter can be proud of."

Carl had, with obvious pride, introduced his daughter a few days earlier. Gretchen was a beautiful girl, a golden girl, with shiny blonde hair and gorgeous green eyes. Gretchen, apparently considering Brenda to be unworthy of her attention, barely acknowledged her.

"She's already in sixth grade. That means it won't be long before she's driving," Carl had said with an exaggerated sigh. "Then she'll show some interest in these beautiful vehicles."

Brenda felt sympathy for Carl, but she had dreams, too.

"I'm not selling, Carl," she said. "I'm sorry. You'll have to figure something else out." She struggled to keep her chin high and firm.

He offered her a smile, but it was not a pleasant one.

"Oh, I'm not giving up yet," he said. "Have a nice day." After saluting her with his soda can, he was gone.

CHAPTER ELEVEN

There was a mailbox at the edge of the parking lot and Brenda had been appreciating the convenience of home delivery. The next morning, when she heard the mailman's car idling, she put down her scrubbing brush.

The May day was lovely. The air was crisp but held a promise of summer. Brenda took her time walking across the lot, her step light. She was glad for the excuse of a mail break, for it was shaping up to be a busy day.

Already this morning she had contacted an electrician who would come over later in the day to give her an estimate, and she had spoken with Kurt Clayson, the owner of the laundry service her aunt and uncle had used. His rates were reasonable, and included pick up and delivery. Brenda had stripped all of the beds and one of Kurt's teenage sons was coming to collect the pile of linen.

The motel's simple aluminum mailbox was overshadowed by Carl Levy's adjoining larger, more flamboyant box, painted to look like a yellow 1957 Chevy with a white insert. The chrome trim surrounding the insert gleamed. Brenda expressed her disdain with a quick flick of the tongue. Shaking her head at her own childishness, she opened her box.

There was only one piece of mail today, a simple white envelope. Brenda fingered the envelope and bit her lip as she read the name in the upper left corner. Mrs. Canfield? Where had she heard that name before? Oh yes, that was the name of the lady who had taken care of the motel after Aunt Ruth had passed away. Brenda stuck her finger inside one end of the flap and pulled, ripping open the envelope.

May 9, 2011
Due immediately to Mrs. L. Canfield.
Payment for Managing the Motel.
Seven Weeks, at Five Hundred Dollars Per Week.
You owe $3,500.

A bill! Brenda's heart jumped. She could not believe it. When she and Ellie had come to the motel, Mrs. Canfield had said she had been helping Ruthie out....no mention of payment. Besides, she was not Brenda's hire.

Brenda, now oblivious to the beauty of the day, hotfooted it down to Kevin Schneider's office, where she thrust the paper on his desk. "Is this for real? No one said anything about paying her, she said she was glad to do it for Ruthie."

Kevin held up a hand as if attempting to staunch her flow of words. He read the sales bill, turned it over to see if there was anything written on the back, reread the front. He stood.

"Let me check the legal documents. I don't recall any mention of recompensing Mrs. Canfield for her services." He walked to a cabinet, extracted a file.

"She got free room and board!" Brenda knew she could not

pay the woman the sum she requested. She'd be hard-pressed to come up with any amount.

Kevin ignored her, shuffling through papers. Finally he shook his head. "I don't see it as part of the agreement. There's no legal ties to bind you."

"But I'm glad you stopped by," he continued. "Your neighbor Carl was here earlier this morning, informing me that your property is ripe to be condemned. What with the boarded up windows, the trash, and the rodents running rampant. A health inspector will be checking out your motel in the next day or so to see if there is any credence to his claim."

"There isn't." But Brenda wasn't so sure.

"We'll be in touch," said Kevin.

She walked back to the motel, her head filled with thoughts of bills, inspectors, and unfinished projects. She operated on autopilot the rest of the day: dealing with the electrician, heating canned beef stew for the evening meal, washing up the dishes in the bathroom sink, helping with homework, nodding and commenting in all the right places when Ellie chattered on about doings at school.

All night Brenda tossed and turned, fretted, sleeping off and on, her scattered dreams centering around a dragon of a man, scowling and filling a legal pad with heavy scribbles as he tramped from one end of the motel to the other.

***

When Brenda returned from driving Ellie to school the following morning, the health inspector was waiting for her.

"I am Jason Cordell," he told her. "Let's take a look."

Jason Cordell was not a dragon. He was young and businesslike, and carried himself with unnatural erectness, clipboard in hand. Grimly, braced for the worst, Brenda unlocked each door for him, and he scanned each room, making notations from time to time. When they reached Unit Ten, she was glad to discover that the skunk smell was barely discernable. Jimmie must be fond of tea tree oil, she thought, her nostrils twitching.

"Well?" Brenda was blunt.

"Well." Jason glanced up from his clipboard. "You'll need to update your smoke detectors. And take care of those boarded up windows, won't you? Of course, you cannot rent out those rooms until you do. Your roof is in good shape, I didn't note any water damage. And your exits are clearly marked and easy to access. You shouldn't have any trouble bringing this place up to code." He handed her a sheet of paper. "You'll get my formal inspection next week."

Brenda was so relieved her knees felt wobbly. She thanked Jason for coming. Take that, Carl Levy, she thought victoriously.

There was still the bill from Mrs. Canfield to deal with, however.

One hurdle at a time, she schooled herself. She examined the boards covering the windows and found she'd need to replace the broken glass before she removed them. Brenda did not think she was capable of that project. But she could install some new smoke detectors and fill in the potholes that pitted the parking lot...if she had some dirt.

Brenda glanced around the parking lot. Her eyes narrowed as they rested on the small heap of gravel on the edge of her lot, where the pavement adjoined with Levy's. Couldn't she use that to fill in the holes? She'd still need to cover them with tar or asphalt or something, she knew, but at least cars would not dip down and clunk when they crossed the lot. It would be an improvement.

Brenda hurried out to Ed's shed and upended a wheelbarrow that was tipped against the wall. She found a shovel, propped against a rotary lawn mower. Balancing the shovel on the wheelbarrow, she awkwardly trundled over to the pile of small stones and sand. It must have been there for quite a while, for it was settled and packed, making scooping difficult, but Brenda persisted.

By the time she had the worst of the potholes filled, the heap of gravel was down to a scattering of pebbles. Brenda straightened her back, satisfied with her efforts. As she stretched, Carl Levy bustled toward her, a finger in the air.

"What do you think you're doing with my gravel?" he blustered.

"Your gravel? It was in my parking lot."

Carl shook his head, once, definite. "Lady, you need to learn where your boundaries are. That is my gravel, and I have plans for it. Sooo you'll need to put it back. Put it all back in the pile where it was."

She had seen him roaming between the cars when she was fetching the wheelbarrow and shovel. Now she was angry with herself that she hadn't checked with him then.

Why didn't you tell me an hour ago?" she asked.

Carl displayed his too-square teeth.

"And miss watching you huffing and puffing out here? Not a chance."

His attitude was despicable. Brenda tamped down her irritation.

"I'll get some to replace it. You won't," she added shrewdly, "be so childish as to insist that you need that very same gravel, will you?"

"It was exceptional gravel," Carl said stiffly, but he did not insist.

Later, after stopping at Walmart to pick up ten smoke detectors and fetching Ellie from school, Brenda returned to the doorway of Unit Nine to stare at the ceiling. It was stained yellow and gray, probably from cigarette smoke. She inhaled deeply, then coughed. Definitely cigarette smoke!

Jimmie drove up on his motorcycle, parked in front of Unit Ten, and joined her. His shoulders were sprinkled with a fine layer of sawdust, as was the scruff on his cheeks and chin, but the stain that had adorned his vest was gone.

"See you got them potholes filled, ma'am," he greeted her. Brenda nodded and held up her hands, displaying a couple of calluses and a blister.

"Not used to that kind of work." Her tone was rueful. "How's the ramp coming?"

"We finished today. So I'm on the lookout for a new project." Jimmie stuck his head into the room, followed her gaze upward. Tentatively, he suggested, "If you put BIN on it first, that will cover up them stains." He coughed into his fist.

"I have a proposition, ma'am."

"Please, call me Brenda," she interrupted.

With a slight smile, he tried again.

"I could hang out for a while, *Brenda*, do some fixin' to offset my room fee, that'd be fine."

"Don't you have a home?" Brenda asked. She flushed, added, "I'm sorry. It's none of my business."

"Nowhere is home if you don't got love. And my love is six feet under." Jimmie's sad blue eyes grew sadder. "Since my wife, my Angie, passed on, I've been driftin'. Lookin' for things to fill my days. I could help you out for a while, if you want."

Brenda met his eyes.

"I'm sure we could work out an arrangement. There is certainly enough to do here."

"I can give you references."

"I can't pay you much."

"What I need, money can't buy. Helpin' you out gives me a purpose, and I reckon that's what I need right now. But could I make a suggestion?"

"By all means."

Jimmie placed a hand on the small of her back and guided her outside where he pointed at the boarded up windows.

"Let me start by takin' care of them. I reckon that'd make this place seem a bit more up-and-coming. And then, how 'bout us scrubbing the siding, so's it looks better from the road?"

"Good ideas," Brenda acknowledged. "The inspector who was here this morning, he wants the boards gone."

"I'll get at 'em tomorrow," Jimmie promised. He winked, and she, unaccountably, blushed. She made an excuse and ran for her legal pad. Scarcely able to believe her good fortune, she started a list for Jimmie. A handyman would be worth his weight in gold.

And he was kind of cute, too.

CHAPTER TWELVE

Progress on the motel was slow but steady. Jimmie was proving to be a skilled worker: replacing the glass in the windows, negotiating with the electrician and minimizing that bill by doing much of the labor, installing the smoke detectors in all of the units, capping her potholes with a quick mix, delivering a mound of gravel to Levy's Lot.

After that, Brenda and Jimmie tackled cleaning the siding on the motel. Armed with long soft-bristled brushes, they scrubbed from top to bottom with bleach water. This got rid of much of the grime, but several stubborn patches remained.

"We'll need to bring out the big dogs," Jimmie said, raking his hand through his gray curls. He disappeared on his motorcycle, returning a half hour later with a package of trisodium phosphate. After donning protective eyewear and long rubber gloves, he mixed up a batch of heavy duty cleaner and worked with a will, succeeding in eliminating almost all of the stains. He would not let Brenda help with this part of the project, saying it had to be done just so. She did not insist. Her back ached and her arms protested when she lifted them over her head. She was not accustomed to such vigorous work.

It was worth it. The upper three-quarters of the building, at least, were respectably clean. Much of the bottom quadrant of siding had loose or missing strips.

"Lemme think on how to handle that lower section," Jimmie said.

***

Wednesday morning was so beautiful that Brenda couldn't bear the notion of being inside. Despite the fact that the interiors of the rooms were calling her name, she resurrected some gardening tools from Ed's shed and knelt in front of Unit One. She had purchased marigolds—hardy things that she should be able to keep alive—and intended to plant the flowers in the narrow flowerbeds outside of each door.

The bright blooms, along with the paint soon to be applied to the doors, would go a long way in making the motel appear to be a thriving establishment, she hoped. The sun was warm and the smell of last night's rain lingered. Engrossed in removing the weeds from the rectangle of earth outside of her unit, she was startled by an ostentatious throat-clearing.

"Sorry to bother you," said Violet, who did not sound sorry in the least, "but we need to talk to you."

We. Brenda extended her gaze to take in Rose, and—strangely—Mrs. Canfield. The three women were dressed in coordinated flowered dresses. Violet had taken the time to line her thin lips with an unflattering shade of coral lipstick, and Rose had a scarf draped over her dress. An artificial pink carnation was pinned to Mrs. Canfield's ample bosom. Brenda, in her faded T-shirt and well-worn blue jeans, felt at a distinct disadvantage.

Warily, she set down the trowel and rose to her feet.

"How can I help you?" she asked.

"You owe me money," said Mrs. Canfield. "For services rendered." She smiled as she repeated a phrase from the bill she had sent to Brenda.

Brenda looked at the gap between her front teeth, to the matching one in Rose's mouth.

"Are you related?"

"Oh, didn't you know?" Violet was all innocence. "We're sisters."

"You've met Lily," said Rose. "We're flowers in Mother's garden." The three exchanged smug glances.

"I'll make it easy for you," said Lily. "You can pay off the money you owe me by letting my sister and nephew stay at the house."

The three women beamed. The contentment Brenda had felt while she was working the soil evaporated.

"In lieu of rent," Rose clarified.

Brenda focused on her marigolds. Their strong yellow blooms lent her courage. "My lawyer said that it wasn't part of the agreement. To pay you, I mean."

The three women exchanged glances, clearly affronted.

"You agreed to the rate I charged before you moved in," Brenda persisted, looking at Violet.

"You don't know a hill of beans from a corn row," Rose said. "Right is right."

Brenda's resolve weakened. The three sisters stepped closer.

"Why, hello, Lily!" Teak, carrying a plate wrapped in tinfoil, entered the parking lot and the conversation. "It's so good to see you again." She unwrapped the plate and held it out, offering fresh chocolate cookies. "I had the morning off, thought I'd do some baking."

As Lily reached for a cookie, Teak asked her, "Did you stop by to thank Ruthie's niece for letting you stay at the house after you had that spat with your husband?"

Lily's hand stopped and dropped to her side. She shook her head vaguely.

"I helped out with the motel. She needed help with the motel."

"Yes, she did," Teak agreed. "She sure did, and fortunately for both of you, you were in a pickle and you needed somewhere to stay. Worked out so perfectly for both sides. God is good."

The three sisters had nothing to say to that. It wasn't long before they retreated to the house, to sit on the porch and watch while Teak gave Brenda a hand with her marigolds project.

"Thank you," said Brenda in a low tone. "Thank you for coming over just now."

"The Holy Spirit nudged me," Teak replied. "And I've learned to respond to those nudges."

Holy Spirit? Nudges? This was not familiar territory. Sometimes Teak seemed too holy to be real. Still, Brenda was grateful that she had come to the rescue when she had, and she thought maybe she might want to find out more about the Holy Spirit.

***

"Well, what's the plan for tomorrow?" asked Jimmie as he came into Unit One later that afternoon where Brenda sat at her little table, reviewing records and receipts. He went over to the counter, found his cup beside the coffee pot, and poured himself a cup of what Brenda knew would be overcooked coffee.

Jimmie took a sip, winced, and reached for the saltshaker. A quick shake, another sip, a nod. He had his own method of freshening his coffee. Brenda didn't ask. She tapped her pen on the top page of her legal pad. The once pristine page was now filled with cross-outs, additions, stars, arrows, lines, exclamation marks, and wet splotches.

"Tomorrow? Well…"

"How 'bout we get going on paintin' the doors? A fresh coat of paint will spruce them right up. Course, I'll have to sand some of them." Jimmie took another swallow of coffee and looked over her shoulder at her list. "And after that, you want me to go with you to pick up furniture?" he said. "I can drive the truck if you like."

"Good," said Brenda, relieved she would not have to drive. She had been putting off asking him, shy for some reason she could not fully understand, did not want to explore. "Monday sound okay? I'll see if Ellie could walk home from school with Hailey then. In case we are late getting back."

"Never can be too sure about the traffic," Jimmie agreed. "I'll go on down to that gas station that rents out U-Hauls and reserve a—what size would you say? Mid-sized truck? And we can leave first thing Monday morning?"

"Sounds great. Right after I drop Ellie off at school." Brenda made a note to call Teak and see if Ellie would be able to hang out with Hailey that afternoon. Already she was looking forward to Monday.

***

On Saturday morning after she had shared a cup of coffee with Jimmie and heard his motorcycle leave the parking lot, Brenda extracted the quart of milk from the tiny refrigerator. It was very light, nearly empty. She called Ellie's room.

"I'm running down to the grocery store. There's not enough milk for our cereal."

"Wait for me. I want to come."

When they met at the car a few minutes later, Ellie had a proposal.

"Let's go to the thrift store first!"

Brenda checked her wallet, counted bills.

"We can't get much," she cautioned.

Despite her caveat, they had a good time browsing through the odds and ends at the thrift store. Ellie loaded a basket with all things pink: pink plastic flowers, a pink wall décor suitable for the bathroom, pink placemats, a pink vase trimmed in gold. She stuck the plastic flowers into the vase, set it on a placemat, and declared it perfect.

Brenda looked at the display, the price tags, Ellie's eager face, and swallowed.

"You may choose three of these things," she said. "That's all we can afford right now. Anyway, we don't want the room to look gaudy."

"Let me just look at the pictures," Ellie begged. "I want to find a picture that is pink. Teak did say it would be a good idea."

"Fine," Brenda said again. "You look. I want to see if there's any cheap shelving units here. I'd like to get some of my stuff up off the floor."

But Ellie had already skipped off, headed for the artists' corner of the store. Brenda searched but could not find any suitable shelves. Ellie mourned the absence of any primarily pink pictures, but she did spot a lovely pastoral scene.

"We can hang this in the green room," she suggested.

Brenda liked the picture.

"We'll take it," she said. "And I'm hungry, aren't you? Let's stop at the grocery store quick and go home and have some breakfast."

"I'm starved," said Ellie, and so it was decided.

"After we eat, we can go over to Teak's house," said Brenda. "I want to ask her if she—or Hailey—can keep an eye on you while I go to the cities Monday."

"Did you get a truck?" Ellie kept abreast of all that was going on in the renovating and knew about Brenda's potential trip.

"Jimmie did." They pulled into the parking lot of the motel, the lack of potholes making their entry smooth. The newly painted black doors gave the place a stately air, although the siding looked extra dingy in comparison. All in good time, Brenda schooled herself as she rooted around in her purse for the keys. Finding them, she unlocked the door to Ellie's unit, and then her own.

"I'll just set my pink stuff in my unit and come over for breakfast." Ellie clutched the bag in both hands. "It's gonna look so good!"

When Ellie rejoined her grandmother, giggles were burbling out of her. "Granda, that chair in there, now it's squeaky when I sit on it. It sounds so funny!"

"Squeaky how?"

"Squeak-toy squeaky. Like you'd give a dog…if we had one."

Brenda thrust a bowl of cereal at Ellie. "Stay here." She went into Ellie's unit and examined the cushion in question. Threads had been nibbled and the stuffing of the cushion disturbed.

A nest.

Her head swung back and forth, hunting for a way to avoid dealing with it. Nothing. She clamped her jaw and returned to her unit where she ripped a couple of baggies off of the roll on the counter in the kitchen area, stuck her hands in them, and then, with makeshift gloves in place, carried the chair outside of the motel.

It started squeaking as soon as it was disturbed. Heart pounding, she lugged the chair to the end of the motel, out of sight, she hoped, and tipped it over. She watched in horrified fascination as a cluster of tiny, hairless mice dripped out of the hole in the cushion and down onto the grass, where they wriggled out of sight.

She swallowed the scream rising in her throat and, leaving the chair upside down in the grass, returned to her unit where she threw away the plastic bags and scrubbed her hands.

Ellie was finishing up her cereal.

"Did you find out what was squeaking?"

"All taken care of," Brenda said lightly. "Ready to go over to Teak's now?"

"Let me go by myself. I'll ask them."

Brenda hesitated. After the mice incident, she felt depleted and would cherish a few minutes alone to regroup. And it was good to see confidence growing in her timid little Ellie. "Be sure and tell her thank you, won't you?" And I will have to think of a way to repay her for her many kindnesses, she thought.

CHAPTER THIRTEEN

"Very profitable." Brenda was still gloating over the bargains as they reached the outskirts of Minneapolis. "Thank you so much for all your help, Jimmie."

Jimmie's right hand left the wheel and rested next to hers on the bench seat, the contact slight but electric. His hand moved momentarily to the shifter before returning to settle against hers. Brenda swallowed, tamping down dormant feelings, both strange and pleasant. She breathed in his now-familiar scent; lavender, with an undertone of tea tree oil. She did not look at him.

"The moon's pretty tonight," she mentioned. A high giggle escaped.

"Gotta love a full moon," Jimmie agreed, nudging her hand ever so slightly. His words were punctuated by the wail of a siren, and a sudden sea of red lights in front of them sent silent warnings.

"Accident," Jimmie said. He braked sharply and pulled over to allow a police car, in full emergency mode, to zip past.

The traffic came to a standstill. Jimmie's whistle was long and slow.

"Bad one."

Brenda felt nauseated. She kept her eyes averted from the scene and took slow, shallow breaths.

"If we're stuck here, at least the company is good." Jimmie fully laid a gentle, callused hand on top of her rigid one.

Brenda barely heard him. She was once again fifteen years old, and staring at the flat broad front of the Mack truck, the headlights so close, hearing again the horror in her mother's scream, a scream that terminated mid-note. Brenda stiffened and closed her eyes, attempting to block out the memory.

It was not easy. Although the crash itself came to mind in blurred disconnected pieces, like shards of broken glass, one cruel retort during the aftermath remained vivid.

"She's dead because of you," Father had told her as they stood graveside. "If it weren't for you wanting a new outfit, I would still have my wife." He had retreated to nurse his bitterness and Brenda, wracked with guilt and grief, had been left alone.

Now she huddled into herself, concentrating on scrubbing away the trauma of the past and setting her mind on the happier present.

Jimmie withdrew his hand.

"Shouldn't be long," he said, his tone formal. "There's a police officer waving vehicles on."

They rode in silence for several miles. As Brenda regained her composure, she became aware of the tension in the cab. Was something bothering Jimmie?

"Thanks so much for driving, Jimmie."

"Not a problem." His tone was cool, but she felt him relax beside her and in a moment started to whistle softly. But even though she kept her hand invitingly near, he did not reach for it again.

***

It was later than Brenda intended when the truck finally pulled into the parking lot of the motel.

"I hope Ellie's—"

A police car was parked in front of Ellie's unit.

Brenda bolted from the cab and was halfway to the door before Jimmie had the vehicle completely stopped. Her hands slipped on the doorknob and she staggered inside, dread assailing her.

Ellie sat on her bed, eyes bright. A police officer, his jaw set beneath a dark clipped moustache, stood by the window. His eyes met Brenda's.

"Are you the grandmother?"

"Yes! What's wrong?"

"I was all alone and I called your cell phone and when you didn't answer I got scared and called nine-one-one." Ellie was quick to explain. She hopped off the bed to encircle Brenda's waist with two skinny arms, hugging fiercely.

"But I thought—isn't Teak—?"

"Hailey and Teak aren't home. I got scared so I called nine-one-one," Ellie repeated, blinking.

"I've been sitting with her for the past two hours." The policeman sounded aggrieved. "Been trying your cell phone. Over and over. Kept going right to voice mail. Just about to call Child Protection Services. We take child abandonment seriously." He adjusted his belt.

Jimmie stepped into the room.

"Everything okay here?"

Brenda turned to him.

"I thought Ellie went home with Hailey after school today, I thought Teak was taking care of her, I didn't know she was alone, oh, poor girl!" She shifted her attention to Ellie. "Are you hungry, honey?"

The policeman indicated a grease-stained bag.

"I bought her a hamburger. Didn't see any food here. Poor kid."

"We eat in my unit," Brenda explained. "But Teak? I thought you said she was fine with watching you, honey."

"Your unit?" asked the police officer. "You make her sleep alone in a motel unit?"

Ellie examined her nails.

"Granda, I forgot to ask her."

"Ellie! You went over there Saturday to ask her."

"But Hailey was outside with Smokey and–"

Brenda's hands covered her face. She heard the police officer's voice rising and falling. She heard Jimmie respond. She pulled herself together enough to murmur phrases of apology and recrimination.

The officer left with, "You'll be hearing from Child Protection Services."

Jimmie broke the awkward silence.

"Well, let's unload the truck and then I can drive it back to the rental shop so it'll still be only a one-day charge."

The happiness of the day and the satisfaction of the good buys had long evaporated. Brenda helped Jimmie unload the bed frames, headboards, dressers, and chairs and crammed them into Unit Six for the time being. She had purchased three TVs, too, and she let Jimmie pick out the one he wanted to use in Unit Ten.

Jimmie left to drive the truck back to the rental shop. She heard him returning on his motorcycle while she was sitting by Ellie's bedside, rubbing her back, listening to the child explaining and exclaiming about looking for Brenda's car after school, and then walking all the way home by herself because she didn't see Hailey and not knowing what else to do.

Brenda blamed herself. For something this important, why had she trusted Ellie to make the arrangements? If anything had happened to that little girl, she would not be able to go on.

And her cell phone! Again she berated herself. How hard was it to keep the battery charged? Eventually Ellie drifted off to sleep and Brenda went back to Unit One where she plugged in her cell phone and readied herself for bed. Then she returned to Ellie's room where she stretched out on the other bed, keeping guard, thankful she was safe and well.

CHAPTER FOURTEEN

Brenda slipped out of Ellie's room just before six the following morning. Her eyes felt gritty from lack of sleep. Back in her own unit, she started a pot of coffee, took a shower, settled on a black T-shirt and tan capris. Then she set to sprucing up. If someone from Child Protection Services came by, she wanted her place to be beyond reproach. And keeping busy was an antidote to her feelings of inadequacy and self-recrimination.

"If this is going to be where people sign in, I need to make it look more official," she said aloud. She cleared her table of the salt-and-pepper shakers, the napkins, the half-loaf of bread, the jar of peanut butter, the mail, her legal pad. She left the vase with her faded rose, thinking she'd replace it soon with a fresh bloom. That would be a classy touch. She added a calendar, a couple of pens, a registry, her cell phone, and a little box containing the room keys.

Casting a critical eye, she grabbed the table and pulled it closer to the door, where it could act as a registration desk and would block off the rest of the room. The vase tipped over and murky water spilled out over the calendar and registry. A stench of decay rose as the mushy stem of the flower came into view. With an exclamation, Brenda snatched up the vase and drooping rose and got them out of the way.

After she mopped up the water and remaining bits of flora, she checked to see if her stationery items were rendered unfit. If she threw away November and December, she decided, she could use the rest of the calendar. But the registry, which had taken the brunt of the deluge, would have to be replaced. Brenda closed her eyes, wishing that just once, things could proceed without a hitch.

"What's going on?" Ellie, still in her pajamas, stepped inside and approached the table in its new location. "Cool. Is this where we can check people in?"

"Yes." Brenda opened her eyes, somewhat mollified by Ellie's enthusiasm. "Now that we got some better furniture and TVs, I'm going to make Units Nine and Eight available for renting. I'll flip the VACANCY sign this afternoon after Jimmie and I put the new beds and dresser in Unit Eight. And Unit Nine gets one of the new TVs. Hopefully someone will stop." She wiped up the rest of the mess and rearranged her table/desk as she spoke.

"It's good, Granda. Can I help you? If someone comes to stay, I could show them where to go and ask if they need anything."

Brenda remembered how much she had enjoyed helping her Uncle Ed during that long-ago weekend.

"Yes, Ellie," she said with a smile, adding with mock severity, "if you don't work, you don't eat."

The girl giggled.

"You're so funny, Granda."

"And now, young lady—" Brenda said, pointing in the direction of the door, "—march back to your unit and get dressed. You have a half hour before we need to leave for school."

"Okay," Ellie agreed. "I don't want to be late. We are working on writing poems."

While Ellie readied herself for school, Brenda carefully patted her rose with a paper towel before she tied a string to its stem. She hung it upside down from the clothes bar to dry, stroking it with her finger.

"Love you," she whispered, speaking beyond the rose to the suspected giver.

All the way to school, Ellie and Brenda amused themselves by making up ridiculous rhymes. Brenda's spirits lifted.

"Don't forget to crunch your lunch," she told Ellie, who retorted, "Don't forget to drive your car to a star."

As Ellie got out of the car, Brenda called after her, "See you after school."

Ellie was silent, her face screwed up, thinking. Her face cleared and she called back, "That will be cool!"

After Brenda returned to the motel, she trekked out to the mailbox to collect Monday's mail. Holding the thin pile, she eyed the No Vacancy sign. Was she really prepared to open up a couple of rooms?

Jimmie stepped out of his unit, heading over for his daily cup of coffee. Brenda pulled the Office sign out from under the bed and explained to Jimmie where she wanted him to hang it. He thought he could fix the burnt out "ice," much to her relief.

"I'll get to this after I put them beds together," he promised.

Brenda poured herself a second cup of coffee and glanced through the mail. One letter gave her pause. It was from her old employers at Silver Age Manor. She ripped open the envelope to find her final paycheck. She had forgotten–how could she!–that it would be coming. So welcomed it was. So needed. A note from the Director of Nursing, telling Brenda that they missed her so much, was tucked in with the check.

"I didn't realize how many unseen things you did for us until you were

gone," Brenda read. *"And I want you to know, Brenda, that if you ever decide to come back to this town, you will always find a job with us here. We miss you and would love love love to have you back with us."* The letter went on to include the signing bonus that Brenda would receive in that event.

"Well, that's not going to happen," Brenda said defiantly, crumpling the letter and tossing it into the trashcan. Having second thoughts, she fished it out, smoothing it before she stuck it into the back of her yellow legal pad. Someday she might want a reference, and it sounded like her nursing director would give her a good one.

Brenda rinsed her coffee cup and set it upside down next to Jimmie's. Time to get to work. By the end of the afternoon, Brenda had a positive feeling about Units Eight and Nine. The new headboards were much nicer than the old ones and being able to replace the TV in Unit Nine afforded her pleasure.

She had made up the beds, spreading the sheets over the mattresses with careful precision, enjoying the fresh, cottony smell. She surveyed her work and smoothed an almost nonexistent wrinkle from the bedspread. It would do. She peeked into the bathroom, double-checked the tissue and the towels. The towels, while not new, were still fluffy and spotlessly white. These two units seemed like comfortable places for travelers.

When they got home from school, Brenda let Ellie flip over the NO on the NO VACANCY sign.

Together, they walked back to Unit One, where Brenda plugged in the OFFICE sign. Jimmie had replaced the bulbs in the ICE, and though the last three letters burned a trifle brighter than the "off," it was a step up from the sign she had encountered on the porch of the house three weeks ago. They were ready to welcome visitors!

An hour hadn't passed before a woman rapped on the door of Unit One, looking for a room for the night. Ellie wanted to be involved in the process, and Brenda let the excited child slide the registration form across the table so the guest could fill in her information. Ellie also located the key for Unit Nine in the box of keys and handed it to the guest, a thin woman with curly blonde hair and a skittish air.

"You go down to the end," Ellie said. "Your room is the next to last. You can park in front of it. I can show you." Her hazel eyes sparkled.

"Tell her thank you," Brenda prompted as Ellie and the new guest left the room. She lifted her water bottle with a flourish and took a sip. They were in business!

***

Later that same evening, while Brenda was washing up the supper dishes in the bathroom sink, Ellie approached her.

"Can I read you a poem? I wrote it in school today. Ms. Winthrop said it was interesting."

"I'd like that, sweet thing."

Ellie rustled around in her school bag for a moment and then returned to stand in front of her grandmother. Brenda wiped her hands on a slightly soiled dishtowel and gave Ellie her full attention. The little girl had on a red and yellow sundress today. It was a trifle short, and Brenda noticed that the hem in the back had come undone and hung down unevenly. She was growing so and in need of new clothes. Ellie, oblivious, was beaming, enjoying the spotlight.

"Granda and me," Ellie read,

"are a family."

Brenda smiled. Yes, they were.

Ellie continued, *"But we don't live together*

in any weather."

Brenda's smile faded.

"She lives in one unit and
I live next door.
I sleep on the floor.
I hear Granda talking to Jim.
She likes being with him.

Brenda's horror increased.

I sleep with a moan
all alone
and sometimes there's a mouse.
I wish we had a house.
Sometimes I'm cold
but I do what I'm told."

Ellie, flushed with pride, lifted her face. "It rhymes good, don't it?"

Brenda groped for something to say.

"Yes," she managed. "It does rhyme. But, Ellie. It isn't true. You don't sleep on the floor, honey. And you wanted your own motel room. I didn't make you—"

Her phone rang.

CHAPTER FIFTEEN

"Hello, is this Brenda Miller? This is Suzanne Waters from Child Protection Services. How are you?"

"How can I help you?" Brenda skirted the nicety.

"We received a call about a minor in your care." A pause. "Ella? Ellie?"

"Yes?"

"We have actually had calls from more than one contact in the past forty-eight hours. So we are Very concerned. We understand that, ah, Ellie, is not being adequately supervised? Staying alone in an unheated motel room?"

Brenda reached behind her for a chair and sat down.

"She is supervised. She has her own room in our motel, yes, but I am in the unit next door to her. And it's May. That's why the heat isn't on." She sounded defensive even to her own ears.

"Why isn't she in with you?" The voice sharpened.

"Did Ms. Winthrop call you?" Brenda felt betrayed by someone she had considered to be her ally.

"We are not at liberty to say." Suzanne's voice was smooth.

"We are going to need to sit down and talk to you face to face, Brenda. May I call you Brenda? And I need to see just what the living situation is for Ellie. Will you be home this evening?"

"Yes, I will," Brenda said, faltering. She closed her eyes and took a deep breath before she continued, "Truly, there was a misunderstanding, Ellie is supervised. Everything is fine."

"We'll check for ourselves."

After a few logistics were ironed out, Suzanne disconnected the call. Brenda went next door into Ellie's room. Ellie was lying on the bed, watching TV.

"Pick up your things." Brenda reached for the remote. "Clean up. Someone is coming to see us."

Ellie sat up. "Now? Who? Why?"

"Child Protection Services. The woman I spoke to said she doesn't like it that you are living in your own unit."

"But I love having a place of my own," Ellie protested.

"I know you do, sweet thing," Brenda reassured before she disappeared into the bathroom to give the toilet a quick swish.

***

They met in Brenda's unit, Suzanne looking very official with her Child Protection Services lanyard around her neck and her iPad opened to a questionnaire.

Brenda had taken the time to run a comb through her hair and change into a clean T-shirt. She kicked herself for not having Ellie change out of the scanty sundress. Did the child look like a victim of neglect?

Brenda sat stiffly alert at the table, Ellie pressed against her side. The door opened while Suzanne was asking about Brenda's relationship to Ellie. It was the woman staying in Unit Nine, whose long nose twitched while her eyes sharpened in curiosity.

"Can I help you–" Brenda dug through her shaken mind for

a name. "—Clara?" She stood up, holding on to Ellie's shoulders, managing a smile.

Clara did not return the smile. She scanned the crowded room, letting her gaze rest on Suzanne's iPad, the ID on her lanyard.

"Trouble?" she asked.

"No trouble," said Brenda, but Suzanne's "That is yet to be determined" put her response in the shadow.

"I wanted to see if I could get an extra pillow," said Clara. "The one in the room is very thin."

"Ellie will bring one down to your room right away." She thought the pillows were thick and lovely, but was not about to disagree with her guest.

Ellie rejoined them after delivering the pillow.

"Was she satisfied with the pillow?" Brenda asked her.

"Yeah." Ellie perched on Brenda's knee, and Brenda's arm automatically curled around her waist. "She asked me if you paid me for working here, and I told her," Ellie said, giggling, "that you always say, 'if you don't work, you don't eat.'"

"What?" Suzanne's head, which had been bent over her iPad, snapped up. "Is that your policy?"

"It's an old saying." Brenda felt weary. "It's a joke between us."

"That does not sound like a joke. It is a very unkind thing to tell a child." Suzanne pursed her lips. She reached into her bag and drew out a photo.

"I have something else that I have a question about." She slid the photo toward the Millers.

"It's my class!" Ellie squealed. "Look, Granda, there I am." She pointed to herself, one in a group of twenty-odd others.

"I noticed in the photo," said Suzanne, "that Ellie's mouth is swollen. How did it get that way?"

"Bee sting." Brenda's heart was pounding faster. She hadn't

realized that Mrs. Winthrop had been keeping such tabs on her. What else could the teacher have noticed and reported on?

"I didn't get stung by a bee," Ellie said.

Suzanne's lips pursed even tighter. Her head swiveled from Brenda to the little girl, and her brow beetled.

"Did someone hit you?" she asked Ellie, speaking over Brenda's "Yes, you did!"

"It was a wasp," Ellie said. "Remember, Granda? I got stung by a wasp."

Suzanne picked up the photo and looked closer at Ellie's face.

"Can you verify that? Did you take her to the doctor?"

"No," said Brenda tiredly. "We used home remedies. As you can see, she has recovered completely. And she is right. I misspoke. It was a wasp that stung her lip."

Suzanne did not look convinced, but said no more. After making a few notes on her pad, she asked to see Ellie's sleeping arrangement.

Ellie, with obvious pride, led the way and gave Suzanne a brief tour of her space. Brenda hoped the social worker would realize that it was not much different from sleeping in separate bedrooms in a house.

Finally Suzanne closed the cover on her iPad.

"Thank you for your time and your willingness to talk with me." She offered a tight smile. "I do not see any compelling evidence that Ellie is not safe with you. I see no need for immediate removal. There will be unannounced follow-up visits to verify my findings."

"Feel free to stop in any time." Brenda knew it was in her best interest to be cordial. She returned Suzanne's smile and showed her to the door.

CHAPTER SIXTEEN

*H*IDeoUS *Hotel*
    Although the name of this motel is Neat as a Pin, the only pin I know about is the one sticking through my mattress, preventing me from getting a good night sleep—Brenda read, with growing indignation—*The owner is unkempt and lazy and has turned her young granddaughter into her proxy. It is Ellie who fetches and serves, Ellie who checks folks in and out, produces cream for the coffee, while the owner sits and drinks and barks orders.*

This motel is not worth stopping at unless you want to see a place where child labor laws are NOT in place.

Brenda had settled herself at a library computer, planning on researching more furniture options on Craigslist. But first she had checked her email. There was a message from the administrator of the U-Stay website informing her that a review for her motel had posted that morning. Brenda, hoping for a good review, had clicked over to the site immediately.

Reading her review now sickened her. It must have been submitted by Clara, Clara of the sharp nose and the sharper curiosity. Brenda sent a return email to the administrator of the U-Stay site, demanding that review be removed. It was patently false. She hoped it would disappear before too many people saw it. This was not the kind of publicity she needed.

When Brenda, disheartened, pulled into the parking lot of the motel, she immediately spotted her Aunt Ruth's living room couch on the porch of the brown house. What in the world? The pale blue fabric with its stripes of delicate white and green vines was being exposed to the elements. Here she, Brenda, was hunting so hard for suitable furniture for her units, and one of the few nice pieces she owned was being treated carelessly. A vein pulsed in her temple. This could not be allowed.

She wiped her hands on the front of her jeans. Her fingers lingered on the oversized armrest as she passed the couch. Canned laughter blared forth from the living room TV, contributing to her annoyance. Her firm knock went unanswered.

Brenda stuck her head in the door, and called, "Anyone home?" The odor of fried onions and the stench of rotting bananas drifted into the hallway, empty except for the philodendron, brown and forlorn in a corner, and a stack of newspapers on the stairs.

"So now you'll just be walking in on us?" Violet's truculent voice sounded from the kitchen.

Brenda came all the way into the house and let the door shut behind her.

"I don't want you moving furniture out on the porch," she said.

Violet appeared, spatula in hand. Her hair showed evidence of a recent shearing, for it was shorter than usual and free of its customary collection of bobby pins. She raised her voice to summon her son.

Buddy shuffled down the stairs, clad only in blue jeans, and stood beside his mother, demonstrating solidarity. He stuck his hands into his armpits, hairy arms twitching.

Brenda adjusted the limp collar of her blouse.

"You'll have to bring the couch back inside now. I can help you."

Violet shook her head, once, sharply.

"It'll get hot at night. You don't offer AC here. Buddy, he's planning on sleeping out there."

"You can open the bedroom windows. Get a breeze through that way." Brenda's heart pounded. Surely she wasn't being unreasonable, was she?

"It's hard on us having you watch every move we make, running over here all the time to complain about every little thing." She pointed the spatula at Brenda. "The couch stays on the porch."

Don't cause trouble. Don't make waves. Don't upset anyone. Hard-learned lessons thundered in her head.

"Make sure you keep it dry." Brenda's rebuttal sounded lame to her own ears. As she backed toward the door, she caught a glimpse of Buddy's eyes, triumphant, and the beginning of a smirk on his face. Something inside of her twisted. Her backbone stiffened; she dismissed the lessons, quit her retreat.

"Actually, if things are so unpleasant for you here, you should leave. I want you out of this place by the end of the week." Brenda reached for her legal pad, dug into her pocket for a pen. "Here's your eviction notice." She scribbled a few lines and ripped out the page.

"Are you kicking us out?" Violet's tone was shrill. "You can't do that. I'm calling a lawyer. You can't force us out like this." She was already reaching for a phone.

Brenda folded the yellow piece of paper and set it gently on the windowsill. "End of the week. And your onions? They're burning."

When she got back into her unit, she went into the bathroom and regarded her reflection in the mirror over the sink. Two spots of color, sparkling eyes, a firm mouth. Standing up for herself looked good on her.

It wasn't an hour later that Brenda noticed Kevin Schneider drive into the parking lot and stop in front of the brown house. She hurried to join him.

"Show me the lease," he was saying. When Violet looked blank, he added, "If there's no lease, there's nothing I can do for you, Mrs. Baxter. My hands are tied. You will have to do what your landlady demands."

Violet was huffy and filled with words, but eventually ran dry. She flicked a finger at the door, indicating that Kevin should leave.

"I'm going to do a walk-through first, since I'm here," he said. "I want to have an idea of the condition of the house so if there are any acts of retaliation I will have a baseline. Oh, and Buddy? Give me a hand with the couch, won't you?"

Brenda worked to keep the corners of her mouth from twitching upward. Kevin, firm as he was in her corner, was a pleasant surprise.

***

"I didn't think Kevin Schneider made house calls," Teak said that evening as she sat with Brenda on the back steps of the duplex. Brenda kept an eagle eye out for any potential customers entering the motel's parking lot while she relished sharing her victory with her new friend.

"I guess he was done for the day and about to head home," Brenda said. "And Violet can be pretty persuasive."

Teak sighed, leaned back on her hands, tilted her head so her short dark hair brushed her shoulders.

"Brenda. I'm not sure if I should tell you this or not. I hate to spoil your pleasure… But you probably should know."

A rivulet of fear oozed through her.

"What? Tell me." Brenda sank lower on the step, hugged her knees.

"You know Carl Levy."

"Yes. I know Carl. What about him?"

"When I was working today, I heard Doctor Simmons talking with Carl and the banker. Doc was just going off duty and I was clearing up something at the desk. Carl's looking for investors, and he was asking Doc if he'd be interested."

"Investors for what?"

"For–" Teak hesitated, "– a new motel on the edge of town." She touched Brenda's shoulder. "It probably won't amount to anything, but I thought you should know."

Brenda walked back to the motel in a daze, full of new worries. Rather than getting pleasure out of watching Violet and Buddy clearing out of the house, it felt like every step they took was another nail in her coffin. In the exhilaration of booting them out, she had failed to consider what the loss of the rental money would mean to her financial situation.

She would have to sell the motel. She hated the idea, but with no income coming in from the house, the horrible review, the ever-present weight of being under Suzanne's scrutiny, and now, the threat of competition, it seemed like her only option.

Brenda reheated the last bit of coffee in the microwave and took the cup and her legal pad outside. As she sat on the step, scripts from the past, unbidden, sashayed through her mind: Her father, after she had suggested, tentatively, that she'd like to go to college: "You don't have the intelligence, Brenda." And Dale, sneering, "Wiping asses. Perfect job for you," when she triumphantly waved her CNA certificate.

Brenda tipped her cup, letting her coffee, suddenly acrid, spill onto the cement in front of her. She stared at the puddle, as dark and bitter as her mood. She should have known she would not be capable of pulling off motel ownership. It was time to put that dream to rest.

She picked up the legal pad, needing to get her thoughts on paper. The letter from the nursing home pleading her to come back slipped out. Brenda picked it up, reread it. This was an omen, telling her she should go back to Illinois, back to the life she was best suited for.

She watched the Baxters pull out of the parking lot. Buddy made a rude gesture. Brenda stared back expressionlessly. She realized she should go into the house, check it over, make sure that it was left in good order, but right now she didn't have the heart.

***

"Noooooooo," whined Ellie. "Noooo, I don't want to go back to stinky Prairie City. I have friends here, Granda. I'm happy here. You are so mean. I hate you!" Ellie wrenched the door open and flounced out. Moments later, the door to Unit Two slammed.

Brenda could hear Ellie's sobs through the wall. Tears welled up in her own eyes. She'd rest on her bed for a moment, close her eyes for a moment, let everything go…for a moment.

***

Brenda woke with a start. With a slight groan, she rose to her feet, feeling groggy and disoriented. She looked outside. It was dusk. How long had she slept? She looked at the clock. Seven. Was that a.m. or p.m.?

Brenda shuffled into the bathroom and used the toilet. As she washed her hands she called out, "Ellie? Where are you, sweet thing?" It must be evening, she thought. She couldn't have slept the entire night away, could she?

107

"Ellie?" Brenda called again. She left her unit, took the few steps over to Unit Two. "Ellie? I bet you're hungry!" She pushed open the door.

The bed was a tumble of blankets and sheets, but there was no sign of the little girl. And Schmoe was missing from his customary place of honor.

CHAPTER SEVENTEEN

Where could Ellie be? Had she gone over to the Anderson's, looking for sympathy? Brenda ran over to their house. Smokey, curled up on the porch, rose to insinuate herself against Brenda's legs, but no one else was around to answer Brenda's staccato knock.

Brenda hurried back to the motel, with seeking eyes and a growing sense of anxiety. She checked the door of each motel room. Every window was dark, for there were no guests tonight except Jimmie, and his motorcycle was missing from its parking place. She wrenched open the doors of the sheds, scanned the interiors. No little girl.

Growing more desperate by the moment, Brenda hauled herself into her car and began creeping up and down the streets of the town, scanning the sidewalks, the storefronts, the yards. When she came to the birdbath and recognized Ms. Winthrop's house, she jerked to a stop.

Once on the porch, she pounded on the door. Without waiting for an answer, she opened it and yelled, "Ms. Winthrop! Have you seen Ellie?"

Ms. Winthrop appeared in the foyer, her mouth forming a silent O. "Goodness, no."

"Is it morning or night?" Brenda asked, still sleep-confused.

"Are you on something?" Ms. Winthrop's tone was sharp.

"You haven't seen Ellie? Talked to her?"

"No I haven't. How can I help?"

"If she stops here or calls you or something, let me know. Thank you." Brenda lurched away, her heart pounding. Where was that sweet girl? What could have happened to her?

Brenda made an illegal U-turn and sped back to the motel where she parked in front of her unit, looked inside again, checked every inch of Ellie's unit. She walked down the length of the motel, rattling doorknobs, calling the little girl's name. Then she slipped through the cedar bushes and ran towards Teak's house.

Teak and Hailey were getting out of their car when Brenda approached them. Ellie was not with them. In fact, Hailey told her that she hadn't seen Ellie all evening, even before they had made a Walmart run.

"Is it evening?" Brenda wanted to get clear on that point anyway.

"Yes, Brenda, it is evening. It's getting darker, you see?" Teak moved over to stand beside Brenda, patted her shoulder.

It was getting darker. And Ellie was out there-somewhere- in the dark.

"Hailey and I will walk over to the school," Teak said. "Maybe she's on the playground. We'll find her, Brenda."

The rumble of Jimmie's motorcycle could be heard, firing once before coming to a stop. Brenda headed toward him at a rapid clip.

"Jimmie!" she screeched as soon as she was within earshot. "Have you got Ellie?"

"Have I what? Brenda, what's going on here?" He held up a hand. "Whoa, Nellie."

"Ellie is missing. I was hoping she was with you." Brenda's chest heaved.

"I haven't seen her, Brenda. Course, I just got back to town. Remember? I went over to Hudson to pick up some Bondo to –"

She interrupted, heedless of what he was about to say.

"I don't know where she is. I don't know where to look. I don'–"

"I'll loop around, looking for her," he said. "I'll check down the street, the park, whatnot. You wait here. Be here when she comes so's you can give her some TLC." He patted her arm before kicking his motorcycle back to life.

Somewhat reassured, Brenda went into her unit and stared at the groceries on the counter. Ellie would be hungry. She could heat up some chicken noodle soup, add a package of ramen noodles to it. Ellie would get a kick out of extra noodles in her soup. Mechanically, she prepared the simple meal, but it had been heated and cooled before Teak and Hailey, and then Jimmie returned.

They had not seen Ellie.

"Brenda, I think you had better call the police." Teak's brown eyes conveyed her worry.

Officer Rollins, the same policeman who had responded to Ellie's 911 a week ago, took her call. The pressing worry overshadowed, but did not remove, her humiliation in being found negligent. At least, she comforted herself, he knows what Ellie looks like.

"You stay where you are," he told her. "I'll put out an alert. You say you don't have any suspicions of anyone taking the child?"

"I don't think so," Brenda said doubtfully. A thread of a possibility did raise its head, but she batted it down. No, not after all these years. Surely not.

"You don't sound sure."

"I think she was upset and ran away. Got lost. I had to—give her some bad news and she didn't take it well."

"We'll see what we can do. Keep thinking about possibilities though. If we don't find her soon, I'll have more questions for you. See if there's anything that might provide a lead." Officer Rollins ended the call.

Teak, standing by, rubbed the tight spot between Brenda's shoulder blades.

"Let's pray," said Teak.

Brenda closed her eyes, heard Teak beseeching the Lord to keep Ellie safe and bring her home, heard Hailey's fervent Amen, opened her eyes, feeling as if she were in a bad dream.

"Thank you, Teak. But you might as well go on home now. I appreciate you coming and looking and praying but there's nothing else you can do now."

"Let's walk around the motel one more time," said Teak. "I can't think that she'd have gone very far."

"I'll go investigate in between the cars over at the dealership," Jimmie offered. While he scoured the lot, Brenda, Teak and Hailey opened every door, checked every room, every bathroom, every shower stall. They looked in the sheds again, behind the sheds, under the bushes, in her car, in the trunk of her car.

They hunted in vain. After Brenda promised to call Teak and Hailey when there was news, they returned to their home. Brenda sat on the edge of her green chair, twisting her fingers, staring at nothing.

Shortly after ten, Officer Rollins and his partner, a fresh face, knocked at the door of her unit. Their expressions gave the message: Ellie was still missing.

"I'm Officer Kasten." The new officer stuck out his hand. "You've checked all the rooms in the motel?"

"Thank you for your help." Brenda returned the handshake. She felt tears filling her eyes but by holding herself rigid, she kept herself in control. Falling to pieces would not help Ellie.

"Yes. We checked and double-checked all the rooms." Mechanically, she answered the questions he rapidly fired at her.

"Ellie Miller. March 14. 2001. She's ten. She's about four and a half feet tall... She's skinny... Brown hair... Her front teeth are oversized for her face... No braces... No glasses.... Freckles, yes... I think she was wearing a yellow T-shirt and blue jeans... Schmoe is missing... Her stuffed dog... Nothing else that I can tell."

"Any photos?" Officer Rollins interjected.

Brenda rummaged through her purse and came up with a wallet sized school picture. Officer Kasten resumed his questioning.

"About seven o'clock...I was–sleeping...No, I didn't hear her leave...I didn't hear a vehicle."

Kasten stood, finally. "Let us know, ma'am, if there is anything else you think of that might be some help, provide a clue."

The officers departed, and Brenda's tears fell unchecked. She felt her body shaking.

"I'll sit with you, Brenda," said Jimmie. "You shouldn't be alone right now."

She sank back into the green Adirondack chair while he, fumbling, made a pot of coffee. Soon he carried two steaming cups over to the table and sat down across from her.

"Are you thinking she lit out on her own?" Jimmie asked.

Brenda took a sip of her coffee. It was very strong, but she was glad to have it, glad to have something to hold on to.

"Ellie was upset because I told her I didn't know if we'd be able to keep on with the motel," she told him. "So yes. I think maybe she ran away."

"Not keep on with the motel? That surprises me about you, Brenda. You don't seem the type to quit so easy."

"So easy? It's been nothing but trouble since the day I first pulled into the parking lot and clunked into a pothole." She started reciting the obstacles she had encountered, but before she had run out of words, he was shaking his head.

"Brenda, Brenda, stop seein' trouble wherever you look. Them are all things you can deal with. For instance, even if there were another motel nearby, them big chain motels cater to other folk than you do. Believe you me, you can make it real nice here and not charge an arm and a leg. Maybe have a pet-friendly room or two. That'll draw a certain type of folks." His kindly blue eyes regarded her steadily.

"But I need rent money from the house," she reminded him. "I'm almost broke. And what about how the Child Protection people find out about her running away will probably be the last straw?" She was so upset her words were a jumble.

"Let it go for now. Let's talk about other things. Have you been caring for Ellie a long time?" Jimmie's voice was casual, soothing, and Brenda relaxed ever so slightly. She took a deep breath, and staring into the blackness of her coffee, nodded twice. The warm smell was a comfort.

"All her life. I watched her grow up." Brenda could remember gazing into the eyes of the Ellie when she was a tiny pink mite and being overcome with a fierce rush of protectiveness. "I fell in love with that little girl right from the beginning. She was an easy baby to love. But Janna never bonded with her."

"Janna her mother?"

"Yes. She had Ellie too young. And I never did learn who the father was." Brenda expelled a short, mirthless laugh. "I don't even know if Janna knew. But Janna's not in the picture anymore." Brenda took a sip of her coffee, glad it was hot, glad it scalded her lip, her throat.

"I wonder if they found anything yet," she said, standing up, peering through the window into the dark parking lot.

"The police know you're waiting. They'll let us know as soon as they know. Janna, that's a pretty name."

Brenda lowered herself, looked at Jimmie. He was sitting loosely, apparently interested in her story, exhibiting no sign of impatience. She huffed out a breath, releasing tension.

"Her name is actually Joanna. I named her for the Kool & the Gang song so popular when she was born. 'Joanna, I love you...'" Brenda half sang a couple of bars. "But right from the beginning we called her Janna." She lapsed into silence, worrying her bottom lip between her teeth.

Baby Joanna had been colicky, and Dale got upset when she cried. Brenda ended up giving her everything she wanted to keep her quiet, to keep her from disturbing her daddy, to keep the peace.

As she grew out of the infant stage, Janna developed into a beautiful little girl, blonde and flirty, wrapping her daddy around her little finger. He spoiled her terribly. Brenda could see it wasn't good for her, but again, she did not want to cause Dale's anger to flare up, didn't want trouble, so she did not intervene.

Dale could be so nasty when he was angry, so mean. He seemed to derive pleasure from goading and insulting Brenda until she dissolved in tears. She'd thought about leaving him, but where could she go? She had no money, no friends, no family she could count on. And she had Janna to think of. Janna, who took her cues from her father on how to treat Brenda and blamed her mother for her acne-scarred face, for all her young troubles.

It was shortly after Janna turned thirteen that Dale had decided to move on.

"I'm leaving," he had told Brenda.

"I'll do better," she said, cold fear settling in her stomach. Difficult as Dale was, how would she manage without him?

His eyes were blue marbles. "You don't get it, do you? It's not what you do, it's who you are. And I don't like you." He stood tall, important, rocking back and forth on the heels of his expensive black leather cowboy boots.

"I've had enough," he said. "I'm heading for Montana. I won't be back."

"What about Janna?"

"What about her?"

"Can you take her out? Go to Subway or something? Sit down and talk to her, tell her you love her, you're not leaving because of her?"

Dale snorted. "She looks like a freak. I'm not taking her anywhere."

A door clicked shut. Janna had been listening. A flash of shame crossed Dale's face. Then he shrugged. "See ya."

With that, he was gone. Sure, he sent child support for a few years. Brenda had to credit him for that. But she never saw him again. And Janna from that day forward was completely defiant. Wild. Reckless. Pregnant at sixteen. Pregnant with Ellie, sweet, precious Ellie.

***

"Janna was my daughter," Brenda told Jimmie now. "But we grew apart. Ellie, now, sweet Ellie…she's my heart."

By midnight, she was weak and jittery from worry and too much coffee. Jimmie left around 2 a.m., saying he'd catch a few winks and be back in the morning. The room seemed empty without his comforting presence. Brenda had turned on the radio, flicked through a few stations, wondering if she'd hear any references to her missing granddaughter. Weather, sports, someone laughing insanely, a hymn…Brenda's fingers stilled. The music was quiet, soothing.

Abide with me, fast falls the eventide.
The darkness deepens; Lord, with me abide.
When other helpers fail and comforts flee,
Help of the helpless, oh, abide with me.

God again! Abiding with her? She recalled how Teak had said the Holy Spirit nudged her, and she had come over with cookies, effectively thwarting the "flower sisters." Would He help her now? Brenda paced the room, her lips forming an awkward prayer.

"O God, I'm so scared, and Ellie is so little. Help her to feel safe and help me to find her." She added a phrase that had risen from a deep almost-forgotten place, "In the Name of the Father, and of the Son and of the Holy Spirit. Amen."

Emboldened by her prayer, Brenda decided to go out and search once more. She grabbed a flashlight and stepped outside.

She wandered beyond the motel, climbed the knoll. She clicked on the flashlight and swung it from side to side, checking under the same cedars she'd checked countless times. Nothing. No one. She turned her gaze toward the now-empty house.

Pooling in the backyard of the house, in sharp contrast to the blackness of the grass surrounding it, was a rectangle of light that hadn't been there before. Light! Brenda's head jerked upward. An upstairs window glowed.

Scarcely able to breathe, she scurried around to the front of the house, pounded up the porch steps, turned the doorknob. The door stuck, but she put her shoulder to it, and it gave way. She stumbled as she gained entrance.

A low wailing whine greeted her, drifting down from the upper floor. Mournful. Familiar. Wonderful.

"Ellie!" Brenda screeched. She was across the vestibule in three leaps, and took the stairs two at a time.

Brenda followed her ears to the bedroom Ellie had loved, jiggled the doorknob.

"Ellie? Let me in!"

In a thin and reedy voice Ellie informed her, "It's locked and I c-c-can't open it. Oh, Granda," she wept, "I peed on the floor. I'm sorry. Get me out. Please get me out."

Brenda fell to her knees and bawled through the keyhole, "Nobody put you in there, did they? Or do anything bad to you, did they?"

"No, Granda. Schmoe and I came here to visit." Ellie hiccoughed and sniffed. "By ourself. We were mad. And I locked the door, but I can't open it and–Granda, get me out!"

Brenda jiggled the doorknob, pushed and pulled. Finally she said, "Sweet thing, I'm going to go get Jimmie. I'll be right back."

"Don't go, Granda. I've been so scared here by myself."

"Child, I need to go get Jimmie." Brenda didn't wait for a reply. She galloped down the stairs and it was only a minute–possibly less–before Brenda was banging on the door of Jimmie's unit.

He came to the door clad only in red and white checked pajama bottoms and his leather vest, unbuttoned and askew.

"Ellie?" he asked immediately.

"Jimmie, I found her! She's in the house! And locked herself–"

"I'll get my tools." Jimmie cut her off. He stepped around her to fetch the bundle of tools from the back of his cycle, looking up to suggest, "You might-could let the police know."

CHAPTER EIGHTEEN

Brenda collapsed on the bed beside a freshly-showered and gently snoring Ellie. Although exhausted, four o'clock in the morning as it was, Brenda's mind was churning over the happenings. Of course Ellie would retreat to the room she loved. Why hadn't she thought to check it?

As she simmered down, she remembered how she had asked God for Ellie's safe return.

"Thank you," she whispered, and it was a prayer.

It was mid-morning before she woke, becoming aware of a foot wedged against her ribs. Brenda regarded Ellie, sound asleep beside her, sprawled out like a starfish, and grinned. How she loved this little girl!

As quietly as she could, Brenda eased off the bed, dumped out the remnants of the thick black coffee Jimmie has served up the night before and started a fresh pot. She showered while the coffee was brewing. Leaving the little girl to sleep as long as she needed to, Brenda slipped outside with damp hair and settled herself, coffee in hand, on the step.

The morning was lovely: fresh, bright, glorious springtime. A song sparrow lent its voice to celebrate. Brenda closed her eyes and breathed deeply. What should she do? Jimmie, she realized, could be right. None of her troubles were insurmountable. But was she up to facing them, working through them? She knew Ellie wanted to stay, but would that be best for the child?

The crunch of footsteps interrupted her pondering.

"Hey, Brenda." Teak, decked out in nursing scrubs decorated with purple and blue felines, hastened toward her. In variance with her cheery outfit, her brow was furrowed, her eyes telegraphing her concern.

"Any news? Yes?"

"Yes." Brenda smiled, big. "She's sleeping. Teak, she was locked in the house! Why didn't we check the house?"

Teak bonked her palm against her forehead.

"Beats me. Thank God you found her!"

"I did thank Him," Brenda said, low. She met Teak's eyes, and a shared moment of recognizing the goodness of God pulsed between them. Then Brenda continued, "Ellie is fine, tired, still sleeping, but fine." She went on to give Teak a condensed version of what had prompted Ellie to go into hiding.

Teak was silent for a moment before saying, "Correct me if I'm wrong, but I got the impression that you were not happy in Prairie City. Are you sure this is what you want to do?"

"Actually, I'm not at all sure. It would be hard to leave. And you're right, I wasn't happy there. But I don't think I have what it takes to run this place." Brenda ran her fingers through her hair. "I have a buyer right now, but for how long? Carl might lose interest, decide not to buy. Then where would I be?"

"I'd miss you," Teak said. She looked at her watch and bit her lip. "I have to go to work now, sorry, I'd love to stay and brainstorm with you. But here's something someone told me once, and it stuck with me: There's only one thing worse than giving up, and that's the regret you feel when you realize you gave up too soon. And this, too." She took a pen out of the pocket of her scrubs, reached for Brenda's hand and jotted something on the back of it.

"Check it out." She gave Brenda a quick squeeze and was gone.

Brenda was trying to decipher what Teak had written—it looked like 1 Pet 57—when Jimmie came out of his room, shutting the door firmly behind him.

"Morning," he called.

"Morning. Want some coffee?" At his nod, she rose and went into her unit to fetch some, moving silently so as not to disturb the still sleeping Ellie. After Brenda handed Jimmie a steaming cup, she showed him the back of her hand.

"Do you know what this could mean?"

Jimmie set his coffee down on the step before he took her hand and peered at Teak's jotting. His hand was warm, and she found comfort in having hers rest there. Releasing it, he replied, "That's a Bible verse. First Peter, chapter five, verse seven."

"A Bible verse? You don't have a Bible, do you?" She thought not, he was traveling light.

"I reckon I might." He sighed in a way she could not understand before he walked down to his bike and rummaged around in his saddlebag, eventually unearthing a battered paperback with "Hope for the Highway" on the cover.

"Just a New Testament," he said, "But that's all we need." He paged without hesitation through the book, located the verse and handed the Bible to Brenda, his finger poised over a line with a 7 in front of it.

Brenda's head was spinning. She would not have suspected that Jimmie was familiar with that book, let alone have one.

121

"Read it out loud," he urged her.

Brenda cleared her throat and read, "'Casting all your anxieties on Him because He cares for you...' Who's Him?"

"That be God. That verse says, give your troubles to God. He cares." Jimmie nudged the book toward her. "Keep it. You might get some good out of it."

"I don't want to take your Bible, Jimmie."

"I'm not usin' it right now." He set his lips and stared over her head. "Take it."

Her fingers closed over the book.

"I'll give it back soon," she promised. He had already reclaimed his cup of coffee and turned away, but he waved his hand over his head, acknowledging he had heard her.

Brenda sank onto the step, her mind a buzz. You'll always regret giving up too soon...Would she spend the rest of her life wishing she had stuck with this? Did she really want to return to Prairie City with her tail between her legs? And the Bible verse! She reread it. "Casting all your anxieties on Him because He cares for you."

God had been helping her, she realized. Providing friends. Finding Ellie. She continued to sit, paging through Jimmie's Bible, reading verses that caught her eye.

"God," she whispered. "I'll take all the help you want to give me. Thank you."

Ellie poked her head out of the door.

"I'm up," she announced. "Can I have Cheerios for breakfast?"

Brenda rose, gathered her in her arms, kissed the top of her head.

"You sure can, sweet thing."

Soon the two were settled at the table with their Cheerios and milk, having a heart-to-heart talk.

"Do we really have to move back?" Ellie pleaded.

Brenda jabbed at her Cheerios, sinking several into the milky depth, stalling.

"If I can figure out a few things," she said finally, "we'll try to make it work."

Ellie waved a spoon and squealed in approval.

"I might have been too hasty," Brenda admitted. "I shouldn't have said we were going to up and quit. But, Ellie. We have to stick together. You can't run off when things don't go your way." Like your mother did. "All right?"

Ellie agreed, then noticing the time, cried, "11:45? It's 11:45? Can I go to school now? I don't want to miss lunch recess. Our horse club is having a meeting."

Brenda marveled at Ellie's ability to set aside the trauma of the day before and revert to the cadence of an ordinary day. She herself was not as resilient. But in the light of morning, buoyed by Ellie's enthusiasm and the encouragement of Teak and Jimmie, she decided not to abandon her dream—yet. She did not want to be burdened in the years to come with the notion she had quit too soon. Memorial Day Weekend was right around the corner, and if that brought a surge in guests, it might be enough income to see her through the next week or so.

After dropping Ellie off at school, Brenda settled into her customary seat in the computer section of the library and punched in its code. Once the computer was unlocked, she posted an updated ad on Craigslist, stating a house would be available for the summer. She knew she'd screen potential renters with more care this time.

After completing that task, Brenda checked the U-Stay site to see if the negative review had been removed. It was still there, but there was a box below it where she could offer a rebuttal. She hesitated, fingers poised over the keys.

How to explain she had merely let the excited Ellie have the enjoyment of checking in the visitor? And she wasn't barking orders, as the reviewer had assumed, she was giving Ellie directions.

Brenda's eyes lingered on the phrase "lazy and unkempt." Is that how she appeared to others? Unkempt? What precisely did that mean, anyway?

She inputted "unkempt" into an online dictionary and a moment later was reading the definition: "untidy and disheveled."

Brenda looked at her rumpled T-shirt, brushed off some particles of indeterminate origin. Maybe she should choose a certain outfit to wear when she was expecting guests. Brenda googled "motel attire" and was mortified when pictures of scantily dressed women came up on her screen.

A librarian doing the rounds halted behind her computer.

"Not appropriate," she hissed. "This is a family library."

Brenda's face grew hot. Her fingers fumbled as she modified her search to include the words "front-desk," and the images changed to proper ones. The librarian, after a beat, moved on without saying anything more.

After checking out the options, many of which were too fancy for her simple motel, a plain black vest caught her eye. Something like that could be worn over a polo shirt, or even a T-shirt. And it wouldn't cost much, she thought.

Could she have "Neat as a Pin Motel" embroidered on the vest, maybe with a little stylized straight pin beneath it? Pulling her ever-present legal pad toward her, Brenda sketched a vest with the logo on the upper right side. Nice.

Her phone buzzed.

"Neat As A Pin Motel," Brenda, conscious of her surroundings, whispered the greeting. "How may I help you this morning?"

"Is this Brenda Miller?"

Brenda recognized the voice of Suzanne from Child Protection Service. She stood, abandoning her computer to move outside of the library where she could continue the conversation full voice.

"Yes," she said. "This is Brenda."

"We were contacted by the Miskomin Police Department this morning. As well as…another party. Is it true that Ellie ran away last night?" Suzanne was abrupt and cool.

"She's been found. She's fine. She's good."

"She must not be 'fine and good' if she is running away from home. What can you tell me?"

Brenda heaved a sigh. "She didn't run away from home, she ran away to home."

"That makes no sense."

"We are staying in a motel temporarily. As you have seen. We plan to move into the house as soon as we possibly can. Ellie ran to the house, the home we are working toward. She was upset. We talked things over, she is all right now."

Suzanne explained to Brenda that she was Very concerned and would continue to monitor the situation. Brenda murmured what she hoped were appropriate responses and ended the call as soon as she could.

CHAPTER NINETEEN

Brenda was attempting to vacuum some life into the flat carpet in Unit Seven later that afternoon. It was the Thursday before Memorial Day, and she wanted to have another room available for the weekend, if she could manage it. A knock-knock on the frame of the open door interrupted her work. A potential guest? She fixed a welcoming smile on her lips and looked up.

The middle-aged man in the doorway, stout, balding, and genial, introduced himself as "Arnold Williams, head of the Community Club," and explained, "Have you heard about the parade we got going here on Memorial Day?"

Brenda hadn't.

"It's a small parade. Veterans, Scouts, high school and middle school bands. That kind of thing."

"It sounds nice," Brenda said, disappointed that he was not looking for a room and wondering why he was sharing this information with her.

Arnold ran a palm over the top of his head, ending the movement with a tiny flourish before he continued his spiel. "In the past, we ended the parade in the motel parking lot. The groups dispersed from here. Sorry for the short notice. Just realized we probably should get your okay."

"Of course," Brenda said immediately. Any positive PR for the motel was a good thing. Maybe she could fill the refrigerator in the empty house with bottles of water and offer them to the veterans when they finished marching.

"Good idea," Jimmie said when she mentioned her plan to him. "By the way, I won't be around, Brenda. I'm going on a Veterans' Charity Ride. Travelin' from Hudson to Stevens Point. Be gone all day."

"Sounds like a good cause," she said, realizing she'd miss his presence.

***

Memorial Day was sunny and warm. Clusters of onlookers lined the main street and clapped their appreciation for the veterans who marched–or were transported via a small trailer–down the street. As the parade wound to a close, people congregated in her parking lot. Brenda was gratified to see how appreciative they were of the water. A half a dozen of the veterans stood in a tight circle and commenced chewing the fat.

"Thank you so much, this is real nice of you," one of them told Ellie, who was in charge of handing out the bottles of chilled water.

"Thanks for your service," she responded as Brenda had schooled her.

Brenda had seen Hailey marching in the Middle School band, and now noticed her wandering toward the brown house with another girl. The house! Brenda kicked herself. She should have put a For Rent sign on it before the crowd gathered in the parking lot.

At any rate, she was glad she had thought to offer water. It was a great way to get herself noticed and in a positive way. Brenda's eyes drifted to an older fellow who seemed to be searching for something and she headed toward him, a spring in her step.

Hailey and her friend intercepted her to toss their bottles into the trash bag she held.

"Thanks for the water," Hailey said.

"You're welcome," Brenda responded with a smile. "Who's this?"

"She's Lizzie. Lizzie, this is Brenda who owns the motel."

"It's nice to meet you, Lizzie."

Lizzie, a slender girl with brown pigtails, nodded in return and dipped her chin toward the dealership. "What's Princess Gretchen up to now?"

Carl and his daughter had appeared at the edge of the lot in full showmanship mode. Gretchen was displaying a bottle of Mountain Dew and a Snickers bar. Carl held a megaphone.

"SODA POP AND CANDY BARS!" Carl's magnified voice boomed. "RIGHT NEXT DOOR. PLENTY FOR ALL."

"Classmate?" asked Brenda, her heart sinking as she watched the crowd in her lot gravitated toward the car dealership.

"I guess you could call us that. But she's so much more mature," Hailey said with a cattiness Brenda hadn't heard from the girl previously. She and Lizzie drifted away. Brenda and Ellie and several abandoned bottles of water were alone.

"Well, that's that," Brenda said into the sudden silence. "Let's clean up, shall we?"

Ellie, without enthusiasm, joined Brenda in picking up the discarded water bottles. As they were finishing their task, a car pulled into the parking lot. A broad smile crossed Ellie's face.

"It's Gabby!"

An apparent mother-and-daughter team slammed their doors

in unison and headed toward them. Ellie raced toward the girl and the two hugged.

The mother smiled at Brenda.

"I'm Stacey Bornson." Stacey was relaxed, tall, her blonde hair pulled back in a messy bun. She extended a hand. "My Gabby just loves your Ellie."

Brenda squeezed and released the proffered fingers. "I'm Brenda. It's nice to meet you. Ellie thinks a lot of Gabby, too."

"You live in this motel, Gabby said?" Stacey perused it briefly. "You've done a lot with it. Nice. We came into town to watch the parade, get a few groceries, and Gabby saw Ellie here and got to wondering if she could come home with us? Spend the afternoon?"

Ellie stuck her head under her grandmother's arm and hopped twice. Her eyes were shining. When was the last time Brenda had seen her so excited? And when had Ellie ever been so confident with a friendship before?

Brenda nodded her permission.

"Of course she may. Thank you for thinking of her. It would have been a real quiet afternoon for her here."

"We'll be fishing off our dock," Stacey said. "And the girls will have life jackets on. We are very safety-minded. When would you like her home?"

"Five?" Brenda suggested. "There is school tomorrow, so I'd like to keep her on a school-night schedule."

"Five is perfect," Stacey said. "I'm with you on keeping to a schedule. Two more weeks."

At Brenda's bidding, Ellie raced into her unit to get a sweatshirt. She gave her grandmother an exuberant hug, and she was gone.

Two more weeks. Once school was out for the summer, she'd

have to find something to keep the child busy. Brenda did not want her lying in bed all day watching TV. She rounded up her legal pad and on a clean page, started a new category: Ellie-Summer.

Brenda was toying with possible activities for Ellie when an activity she'd like to try herself drifted into her mind. What would it be like to ride a motorcycle? She wondered how it would feel to wrap her arms around Jimmie and experience the freedom of zipping off somewhere with him.

She shook her head, realizing this line of thinking would get her nowhere. Jimmie was still mourning the loss of his wife. He would not be interested in a slightly overweight, unkempt woman. Anyway, riding a motorcycle might trigger her own unpleasant memories.

Restless, Brenda put away her legal pad and pen. She needed a diversion. She'd go over to the house, be sure it was ready for new renters. On the short trip across the lot, she spotted Teak sitting on her front steps, a large book open on her lap, face lifted, eyes closed. Brenda hesitated, torn between being rude by not acknowledging her and being insensitive and intruding in her private moment. Her quandary was solved when Teak opened her eyes, waved, and beckoned.

Brenda climbed the knoll, slipped between the cedar bushes, and crossed the alley.

"I don't want to bother you if you're in the middle of something," she said, noticing that the book Teak held was a Bible.

"I was finishing up my quiet time," Teak replied. "I was reading in Colossians. Listen: 'You are chosen by God, holy and dearly loved.'"

Chosen. Holy. Dearly loved. Brenda made a sound she hoped signaled appreciation. The phrase fit happy, helpful, capable Teak well. But it certainly would not apply to her, Brenda.

"We have a good, good God," Teak said with a sigh as she closed the Bible and set it carefully aside. "What are you up to?"

"Oh, not much. Business had been good all weekend, but today things have slowed down considerably. And Ellie's gone to a friend's for the afternoon." A wisp of unease niggled at Brenda. In her pleasure at Ellie's excitement, she had not considered the ramifications. She did not know the Bornsons. Would Ellie be okay?

There was nothing she could do about it now. Thinking she might as well keep herself busy, she broached a subject that had been on her mind ever since Teak had whipped up the set of curtains for Unit Two.

"I was wondering," she said to Teak now, "if you could show me how to make curtains. Ellie's don't seem too complicated. Ruth has so much material, you know, and if you wouldn't mind give me a tutorial, I would think I could learn—"

Teak cut her off mid sentence. "Of course," she said warmly. "A very good idea. Handmade curtains would certainly freshen up all of the rooms, and set them apart from a chain motel. Let me show you what I did with Ellie's curtains."

She started to move toward the motel. Brenda stayed put.

"Are you sure? I didn't mean today. You must have something more fun to do on Memorial Day."

Teak shook her head.

"Hailey is spending the afternoon with her friend, Lizzie Gordon. Did you meet Lizzie?"

"Yes, Hailey introduced me to her today."

"She's been a good friend for Hailey. I'm glad for something to do, Brenda. And this will be fun."

Soon the two women were up in Ruth's sewing room choosing fabrics. Teak lifted the cover from Ruth's sewing machine and inspected it.

131

"Let me oil this for you," she offered. "And then we can go ahead and start."

From the sewing room window, Brenda watched for cars coming into the motel's lot. She ran down to the Unit One Office in the late afternoon to register an older couple. They would occupy Unit Nine for the night. As luck could have it, a shy young man stopped by while she was finishing up with them. He did not make eye contact with anyone and kept shifting from foot to foot. Brenda put him into Unit Eight.

"There's not a coffee pot in the units," she told them all, "but you can come down here in the morning and get a cup of fresh-brewed coffee if you like. And please let me know if you need anything. I want you to enjoy your stay."

Don't be too gushy, Brenda schooled herself. You'll scare them off. After the guests had made their way to their rooms, she returned to the sewing room, where, under Teak's tutelage, she finished a set of curtains for Unit One.

"I think I can tackle the next set." She had the necessary confidence now, as well as measurements and a few jotted notes in her pad. "Thanks so much, Teak."

"Be sure and call me if you have any questions." Teak rose from the chair and stretched. "Guess I'll head on home now."

"Yes, me too. I'll hang these curtains and see if Ellie notices." She looked at the clock. It was ten minutes past five. Where was the child? Her phone buzzed, stirring up a jolt of dread.

"I'll see myself out. You take that." Teak headed for the stairs.

"Granda? This is Ellie."

Brenda calmed herself by breathing deeply. "Child, are you okay? You were supposed to be home by now."

"I know. I'm fine. Granda, we caught fish! A lot. They want to know if I can stay for a fish supper. Can I?"

Before Brenda could answer, Stacey's voice took over. "We'd love to have Ellie stay for our fish fry. Sorry we didn't call sooner. The fish were biting like mad!"

Brenda was not thrilled about the last-minute change in plans but gave her assent, relieved the child was fine and knowing it would mean much to her.

"She needs to come home right after she eats."

"Absolutely."

Brenda folded the new curtains and carried them over to the motel. She soon realized they were not suitable for Unit One. The color was off just enough to be irritating. She shook her head, realizing she should have brought a sample of the fabric down to the room to check before putting all the work into making curtains. Still, they would not go to waste. There were plenty of other rooms that could use these particular curtains. She pondered. Unit Seven?

They would be perfect. Soon Brenda was inside that unit, exchanging the threadbare old curtains for the fine new ones. While she worked, the guest from Unit Eight pulled up in his sporty red car, and one of the occupants of Unit Nine, the older man, came out of his room. Did they know each other?

Brenda peeked out the window, watching and listening. The shy man had a cardboard container in his hands. He handed it to the older fellow.

"This here is leeches. Carl says to dump 'em in the toilet without Val noticing. Then when she goes in there—her reaction will be natural."

"I can't wait," said the older man, chuckling. "Poor Valerie."

"When you stop over to the dealership tomorrow, Carl's gonna ask Valerie how the night's stay went."

"Everyone in the place will get an earful, that's for sure!"

The two men snickered, and the younger man warned, "Be sure you don't leave the container in the room."

Brenda had heard enough. She pushed the door open and stepped outside. The expressions on the two men's faces when they realized she had heard their conversation would have amused her greatly if she were in the mood to be amused.

"I'll take the container for you right now," she said, reaching for the leeches. The shy man reddened and studied his shoes. The older man made an awkward reference to it being just a joke, a prank.

"But why?"

"Carl asked us to do this for him. A gag, he said."

"I'm not laughing," Brenda replied. She took a deep, steadying breath. No ambitious car dealer was going to get in her way. She spotted Carl in his lot, polishing cars. She headed toward him.

"All those kids over here this morning, sticky fingerprints on my cars." His tone was agitated as he bent over his work, much too busy to give her the time of day.

"Carl."

He ignored her, moving his polishing rag in ever-increasing circles.

"You planted people in my motel to try to sabotage me."

"Lady, I don't know what you're talking about."

"Don't try to worm out of it," she said. "You should be ashamed of yourself." Fueled by building outrage, she continued, "That was just plain mean. You need to accept the fact that the motel is not for sale and is not going to be for sale." She turned on heel and marched back to her motel, ignoring Carl's sputtering remarks.

It was almost six-thirty before Gabby and her dad brought Ellie back to the motel. Ellie handed Brenda a fragrant, foil-covered plate.

"Stacey sent some fish for you, Granda!" Ellie was filthy but triumphant. "I caught seven fish, Granda. Seven!"

Gabby's father was pleased to take the live bait off of Brenda's hands.

CHAPTER TWENTY

Jimmie settled himself in the Adirondack chair, his coffee, steaming hot, in hand.

"Ya know, I've been thinking about the busted up siding on the bottom out there. Needs a little TLC."

"Don't I know it," Brenda sighed. "Any ideas, Jimmie, that wouldn't cost an arm and a leg?"

"Well." He sipped his coffee. "Have you thought about maybe ripping it off and replacing it with, oh, faux stones or something?"

Brenda tried to visualize what he was talking about.

"How do you install them?"

"Comes in panels. Three by four foot panels. We'd screw 'em into the studs. Over to Cumberland, not so far from here, you know, there's a café that has that type of skirting. Would you–" Jimmie took a sip of coffee, uncharacteristically at a loss for words.

"What are you getting at? Would I what?" Brenda had been emptying the dish rack, putting away dry dishes but she quit the task to focus on Jimmie.

Jimmie's face was reddening, but he looked at Brenda directly.

"Would you like to take a cycle ride over there with me, take a look at it? Maybe have lunch? Course, I'd round you up a helmet."

Heat crept into her own face.

"It sounds tempting...is it safe?" She clasped and unclasped her hands.

"Course it is. Why so jittery? You have a run in with a cycle?"

"No, I ...." Brenda trailed off, not wanting to bring up the accident that was the basis for her agitation.

"Go on," Jimmie said. He saluted Brenda with his coffee cup. "I'm all ears." He assumed a listening posture.

"I was in a car accident," she heard herself saying. "That's why I get freaked out sometimes."

"Brenda." Jimmie put down his cup, wrapped an arm around her shoulders.

"My mother was killed. We were going into Chicago. Shopping. For my concert." His warmth comforted. She sniffed and gulped.

"Father said if it weren't for me we wouldn't have been travelling on a bad night."

"You were how old?"

"Fifteen. I still miss her."

"Course you do. But it's not your fault. Accidents happen."

"I try to believe that. But his words still haunt me."

"He was most likely dealin' with his own pain and not being rational. How's your father nowadays?"

She shrugged.

"Not sure. He moved to Florida, oh, probably twenty years ago now. We aren't in contact." She glanced at Jimmie's motorcycle, back at his kind eyes, his messy curls.

"Maybe...it would be healing for me...if I let you take me for a ride."

His smile transformed his face.

"Good for you, Brenda."

And so it was the next morning, after Ellie was settled at school, that Brenda, having checked and rechecked the battery on her cell phone, donned the borrowed helmet and stiff gloves and approached Jimmie's motorcycle.

"Left side," said Jimmie, "if you please." Brenda placed a palm on his narrow shoulder and stepped up on the peg. She threw her right leg over the leather seat.

Jimmie revved up the engine.

"All set?" He glanced over his shoulder, and at her nod, added, "Hang on." Tentatively, she placed her fingers on his waist. When the cycle lurched forward, she grabbed him fully, decorum out the window.

Jimmie started slowly, as if to give her time to acclimate to the ride. Brenda's view was concentrated on the brown leather of Jimmie's back. She was in a bubble consisting of the white noise of the cycle, the roar of the wind, and the solid sense of the man in front of her. Various smells rose up sharply and departed as quickly: the earthy smell of manure, new-mowed grass, motor oil.

It was a grand day, sunny with a bit of a breeze. Brenda knew she was not dressed for a cycle ride, as she was wearing her mustardy pea coat, but that was her best option, and it offered some protection from the wind.

Brenda had never experienced a motorcycle ride before and she found driving without walls intoxicating. All of her cobwebs and worries flew to the four winds. By the time they had covered the 40-odd miles and reached Cumberland, her smile was continual and unforced. She caught Jimmie looking at her as if he liked what he saw, and a fluttery feeling rose up in her tummy.

Jimmie parked in front of the small café. He got off the cycle and extended a hand for Brenda. They walked over to get a closer look at the simulated rock skirting. Brenda ran her hand over the stones, appreciating the texture.

"It looks natural," she said. "Something like this would be perfect for our motel."

"These panels go up three feet. Good height. It's all made from polyurethane so it is light and easy to work with. We can check what they have down to the home improvement store." Jimmie, sounding like an excited schoolboy, was obviously sold on the idea.

Brenda was, too, provided it wasn't too expensive.

"Let me get some tenants back in the house first," she said. "Once I have that rent money coming in, I can pay for the panels. I hope."

"We can go inside here, sit down." He nudged her toward the door of the small café. It was early, a few minutes after eleven, and most of the tables were empty. They seated themselves at an oilcloth-covered table near the rear of the room. Brenda, feeling awkward, studied the laminated menu in front of her.

A heavily-tattooed waitress came by and set a couple of red plastic glasses of water in front of them as well as two sets of silverware wrapped in paper napkins. Her hello was cordial. Brenda took a sip of water and schooled herself to relax. This was Jimmie, just Jimmie, the same fellow she'd been drinking coffee with every morning. There was no reason to be uptight.

"You did okay on the ride, then," he stated more than asked.

She nodded, and a slow smile spread across her face.

"I'm so glad I did it. It was wonderful."

"My wife, my Angie used to say, 'Sometimes we gotta do the hard things.'"

"And sometimes they end up not being so hard after all."

Brenda was still reveling in the freedom of the ride. With an effort, she turned her attention to her menu.

"I feel like a burger," Jimmie mentioned. "And you?"

"I feel like a human being," she replied tartly. "A human being who would love a grilled cheese sandwich." Decision made, she pushed the menu aside and suggested, "Tell me about Angie."

"Angie." The name sat soft in his mouth for a moment, and a bit of a smile played on his lips. "She was a sweet gal, that's for sure. Loved herself a mason jar of peach sweet tea. Always good spirited. She was one to have vases of wild flowers sprinkled throughout the house. I never paid them no mind till they weren't there anymore. And whenever there was the slightest breeze, she'd open up the front and back doors, encouraging the outdoors in."

His words came slowly at first, and then more rapidly, as if anxious to be set free. The waitress, returning to take the order, did not distract him for long. Brenda learned that Jimmie and his Angie had been married for almost thirty years before she died.

"Cancer," he said, brushing over that part of the story as if it were too painful to relate. He brightened as he shared that they had a son, "a real bright kid" who was living in the home Jimmie owned in Columbia, South Carolina.

"Sam's finishin' up college," he said. "He's occupyin' the house, him and a buddy." He paused, unwrapped his silverware from the confining napkin. "I can't bring myself to go back there. It's just not home without Angie." He looked at Brenda, his eyes tortured.

"So you've been traveling," Brenda said.

"Running," Jimmie corrected. "It's been a year and a half, and I'm still running."

"Sometimes," she reminded him, "you gotta do the hard things."

Their meals arrived then, and the conversation turned to other topics.

"There's supposed to be a good meat market in this town," Jimmie said, scooping up ketchup with a final French fry. "Louie's, I think it's called. Want to go check it out?"

Brenda was willing. The rich smoky aroma met them in the parking lot and helped convince Jimmie to purchase a couple of packages of Louie's award-winning sausages.

"Not sure how I'll cook these," he commented as he stowed his package in one of the saddlebags on his motorcycle.

"We have that fire ring in the back yard of the house," Brenda remembered. "If you could find us some wood, Jimmie, maybe we could have a wienie roast."

Jimmie's eyes lit up.

"Oh, I'll find some wood," he promised. "These dogs will be delicious cooked over an open fire."

Ellie was excited at the prospect of a campfire. She helped Brenda set buns and condiments, cans of soda, a bag of chips and some baby carrots on the picnic table. Although the bricks surrounding the backyard fire pit had tumbled, Brenda and Ellie had been able to stack them well enough to provide a safe haven for the chunks of wood that Jimmie produced and set aflame. He had found some roasting sticks, too, and soon all three were enjoying their meal. Ellie explained, not for the first time, the rules of her Wild Horses Club. Brenda observed Jimmie who was listening with a slight smile on his face. He seemed almost happy, she thought, and it was good to see.

He was roasting his third hot dog, and Brenda was selecting the perfect potato chip, when Ellie, who was preparing a second hot dog and chattering nonstop, interrupted herself to exclaim, "Hey!"

None of them had noticed the small brown and black dog that had sneaked into the yard until she jerked the hot dog from Ellie's dangling stick. The pup trotted under the cedar bushes and ate her bounty in worried haste.

"You punk," growled Jimmie, directing the remark to the little dog. "You git, now." Despite the words, his tone was affectionate, and the dog inched out of the security of the bushes and rejoined them. Ellie offered pieces of her empty bun and lavished her with pats and belly rubs.

"Granda, this is a nice dog," she said. "She don't got a collar, either. Maybe she needs a home."

"Ellie, I know where you're going with this and it's not going to happen," warned Brenda. "We are not equipped to take on a dog right now."

"But Granda, she loves me," Ellie said. She scratched behind her shaggy ears. "Don't you, girl?" The little dog thumped her tail.

"Ellie, a nice dog like this, I reckon she has a home," Jimmie said. He wiped his fingers on a paper napkin, reached for a can of Coke. "Probably just out exploring the neighborhood. But Brenda. Do you have a bowl or pot or something? We need to give this punk some water. She's probably dying of thirst."

The dog lapped up the proffered water appreciatively and hung around while they cleaned up the remnants of their cook out. Despite Ellie's objections, the dog was left to her own resources when they retired to their units in the motel.

***

Ellie spotted the little dog curled up on the front porch of the brown house when she came outside the following morning. She ran over to her, greeting her as if she were a long-lost friend. It was with reluctance that the little girl broke away to go to school.

The dog stayed nearby all day while Brenda and Jimmie

worked in one of the units. Jimmie re-grouted the bathtub and tile and performed some magic on a clogged sink while Brenda washed down the woodwork and walls and considered repainting them. Butterscotch, she thought. Light, light butterscotch would be lovely. She'd match the paint to one of the fabrics from Aunt Ruth's stash, and make up another set of curtains for the room.

"I reckon," said Jimmie, coming out of one of the bathrooms, a streak of white across one cheek, "that punk could stay with me until we find her home."

"Jimmie, I don't want dogs in the motel. They might bark and disturb the other guests."

"Just one unit? It'd be a draw, like I told you before. You might-could charge extra for a pet. You can make the room I'm using be the pet-friendly one. It's down at the end, any barking wouldn't be as noticeable."

Brenda considered. The fact that a residue of skunk stink hovered in the corners of the room sealed the deal in her mind, and she sighed her consent.

"She'll need a dog run or pen or something. She can't run loose, with that busy road out there. Plus think about the parking lot. We can't have our guests having to dodge a dog."

"I'll make a dog run," Jimmie promised.

"And if an owner shows, the game is up," she added, still not excited about the idea.

"Absolutely." Jimmie snapped his fingers, and the little dog scurried to the man. "You're in, Punk. You're in."

Ellie was thrilled when she came home to find that the little dog–Punk–was still with them. She spent the evening throwing sticks for her to fetch and acquainting her with the dog run that Jimmie had set up in the grassy area between the motel and the sheds.

"Tomorrow," warned Brenda, "we'll check to see if there's any LOST DOG notices in the paper."

Punk spent the night in Jimmie's room, even though Ellie had pleaded to have the dog stay with her. But Brenda was firm.

"No, Ellie. I had enough trouble ridding your room of all the hair Smokey shed while she was there. I'm not going through that again. If we have a pet room for our motel, it will be down at the far end. Period. End of story."

In the morning, after Brenda dropped Ellie off at school, she stopped at the Kwik Trip in town and fueled up her car. She went inside the station to pay for her fuel and an unnecessary doughnut when she spotted the local weekly paper, hot off the press. Brenda added a paper to her purchases and carried it over to one of the tables near the coffee station. Munching on her doughnut, she turned directly to the classifieds.

LOST IN MISKOMIN

Brown-and-black dog
Nine months old
30 pounds
Answers to "BELLA"

A phone number completed the entry.

Ellie was bitterly disappointed when she came home to school, ready for puppy fun, to find the dog gone. She retired to her bed to hug Schmoe and sulk.

She's getting too old for that thing, Brenda thought. But this was not the time to bring that up. Instead she said, infusing cheeriness into her voice, "Bella's owner was thrilled to get her back, Ellie. It wouldn't be fair for us to keep her. Once we are living in the house, we'll get us a dog for keeps."

"When's that gonna happen?" muttered Ellie, still peeved.

A car pulling into the parking lot distracted them, and soon Ellie, her sulks forgotten at least for a time, was busy helping Brenda register a tall, thin man and a short, round lady for the night.

"Unit Eight is a real fine room," Ellie assured them.

CHAPTER TWENTY-ONE

"Hi Brenda!" Hearing a familiar voice, Brenda glanced up from watering the marigolds outside of the motel to smile at Hailey and her companion, tousle-headed Lizzie.

"You girls are up and about early for a Saturday," said Brenda. "Ellie's still asleep. And, yes, she does want to go to Kids' Club with you tonight."

"Good! We'll pick her up at quarter to seven. But that's not why we're here. Lizzie stayed overnight last night and we were talking and got an idea we want to ask you about." Hailey's words tumbled over themselves.

"Shoot," said Brenda, curious now. She set her green plastic watering can on the step.

"Hailey said you might need renters." Lizzie needed no coaxing. "And my sister is looking for a place to stay for the summer."

"Just for the summer?" Brenda could hardly believe her ears.

"Yeah. See, Mary, my sister, she and her two kids have been staying with us while her husband, that would be Joe, was deployed."

"His tour got done early and he's home now," Hailey spelled

out. She leaned against the door and looked from Lizzie to Brenda.

"I'm not sure I follow," said Brenda. But a spark of hope kindled within.

"Mary and Joe want to find their own place," said Lizzie, pulling on a braid, "Just until their apartment opens up. We're kinda crowded."

Brenda learned that Joe and Mary had subleased their apartment and their tenant wasn't planning on moving out until the end of the summer.

"This might work." Brenda was cautiously optimistic. "I'll give them a call, see if they want to take a look at the house."

They did. When a white Subaru entered the motel parking lot that afternoon, Brenda, who had been keeping the door and her ears open for their arrival, came out of Unit Nine. She had been erasing evidences of the previous night's occupant, freshening it up for new guests. Now she wiped her right hand on her jeans before offering it to the young couple approaching her.

"Hi, I'm Mary Fields." Mary, who Brenda reckoned was about the same age as her Janna would be, shared Lizzie's dark blue eyes and shy smile. "And this is Joe."

The straight-backed young man gave Brenda's hand a firm, brief pump.

"The in-laws are great," Joe said, "but we need a place of our own. Start rebuilding our little family unit."

"I understand." Brenda nodded. "Come on and see the house. I hope it will work for you."

Mary and Joe loved the house and cozy backyard. The three adults stood on the porch and talked logistics.

"Caroline's semester ends mid-August," Joe said, referring to his sister who was sub-leasing their apartment in the city. "And then she'd be graduating and moving on. So could we stay until

Labor Day?"

"Then Ollie can start pre-K in the city school," said Mary.

The entire summer to get the rest of the motel in shape and three whole months of rent money.

"That would work out just fine for me," Brenda said, pleased. "You can move in whenever you want."

"Roger that," Joe said. "We'll start moving in after church tomorrow."

***

Shortly after noon the next day the Fields family pulled up in front of the brown house, their Subaru filled to bursting with two young children and their trappings. A pickup truck followed, a crib and a scattering of suitcases and plastic totes piled in the back. Hailey's friend Lizzie jumped out of the passenger's side of the cab. With Ellie's enthusiastic assistance, Lizzie kept the little ones entertained in the back yard while Mary, Joe, and the driver of the pickup carried in their belongings.

Brenda brought some juice boxes and crackers over to the backyard and was greeted with happy cries. She was introduced to curly haired Allie, who was just two, and Oliver, almost five and continually in motion. He held a cracker between his teeth and jiggled it up and down, to the amusement of his little sister, until Lizzie told him to "cut it out."

"Patience, Lizzie," the driver of the pickup called, opening the back door a crack. It was a woman, Brenda realized, with short hair tucked up inside a ball cap. "Remember, 'be patient with kids, they are just beginners.'"

"Okay, Mom," Lizzie sighed. "Come out and meet Brenda."

Katie Gordon did just that, and Brenda felt comfortable with her at once. She was a plain-faced woman, about her own age Brenda reckoned, with a no-nonsense demeanor. The two cooked up the plan for an impromptu housewarming picnic. Brenda had assembled a pasta salad earlier and it was chilling in her little refrigerator. She'd love to share it, she said, and Katie ran down to the store for deli meat for sandwiches and "whatever else I see that looks good." Lizzie spotted Hailey coming out of her house, and the Anderson's were invited as well.

Teak smiled at her daughter. "I knew we bought that watermelon for a reason!" she said.

Brenda impulsively invited Jimmie to the gathering too. By the time the Fields family had all of their possessions in their zones of approximated use in their new home, Katie had returned from the store with two bags of picnic essentials.

Jimmie and Joe built a small fire in the fire ring, while little Ollie watched in fascination. Mary relaxed and held baby Allie and the other women spread out the food and opened a package of paper plates. Soon everyone was enjoying the meal.

When a car came into the parking lot and stopped in front of the house, Brenda, whose ears were attuned for potential motel guests, got up at once to see who it was. She returned to the backyard leading a man and two teenage boys.

"This is my husband Bill," Katie made a general introduction, "and our two sons, Josh and Kyle. Are you guys hungry?" She gestured toward the remnants of the repast.

Bill revealed that they had stopped at a McDonald's on their way home from—Brenda did not catch what they had been up to—but "would sure enjoy a piece of that watermelon."

Everyone lingered around the fire. Hailey ran back to her house and returned with a half-bag of marshmallows. Ellie was excited to roast them. Lizzie's brothers got Ollie involved in a Frisbee toss. Soon Ellie abandoned her marshmallows and joined them. Bill Gordon and Jimmie, who had both served in the Navy, became immersed in an animated discussion with Joe, still enrolled in the National Guards.

Brenda was quiet, noticing the bonds between the couples. Katie and Bill, while seated apart, exchanged frequent smiles; Joe and Mary held hands. What would it have been like if she and Dale had stayed together? If it were Janna and a husband who sat where Joe and Mary did? She shook her head slightly, dislodging thoughts of what wasn't to be.

"Brenda, throw over the marshmallows, will ya please?" asked Jimmie. "These embers are too good to waste." He gestured to the bag at her elbow, and Brenda passed it over. His "thank you" conveyed more than the simple words, and his smile was for her alone.

CHAPTER TWENTY-TWO

"I got good news, Granda!" Ellie greeted her grandmother on the last day of school. She tossed her stuffed backpack into the backseat and slid in next to it. After her seatbelt clicked, she added, "Gabby is having a "School's Out!" party."

Brenda slid away from the curb in front of the school, and caught Ellie's eye in the rearview mirror. Her smile invited the little girl to go on.

"We are going to ride on a train where you get pizza." Ellie was quick to oblige. "Gabby's mom said she could have four friends, and I'm one of the four friends!" She flipped her hair. "Karen is coming, and Lilly, and Meg."

"Did you give Ms. Winthrop my thank you card?" Brenda asked when Ellie paused for a breath. She had sent a card to school with Ellie that morning. Included with a thank you for the teacher's help in making Ellie's transition to a new school so painless, she had also asked about any tutoring opportunities, for Ellie's reading skills were still shaky.

"Yes I did, and she said thank you and she'd call you. What is she going to call you about?" Without waiting for an answer,

Ellie returned to the topic of the party and Brenda learned it was scheduled for the next evening.

***

All day Thursday Ellie was nearly bursting with anticipation.

"We are going to have the final meeting of the Wild Horses Club on the train," she said soon after she woke up. She interrupted the brushing of her teeth to remind Brenda, "Gabby says to be at her house before four-thirty so we can get to the station on time." And even while she was helping Brenda refresh a couple of the rooms that had housed guests the night before, she could talk of nothing else but the upcoming train ride.

"I've never ridden a train before. And this one serves pizza! Gabby's mom will bring me home, she said to tell you. It might be late, though. Is that okay?"

Brenda, not for the first time, said that it was, and added, 'You might as well change now, sweet thing, and I'll drive you out to Gabby's house." It would be good to get the excited child on her way. She pushed the cart of cleaning supplies down to the shed and was walking back to Unit One when her phone rang.

"Hello, Mrs. Miller? This is Ms. Winthrop. Do you have a moment?"

Brenda said she did, and, standing in front of Ellie, pantomimed combing hair and brushing teeth while listening to what Ellie's teacher had to say. Ms. Winthrop agreed that, although Ellie had made progress, she was not where she should be as a reader.

"I'd love to tutor her a couple days a week myself," she offered. "If she would like to meet me at the library-or on my front porch-through June?"

Brenda dug in the front pockets of her jeans, searching for her keys while she continued the conversation. She finally spotted them on the counter in Unit One, half-hidden by her coffee cup.

Ellie by this time was sitting in the back seat of the car, her hair carefully combed and her seatbelt on, gesturing frantically.

After settling on a nominal fee, Brenda ended the call. Moments later, she was behind the wheel of the car, but even during the initial backing up, knew something was wrong. She got out and discovered that the front driver's side tire was flat and—she circled the car to discover—so was the rear tire on the passenger's side.

"Let's go," Ellie sang out. "It's already after four."

Brenda kicked a tire and opened Ellie's door. "Get out, sweet thing. I'm going to see if Teak can bring you. This car has two flat tires!"

Ellie tumbled out of the car and checked the tires for herself. She stared at her grandmother, mouth open in consternation.

"How'd that happen?"

"Beats me. It will take a while to get two tires fixed. Time we don't have. Let's run over to Anderson's."

But Teak was not home, and Hailey wasn't sure when her mother, who had taken the car, would be back. There was no sign of any of the Fields family or their vehicle. Jimmie's cycle was nowhere in sight either, not that Brenda would allow Ellie to hitch a ride on the back of a motorcycle all the way out to the Bornsons, but maybe he'd have a suggestion.

Ellie started to whine. Brenda stared into middle space, trying to formulate a plan. She took out her phone, thinking that perhaps Gabby's mother would be willing to drive in and pick up Ellie.

Ellie grabbed her arm before she punched in the number.

"Look at all the cars next door. I bet Carl would let us borrow one. It's an emergency!"

Maybe Carl had something to do with the two mysteriously flat tires. Brenda reached for her purse.

"Let's go ask him."

Carl was busy with another customer and so intent that he did not seem to notice her. She looked for his receptionist, but Carl appeared to be working alone. Brenda and Ellie hovered in Carl's peripheral vision, where they could not remain unnoticed. Carl continued to extol the relative virtues of two of the cars in his showroom. Finally, the customer, an indecisive fellow wearing a Twins ball cap and a Milwaukee Brewers T-shirt said, "Lemme think about it while you help out these gals."

Brenda shot him a grateful look before turning to Carl. Four-thirty was drawing closer, and Gabby lived several miles outside of town. She was abrupt.

"Could I please use one of your cars to run Ellie out to Bornsons? My car has flat tires."

"I run a dealership here, not a car rental."

Carl paused to inhale sharply.

"Anyhow, if you don't take better care of your car than that, why should I trust you with one of mine?" he added.

"Please. I don't know why the tires went flat. Maybe a prankster." That was as close as Brenda dared come to accusing Carl. She had no evidence.

But Carl's lips remained firmly pressed together, and there was no indication from his posture that he was considering helping her out.

Growing desperate, Brenda turned to the sports fan and asked, "Could we hitch a ride with you? I'll pay you."

"Please," added Ellie. "I don't want to miss my train!"

He dithered. Carl interrupted, offering Brenda the use of a car, but only if she'd fill out a couple of forms. They were time-consuming, and the hands on Brenda's watch moved with rapidity. Her cell phone buzzed. She walked a few steps away to take the call.

It was Stacey, Gabby's mom.

"Are you ladies almost here?" she asked. "We really need to get going!"

"Can you swing through town and pick Ellie up?" Brenda hated to ask.

"Oh shoot! I wish you would have called sooner." Stacey was regretful but firm, not wanting to risk missing the train to drive in the opposite direction to pick up Ellie.

Brenda ended the call and faced Ellie who connected the dots. Her face crumpled and she ran out of the dealership without a word. Brenda abandoned the nearly completed application on the counter and followed her granddaughter. The customer's, "That's one ticked-off gal," and Carl's amused snort accompanied Brenda's departure.

Brenda caught up with Ellie and wracked her brain trying to come up with an alternative to mollify the child, something that might temper her deep disappointment.

"Let's call the pizza place in town," she suggested, "and have pizza delivered here for us." Although this was a real extravagance, one that normally would have Ellie squealing in astonished delight, now the notion only sent her lips into a deeper downward curve.

"You don't get it, Granda," she said. "It's not the pizza I'm sad about." With that, she disappeared behind the door of her unit.

When Jimmie got back, he checked out Brenda's tires and discovered that the valve caps had been tampered with. The tires themselves were fine, so he was able to air them up for her. Afterwards, with Brenda's permission, he coaxed Ellie into accepting a motorcycle ride. It was a brief, sedate ride, but served to placate the child somewhat. While Jimmie and Ellie were on their ride, Brenda went ahead and ordered a pizza. Ellie, while still visibly subdued, managed to eat three slices.

The next day, Brenda suggested they invite Ellie's friends over for a chocolate party at the motel.

"We can melt chocolate chips in the crockpot, add a little cream, and you girls can dip marshmallows, or graham crackers, or strawberries, whatever you want, into the chocolate," she proposed. She knew she'd have to spend money she didn't have for the frivolity, but was desperate to make up for Ellie's loss. Ellie showed mild interest, but after two rejections, didn't want to pursue it.

"Lilly has a dentist appointment and Gabby's having a spa day with her mom."

Brenda was not sure what a spa day was, but offered, tentatively, "Do you want to have a spa day with me?"

Ellie shook her head.

"It's something you do with your mom, not your grandma," she said dismissively. "They had a lot of fun last night," she added.

Brenda's heart pinged. She hated seeing the little girl miss out on a fun experience with friends. And while Brenda tried to be upbeat and cheery, Ellie remained down in the dumps for the next few days. Watching the Fields insinuate themselves into the brown house did not improve her mood.

"Allie has the bedroom that you told me would be mine," she informed her grandmother as she picked at the smoked sausage, potato, and kraut dish Brenda had assembled in the crockpot that morning. "And this is a dumb supper."

An incoming guest staunched the litany of complaints. As Brenda noted the fluttering nostrils of the new arrival, she realized Ellie was right: cooking kraut in the room used to greet guests was a dumb idea.

Even the idea of spending time with her beloved teacher did

not suit Ellie. As Brenda and Ellie walked toward Ms. Winthrop's house the next morning for Ellie's first session, Ellie tried, "Granda, it's vacation time. Can't I have a break?"

"I love you too much to let you sluff off," Brenda responded. "And you'll have fun with Ms. Winthrop."

Ellie's expression remained sulky until they came in view of the Winthrop house. Ms. Winthrop was waiting on her porch with a pitcher of something cold–Brenda could see the condensation on the outside of the pitcher–and two tall glasses. Despite herself, Ellie smiled.

Ninety minutes later, Ellie burst through the door to Unit One and presented Brenda with a copy of *Shiloh*.

"Every night, you and me are supposed to read a chapter. When we finish, Ms. Winthrop said she'd rent it, it's a movie, did you know that? And I can go over and watch it and she said I could bring a friend that time. And she said, if you wanted to you could come too."

Ellie's excitement put Brenda's mind to rest. It was good to have her exuberant jabberbox back. Silently, she blessed Ms. Winthrop.

CHAPTER TWENTY-THREE

Even with the rent money coming in, Brenda's funds were dwindling rapidly. Repairs cost more than she had dreamed. And she could not put off ripping out the carpet in a couple of the rooms, for they were soiled and worn. The carpet in Unit Four, especially, stank of cigarette smoke and had burn holes in it.

"You might-could take out a small business loan," Jimmie suggested when he came upon her in tears the next afternoon, kicking herself for not bailing when she had wanted to. "Talk to the banker. I think there's decent rates available right now."

Brenda made an appointment with a loan officer at a local bank to coincide with Ellie's next tutoring session on Thursday. Before they left, Brenda took pains with her appearance, slipping into her nicest black slacks and a fresh turquoise sleeveless top. She put her hair up, did her nails, and applied a bit of makeup.

Ellie was watching. She disappeared into her own unit. When she came out, she, too, had freshened her appearance. The two walked through the warm sunshine to Ms. Winthrop's house where Brenda exchanged a few words with the teacher before she went on to the bank.

Brenda stepped inside the cool, open bank lobby. A business-like young woman directed her to a chair. Brenda had to wait a considerable time before the loan officer was ready to see her. Her palms were damp and her cheeks hot when she followed him into his small office.

Haltingly, she made her request, but the officer was shaking his head before she had finished speaking.

"Carl Levy's a good friend of mine. He warned me about the possibility of you looking for a handout. I hesitate to advance you any money," he said ponderously, "considering what he tells me about your lack of business expertise."

"It would only be a small loan," she said, surprising herself with her boldness. "And isn't the motel collateral enough?"

The loan officer slid a proposal across the table.

"Fill this out and bring it in on Monday. I'll look it over." He gathered together the papers on his desk, effectively dismissing her.

Brenda was relieved to escape. She did not have high hopes for a favorable outcome on Monday.

When she got back to the motel, Jimmie was wedging a roll of worn carpet into a dumpster.

"How'd it go?" he asked, turning to her.

"It doesn't look too promising," Brenda said with a sigh and shared the details of the encounter with him.

Jimmie leaned forward, listening intently. He frowned.

"Sounds like a good old boys club." He stuck his thumbs into his rear pockets. "If that dog don't hunt, realize you got other options. The Community Bank, fer instance."

Brenda wasn't eager to face another rebuff.

"That's the bank I use, they got branches all over." He gestured toward Unit Four. "And I reckon you'll have to put some of the money in here. Look at what that carpet's been hidin'.""

On Monday when Brenda went back to the bank, she was not surprised to learn that a loan was "not feasible at the present time." But she took Jimmie's advice and called the loan officer at The Community Bank, and was gratified when she was treated with a certain amount of respect and the guarantee of money for her remodeling efforts.

Once the loan had been secured, she ordered new underflooring and carpet for Unit Four as well as the faux stone panels for the front of the motel. Jimmie spent three days ripping out the bottom rows of siding and replacing it with the new panels. He added a border of pine boards on top of the panels and secured them into place. The motel had an elegant air, transformed by the new materials.

***

Gabby and Lilly were excited to join Ellie in spending time with their well-loved third grade teacher and viewing the *Shiloh* DVD. Brenda, who had enjoyed reading the story with Ellie, decided to sit through the show as well. She brought juice boxes for everyone, and Ms. Winthrop produced a large bowl of popcorn. The girls were weeping halfway through the movie, and Brenda felt tears prick her own eyes.

This activity marked the end of Ellie's tutoring sessions, but Ms. Winthrop lent them a couple of other short novels, and Brenda continued reading with Ellie before bed every night.

She also developed the habit of reading a chapter from Jimmie's New Testament every morning. She got up early before Ellie was stirring, made a pot of coffee and read, jotting questions in a designated section of her legal pad. Much of what she read either confused or challenged her. She was tempted more than once to throw the book across the room but she persisted in her practice and found comfort in it.

By the first of July Brenda had Units Five through Ten ready for guests. Over that long weekend, all six were filled, and she had Ellie run out and flip the NO down on the vacancy sign. Busy as she was, Brenda took a few moments to walk out to the sidewalk to view and gloat over the "NO VACANCY" sign, and the sight of cars in front of almost every door of her refurbished motel.

Ellie, meanwhile, enjoyed playing with four-year-old Ollie and two-year-old Allie. Shortly after the Fourth of July their mother Mary came up with a plan. If Ellie kept her kids amused for a couple of hours, Mary would pay her five dollars. Mary would be home, but she was finishing up an online college degree and having Ellie keeping an eye on the little ones made it possible for the young mother to concentrate on her studies. Brenda was glad for Ellie have something worthwhile to do, for she had been fretting over filling Ellie's summer.

Brenda continued to do business out of Unit One and was increasingly looking forward to the day that she and Ellie could move into the house and not be confined to the two motel rooms. How she missed her kitchen!

When she mentioned it to Jimmie, he had a suggestion.

"I could redo this now." He gestured in the direction of the makeshift cupboard, the tiny chipped counter, the elderly microwave. "Before you rent this room out, you'll want to upgrade all this. Might as well fix it up now so you can take advantage of it."

"I feel like I am taking advantage of you," she countered. "Aren't you needing to find work that pays better than the little bit I've been giving you?" There was something in his expression that made her add hastily, "You can tell me it's none of my business."

"It's none of your business," he said. "But it's kind of you to be concerned on my behalf." He shot her a grin before leaning forward to fish through the cup of pencils and pens on her table, selecting a stubby but sharp pencil. He quickly sketched a scheme on an empty page of Brenda's legal pad: A kitchen sink with a cabinet underneath and a closed cupboard above. A mini fridge would be tucked under an adjoining section of updated countertop, with a new microwave on a white shelf above the counter.

"It wouldn't be fancy," he warned, tapping the page for emphasis. "And I'm not sure about the sink. Gotta check and see how the plumbing is situated."

"Jimmie, this would be so much better than what's here." The notion of a functioning kitchen unit brought a smile to Brenda's face.

Jimmie smiled back.

He had a nice smile.

***

True to his word, Jimmie got right on the kitchen makeover, and Brenda enjoyed sharing her space with him. His gentle teasing warmed her heart, and her tart responses drew soft chuckles.

The finished kitchenette inspired Brenda to run to Walmart where she purchased a set of white dishes with a simple blue border: bowls, plates, cups, saucers. She also bought white and blue kitchen towels and dishcloths and a new drying pad. Ellie carefully arranged it all in the new cupboard. The facelift transformed the whole room.

To thank Jimmie, Brenda invited him to share the inaugural meal prepared in the pristine new kitchen. She fixed her old standby recipe of chicken spaghetti in the crockpot, made garlic toast, and assembled a salad. Jimmie had two pieces of garlic toast, and topped his salad with a crumbled third piece. At Brenda's urging, he polished off two helpings of the spaghetti and crowed when she produced the dessert: baked (actually microwaved) apples with caramel sauce.

Brenda regarded his flat stomach and wondered where he put it all. The apples and caramel sauce were portioned out, and Ellie, Jimmie, and Brenda enjoyed them in silence. Jimmie used an apple slice to scoop up the last bit of caramel from his dessert dish.

"Those apples were dandy, Brenda," he said. There was a spot of caramel on his upper lip, and she had a sudden urge to lick it off. Brenda recoiled. Where did that notion come from?

"Glad you like them," she said, heat rising in her cheeks. She stood, clattering together the little white bowls and shiny new forks and spoons. To cover her confusion, she started jabbering.

"We only have two more units left to update."

She carried the dishes over to the sink, continued talking.

"A lot of the stuff in Unit Three needs to be trashed, and I can't put the service desk back into the house until after the Field family moves out. And then there's that hole in Ellie's wall. After that's fixed, I plan to repaint her walls."

"A hole? How'd I miss that?" Jimmie leaned back in his chair and frowned.

"I'll wash." Ellie sprang up. "I love our new sink."

Brenda relinquished the dishes to her willing granddaughter. Might as well take advantage of her zeal while it lasted.

"Granda covered up the hole," Ellie offered over an enthusiastic stream of water. "With a map."

"I'll take care of that before I go," said Jimmie.

"Go?"

"Couple-three guys I rode with on the Patriots' Ride, we're fixin' to take our bikes around Lake Superior."

"Oh...when?"

"Wednesday." He hesitated. "Do you reckon you'll need to use my room? Planning to be gone for ten days."

Her laugh was rueful. "Not hardly. We're lucky if we have more than two of our rooms filled on any given night."

"It'll come," Jimmie said, and his assurance gave her hope.

CHAPTER TWENTY-FOUR

On Wednesday morning, Jimmie accepted only a half cup of coffee, saying he'd stop in Danbury for breakfast, affording himself a chance to stretch his legs.

She had his New Testament out, ready for him.

"You should take this."

He picked it up, nodded slowly.

"Reckon I will."

"It's not easy reading," she said, "but there's truth there."

He squeezed her shoulder, gave her a half-smile.

"That there is. Keep your chin up while I'm gone, now."

"I will," Brenda said.

Jimmie regarded her for a long moment, his hand still resting on her shoulder. Then he leaned forward and kissed her full on the mouth. His lips were soft and tasted of mint. He gave her shoulder a final squeeze, headed for his cycle.

Brenda lifted her hands to cover her hot cheeks and stood quite still, listening to Jimmie's motorcycle roar out of the parking lot.

***

Brenda could not stop thinking about the kiss, could not stop analyzing its significance. Or, more likely, lack of significance. Finally she told herself the best thing to do was to keep busy, and so, legal pad in hand, she wandered down to Unit Three and took an inventory of the furniture that was tumbled together there. It was a motley assortment, most pieces needing repairing, refinishing, or replacing.

Debra Muldoon, a guest staying in Unit Seven, peered through the open door.

"Look at that desk!" she exclaimed, entering the room, her eyes fixed on the service desk. "It's a beauty." She reached out to stroke the wood. "Cherry, if I'm not mistaken."

Brenda surveyed the desk she had considered clunky and out-sized and revised her thinking.

"It is nice wood," she agreed. "Needs a good cleaning though."

"Tung oil," said Debra at once. She perused the rest of the furniture without comment before adding hesitantly, "I realize it's none of my business, but I was looking at the dresser in my room. I have an idea of what you maybe could do with it." She went on to explain that she had refinished a lot of furniture as a hobby.

"It's good solid wood," she said. "It hasn't been cared for, though."

They walked down to Unit Seven together. Debra indicated how Brenda could remove the damaged bottom drawer and slide wicker baskets into the cavity.

"And maybe sand it down and lay a darker stain over the whole piece. That way it would tie in with your woodwork."

Brenda was delighted with the ideas. "Do you have time to look at another unit with me?" she asked hesitantly. Debra, who by now had become "Deb," smiled.

"I sure do. This is fun."

It was fun for Brenda, too. She opened up the door of the still unused Unit Four and pointed at the credenza with its destroyed top.

"What can I do with that?" Brenda asked.

Deb studied it.

"I'd put a sheet of laminate on it, wouldn't even mess with trying to restore that finish. If you brightened up the handles and hinges, it wouldn't be half bad." She approved of the freshly painted walls, the new carpeting. "Love this color. What's it called?"

"Butterscotch."

"And the curtains are cute. What this room needs—if I can be honest—is a new bedspread. And fresh art." Deb stuck her hands in the back pockets of her jeans. "I usually don't go around telling motel owners what their rooms need."

"I bet most motel owners don't need help as desperately as I do!" Brenda replied. "Thank you."

The furniture upgrading kept her busy when she wasn't dealing with guests, or doing housekeeping after rooms were vacated. Ellie took an interest in the projects too, and decided to fix up a bedside table for her own unit. She unearthed a small square table from the jumble in Unit Three and wiped off the dust, applied tung oil, and buffed with vigor until the pale wood shone. Although Brenda vetoed painting it pink, she did allow Ellie to purchase a pink ceramic knob for the drawer in the table as well as a pink placemat to set on top. The pastor of Kids' Night, the church group Ellie had been faithful in attending, had given her a Just for Girls devotional book with a pink cover, and Ellie carefully placed it on the table.

Jimmie had managed to patch Ellie's hole before he'd left on his trip, and the white plaster patch was crying to be covered. Ellie and Brenda repainted the whole wall, pink, of course, but with an occasional thin strip of yellow for contrast.

Teak stuck her head through the open door while they were finishing up and gave the results a thumbs up.

"You do nice work," she said. "I stopped by to ask you...I have Tuesday off and Hailey and I are taking a quick trip down to Stillwater. Would you guys like to go with us? There's a lot of cute shops there."

An outing would be a nice break.

"Can we be home by four?" Brenda asked, not wanting to miss any potential guests.

The following Tuesday, after she bid farewell to the lone guest from the previous night and placed a "Back at Four" note on her door, she and Ellie joined Teak and Hailey for the sixty-odd mile trip to Stillwater, Minnesota. After crossing the St. Croix River on an ancient lift bridge, Teak parked in the city lot near the river, and they wandered down the historic main street of the town.

Brenda stopped in front of one of the many red brick buildings, captivated by a window display. The others, who had gone on ahead, came back to join her.

"I like that," she said, pointing to one of the posters. Its upper corner was filled with dull gray, textured flakes gradually morphing into a vibrant pink rose that consumed the remaining space.

"Beauty from ashes," mused Teak. "It's terrific."

Beauty from ashes. That was something to ponder.

"I'd get it for one of the motel rooms, but I don't want to stick a poster on the wall."

"Maybe you could put it in a frame," suggested Teak. "That would elevate it to a piece of art."

Brenda was willing to be persuaded. "I'll see how much it costs." The shopkeeper suggested a technique to enhance the appearance of the poster and produced a suitable frame. Brenda, encouraged by the other three, made the purchases, and they continued window-shopping.

Farther down the street, they entered a store where a bin of reasonably priced paintings caught Brenda's eye. Last week had been a busy one and she had a little extra cash. She felt free to spend some of it on updating the art in the units. She chose a few pieces, consulting the swatches of the material from the curtains she had tucked in her purse. She had learned she could not trust her color-matching memory.

At Teak's suggestion, they purchased sandwiches and drinks at the deli in the River Market and carried them out to the grassy area lining the St. Croix River. It was a beautiful summer day with puffy clouds drifting across a brilliant blue sky. As joggers and dog walkers passed, they lingered over their lunch, laughing at the sea gulls and commenting on the variety of boats that dotted the river.

There was something in Teak's grin, the flash of dimple, which reminded Brenda of her last good friend, Denise. She and Denise had been inseparable all through middle school but drifted apart soon after entering high school. There was a boy—Jason somebody, Brenda thought—that Denise liked, but he had favored Brenda. Denise accused Brenda of flirting with him. Brenda didn't think she did, but Denise stopped talking to her and starting running around with other kids, more rowdy kids. And Brenda got a job cashiering at The Dairy Bar where she met Dale, and pretty soon he occupied all of her time…

Brenda halted her flow of thoughts, shaking her head slightly. Why on earth was she thinking of Denise? They hadn't spoken in decades. She looked at Teak who was leaning back on her elbows, her face lifted to the sun. Teak was nothing like Denise. Teak was solid, true.

Hailey and Ellie wandered down to the gazebo near the bank of the river. Brenda followed them with her eyes.

"Hailey sure has been nice to Ellie." She popped her final bit of crusty bread in her mouth.

"She has a big heart. I've been blessed." Teak's brown eyes were eloquent. "Hailey is the wonderful result of an otherwise terrible situation."

Brenda stopped chewing, silently inviting Teak to go on.

"I was a sophomore in college." Teak seemed to want to tell her story. "I was a good girl, Brenda, I really was. I didn't date at all in high school. My freshman year of college was pretty lonely. So when Danny started paying attention to me, I was happy. But I was so naïve. I didn't plan—" She stopped. "By the time I realized I was pregnant, Danny was long gone."

Your generous nature got you into trouble, Brenda thought.

"So what did you do?" Brenda asked.

"Finished out the year, went home. My parents were disappointed in me. They helped me some, but … it was a difficult time."

Hailey and Ellie had finished their tour of the gazebo and were heading back toward them. Ellie was doing most of the talking, commenting on each of the many dogs that were getting walked on this beautiful day.

Teak crumpled up the brown paper that her sandwich had been wrapped in.

"It was all worth it," she said to Brenda. "Hailey is my greatest joy."

Brenda made a connection.

"Beauty from ashes," she said.

Teak's dimple showed, confirming that Brenda had made sense of Teak's earlier comment.

"But you did finish school then?" Brenda asked. "That must have been hard."

"No, I didn't," Teak replied. "I barely managed to assemble enough credits to be certified as an LPN. I want to go back to school to get my bachelor's degree so I can be an RN. It just hasn't worked out yet." She shrugged slightly.

"It took a long time for my parents to warm up to Hailey," Teak went on. "That's why I really admire how you have taken on Ellie. And I'm curious about Janna, and what she went through. She must have been a young mother too. When did you lose her?"

Brenda watched yellow and white butterflies fluttering low, settling on an occasional flower. They were opposite, her situation and Teak's, with Teak's parents apparently shunning Hailey and she, Janna's mother, absorbing little Ellie. She wondered if she had been too grasping, perhaps pushing Janna away from her own child. Could that be why Janna left?

Difficult as it would be, she was tempted to share her story, explore it with Teak. She had never spoken to anyone about those hard days when Ellie was a fussy baby and Janna was a mess, coming and going, until she finally was simply gone.

Brenda blew out a deep breath and took a gulp of air.

"Ellie was about a year and a half the last time we saw her mother." Brenda had barely gotten the words out of her mouth when Ellie and Hailey raced up, clamoring for ice cream cones. Brenda did not know whether to be relieved or sorry that the opportunity to talk was lost. Teak threaded her way up the hill to Nelson's Ice Cream and treated them all to amazing cones, which kept their tongues busy for a good portion of the ride home.

"We'll finish our conversation soon," Teak said quietly as she helped Brenda carry her parcels into her motel unit. Brenda nodded, but was having second thoughts about sharing her story. She did not suggest a time to reconvene.

With reservations, Brenda took the suggestion of the shopkeeper and used a paintbrush to spread a mixture of glue and water over the poster. When she finished, she felt she had ruined it, for the cloudy mixture masked the effect of the art. However, when she checked it in the morning, Brenda was delighted to see the mixture had become transparent and the sheen of the poster quite elevated.

She had planned to put the picture in Unit One, but Ellie latched on to it.

"The pinkness is perfect for me," she claimed, and the framed "beauty from ashes" picture was indeed charming in Ellie's pink room.

Swapping out the other new pictures for the nondescript ones that had hung in the rooms afforded Brenda a great deal of pleasure. She took particular delight in removing the picture of a sad clown from Unit Four and replacing it with a brilliant field of poppies, all gold, red, and tangerine. The tangerine in her curtains picked up the color of some of the poppies, and the butterscotch walls set off the painting perfectly. That night, a young couple was the first occupants of the refurbished unit.

Brenda ordered simple black vests. After they arrived, she took them to a local embroidery shop where the seamstress showed off her fancy machine and assured Brenda she could embroider "Brenda" and "Ellie" on the vests as well as the name of the motel and a stylized pin. Brenda was pleased. The new vests would certainly give them an official air.

The opportunity to have a quiet chat with Teak did not present itself. Teak was working overtime, and the motel's business was steady, keeping Brenda occupied in the evenings.

Even with all the busyness, Brenda's thoughts drifted

repeatedly to Jimmie, thinking about the kiss and what it might mean, wondering how he was faring as he circumnavigated Lake Superior. After he had zoomed out of the parking lot that Wednesday morning, she had not heard a word from him. Two weeks passed, and August was just around the corner. Hadn't he said he'd be back in ten days?

She walked down to the end of the motel, a duster in hand and entered Jimmie's unit where she pushed the duster over the flat surfaces and checked corners for cobwebs. She had changed the sheets and made up his bed shortly after he left so it would be ready for him. Everything was shipshape. But where was he?

The familiar sound of a motorcycle entering the lot had Brenda rushing to look out the window. Her fingers rested on her lips. Jimmie was back! He parked, and she, despite feeling awkward because she was in his room, stepped outside to greet him.

He was tan and had a new air of assurance about him. His gray curls, she noted, while flattened from their confinement inside of his helmet, had been trimmed.

"Hello, Brenda," Jimmie said. "How's the room?"

"Good. I just finished dusting it. Was getting worried about you."

"Don't need to worry about me," he said, stretching. "Ah, that's a long ride. Came all the way down from Duluth without stopping....Do you have time to walk a bit? I need to move. Been sitting too long."

"Sounds good." They fell into step, walked around the motel and down the street a short ways. Brenda kept an eye out for cars pulling into the parking lot, but it was only mid-afternoon, early for guests. She was aware of how hard her heart was beating, how hard she was working to appear casual.

"The trip around Lake Superior was great," Jimmie was

saying. "It's beautiful, with the mist on the water, the granite cliffs in Ontario. And then of course, I stopped in Sinclair Cove for a couple-three hours."

"Sinclair Cove?"

Jimmie stepped off the curb.

"Let's walk on the other side of the street, work our way back." His hand brushed her elbow, guiding her. She tried not to think about how warm his fingers were. "Sinclair Cove is somethin' else," he continued after they had crossed the street. "Last time I'd been there was with Angie. Six years ago." He jammed his hands into his front pockets and stared straight ahead.

When he spoke again, his voice was low, his tone nostalgic.

"Almost seemed tropical…waves lapping on the shore, islands of stone popping out of the water. It was a special place for us. It was hard to be back there without her. Real hard." His voice roughened, and he cleared his throat. "Felt compelled to return, though. And I got some things out in the open. With God," he added. "Told Him how mad I was, how much I hated going on without Angie. I yelled, Brenda. I was all alone, looking at that big ole lake and the tiny islands, and I told God how wretched I felt, and that I blamed Him."

His face contorted, his grief, raw and exposed, so intimate Brenda looked away, studied the sidewalk in front of them.

"But afterwards, I felt cleansed. It was like God took my pain away. I can't explain it. The pain was so terrible, and then it was–gone. The connection between the Lord and me has been restored." His smile was gentle. "I discovered 'the peace that passes understanding.'"

Brenda was listening hard. They had completed a circuit and were standing by the mailboxes now. Idly she rubbed the top of hers, feeling honored that Jimmie was sharing his heart with her, but not knowing quite how to respond.

"What Angie and I had was wonderful and good, but now it's over, and I am okay with that. I am actually okay with that. So I am ready." Jimmie looked straight at her, his blue eyes filled with emotion, and Brenda's heart jumped.

Ready?

"Ready to go home. Back to South Carolina."

CHAPTER TWENTY-FIVE

Brenda was pouring water into her coffeemaker the following morning when a motorcycle roared to life in the parking lot. Carafe in hand, she peeked out her window and saw Jimmie pulling out. Was he leaving without saying good-bye? She hastened down to his room where a mound of stripped bedding greeted her. A Holy Bible, with an envelope peeking out the top of the thick volume, rested on top of the pile of linens.

Brenda picked up the Bible. She stroked its buttery soft cover, extracted the envelope and pulled out five one-hundred dollar bills and a folded piece of paper. Brenda read the brief note twice, not able to get much satisfaction from it.

"Can't do goodbyes. The money might help a little, the Word a lot. Thanks for giving me a place to stay while I was working things out. Your the best. J.S."

She tightened her lips. The money was definitely welcome, but she had felt that giving Jimmie a place to stay offset the pittance she had been paying him. This five hundred dollars negated that payment, and tarnished their budding relationship. And the note! So cold. Jimmie had driven out of her life as suddenly as he had driven into it. This felt familiar.

She shouldn't have let her guard down, shouldn't have dared to think she was worthy of love. Except— she closed her fingers around the bills—with Ellie, her reason for building a successful motel. Her reason for everything.

Brenda wedged the Bible into an opening between a cardboard box and a folded blanket on the closet shelf. She did not think she'd be digging into it anytime soon. After she tucked the money away for safekeeping, she stuck her head into Unit Two, where Ellie was flopped on her bed, watching TV.

"Should we drive out to Round Lake this afternoon?" she asked briskly. "We'll take a chance, step away from the motel for a couple of hours."

After chores and a quick lunch, Brenda put a sign, "Back by four," on the door of Unit One and shepherded the little girl, skinny and jubilant in her swimsuit, to the car.

Wisconsin in late July was beautiful. Brenda plopped down on a bench near the lake, the sun warm on her head and shoulders, watching as Ellie waded into the water. To Brenda's surprise, the beach was empty except for a cluster of Canadian geese. On such a beautiful day, she would have thought there would be many swimmers.

"Come and wade, Granda." Ellie beckoned. Brenda kicked off her flip-flops and picked her way across the strip of sand. She stood in the shallows, the water lapping around her ankles. It was enticing. Brenda waded deeper, lifting the legs of her capris in an attempt to keep them dry.

Ellie disappeared under water and came up, hooting and splashing next to her grandmother.

"Hey!" Brenda smacked the top of the water with her palm, sending a spray toward Ellie, who retaliated at once. It was not long before both of them were fully immersed in the lake, reveling in the warm, sparkling water. Brenda had not planned on swimming, but it felt good, it felt so good, to play.

"We better get back," Brenda said finally, reluctantly. They had only brought along one towel, so they spread it out across the front seat of the car so they both could sit on it.

A blue Ford Focus was parked in Brenda's usual spot in front of Unit One. A customer? Chatter from the car's radio greeted Brenda as she approached the vehicle, a smile of apology on her lips.

"Can I help you?" she called through the open window. An older woman with stiff blonde hair and a mouth set in a straight line clicked off her radio and turned her attention toward the bedraggled Brenda.

"I would like a room for one night," she said.

"Great," said Brenda. "I'm so sorry I kept you waiting. Won't you come inside and register?" She caught Ellie's eye and gestured toward Unit Two. "Go on, get out of that wet suit. And drape it over your tub, won't you?"

Lake water still dripping from her own clothes, Brenda guided the woman, a Donna Johnson, through the registration process with as much professionalism as her apparel allowed. By the time Brenda had Donna established in Unit Nine, Ellie had reappeared, in dry shorts and T-shirt, her wet hair slicked back.

"Granda, I'm itchy," Ellie greeted her, scratching her shoulder vigorously.

Brenda pushed aside the neck of Ellie's shirt, peered at the top of her shoulder and upper chest. A mass of angry red pimples covered the area. Brenda's own skin was tingling, almost burning.

"My butt, too," said Ellie, switching over to scratching her bottom.

Brenda left the little girl in charge while she disappeared into the bathroom to peel off her damp clothes and change into something dry. An itchy rash was forming on her own chest and thighs. She applied talcum powder, hoping to stave off future misery.

What in the world? Was it possible there was something in the water? Who could she ask? Brenda wandered outside and spotted Katie Gordon standing on the porch of the brown house, watching her grandson leap from the second stair onto the sidewalk. Over and over the little boy climbed a stair or two, turned and jumped. He had no end of energy.

"Hey, Katie," Brenda called when she got into earshot. "Nice jumping, Oliver," she added.

"Mary is meeting Joe for dinner," Katie replied by way of greeting. "I get to babysit." She smiled. "Oliver is getting to be quite the jumper, isn't he? Mary and Joe plan to pick up a wading pool on their way home, and Ollie wants to get into shape for splashing in the pool."

"Ellie and I went swimming this afternoon and now we both have itchy rashes," Brenda scratched her underarm.

Katie frowned.

"I wonder if you could have a case of swimmer's itch. That can be nasty."

"Swimmer's itch? Never heard of it." Brenda sighed. She should have known there was a reason no one else was at the beach on such a perfect summer day.

"I think you get it from snails. I'm not sure. Do you have any calamine lotion?"

Brenda didn't, so they worked out a deal. She and Ellie would keep an eye on Oliver and the napping baby Allie while Katie ran a couple of errands for herself and picked up some calamine lotion for Brenda.

"Then I can head straight home after Mary and Joe get back," Katie said, seeming pleased with the arrangement.

As luck would have it, Suzanne dropped in to check on Ellie while she was playing with the younger children. She noticed Ellie's rash right away, for it had spread to cover her thin arms and chin. Brenda was questioned, and Suzanne's fingers tapped briskly on her keypad, using the moniker cercarial dermatitis to describe Ellie's condition, and despite Brenda's explanation about calamine lotion being on its way, added "untreated" to her notes.

The calamine lotion did the trick. But after that Ellie's water play was confined to the Field's new wading pool.

The Fields were great tenants, for not only did they pay promptly, but they were friendly folks who kept the house and yard tidy. No living room furniture found its way to the porch, much to Brenda's relief. And after Jimmie left, Joe took over the mowing of the yard of the brown house as well as the patch of lawn that stretched behind the motel, using Ed's old riding lawn-mower. Jimmie had serviced it, and it ran pretty well. And Katie often visited her daughter's family, and made a point of stopping for a quick chat with Brenda, too.

***

Brenda and Ellie worked together an hour or so before lunch every day to refresh the rooms that had been occupied the night before. Someday, she hoped, she'd be able to afford a housekeeper, but for now, she was managing, and even seeing a slight profit for her efforts, enough so that she felt confident she would not need to rent the house out again after the Fields family departed at the end of the summer.

"Granda," announced Ellie, from under the bed in Unit Seven one morning the first week in August, "I'm going to make a sign." She wiggled out from under the bed clutching a damp towel and a used Kleenex. "It will say, Hang Up Your Towels When You Are Done. And Throw Your Trash In the Garbage Can. We can tape it right by the mirror in the bathroom."

"Oh, child." Brenda shook her head. We can't be doing that, sweet thing. We can't tell our guests what to do. We have to pick up after them, and that is just the way it is."

"You tell me to hang up my towel and throw my trash in the garbage." Ellie wasn't giving up. "Can't we make it a Room Rule? We had Room Rules in school."

"I'll think about it," said Brenda, ending the discussion. Then a thought hit her and she added, "Now don't you be putting any sign in any of the rooms behind my back. Promise me?"

Ellie scrunched up her mouth in a frown and stood mutinously for a moment but eventually nodded. "This housekeeping isn't fun like it used to be. I'll get the mail, okay, Granda?" she asked, switching gears.

Ellie opened the door of Unit One introducing a gust of hot air along with the mail. She handed the small pile to Brenda.

"It was hard to get that outta the box." Ellie indicated a bent manila envelope.

The mailman must have really wedged it in, Brenda thought as she straightened the envelope. When she read the return address, minimal as it was, her heart lurched.

J. Stephens. Columbia, SC.

Jimmie.

Brenda tore open the top of the envelope and pulled out a yellow legal pad. There was a lime green post-it note stuck to the front of it.

"Hey Brenda," she read. "Thought you might be do for a fresh pad. Call if you feel like talking." A phone number was carefully printed beneath his scrawled signature.

A smile curved her lips. Her well-used legal pad was indeed due to be replaced, and that he had noticed how much she depended on those pages touched her. She reached for her phone, started to input his number. It would be good to hear Jimmie's voice again.

But her fingers stilled before she reached the fourth digit. Was there any point in contacting someone who lived over a thousand miles away? She'd be asking for fresh hurt if she attempted a long-distance relationship with him. Brenda closed her phone, crumpled the note and tossed it in the trash. Best to concentrate on little Ellie and her motel.

CHAPTER TWENTY-SIX

Carl Levy beat a brisk rhythm on her door the first Friday of August.

"Knock knock," he sang out, opening the door with a flourish. "Beautiful day, isn't it?" Without waiting for a response, he extended a small white paper plate with two sugary doughnuts on it. "Time for a mid-morning snack."

Brenda took the offering, said a guarded thank you. She had not had any encounters with him in a few weeks, and his absence was not unpleasant. She did not appreciate his visit now.

"Today is National Doughnut Day." Carl indicated the pastries. "Over to the dealership, we take notice!"

Brenda, not knowing what to add, said nothing.

"Do you have a pencil I can borrow for a quick second?" he asked.

Brenda handed him one, and he withdrew a notepad from his pocket and scribbled a few lines.

"Here you go," he said, handing her back the pencil with a big smile. "Well, I'll be getting back to work. Have a good one."

Brenda watched him go, her eyes narrowed. What was he up to now?

Carl returned three days later with a cup of iced coffee. This time, after he offered it to Brenda, he sat down in the green Adirondack chair and stretched out his legs.

"I'll take a load off," he said. "We've been real busy this summer. How about you?" He folded his hands behind his head, his elbows winging behind his ears, and smiled broadly.

"Busy enough." Brenda was noncommittal. She hadn't heard any chatter about the new high-end motel Teak had mentioned in May. Was he here to tell her that they were breaking ground, and she might as well start packing her bags? She took a sip of the coffee, waited.

"You're a hard worker, I'll give you that."

"I want to be an inspiration to Ellie," she said. "She's my driving force."

Carl was silent for a beat, observing her.

"She means a lot to you, don't she?"

"Everything," Brenda said simply. Eventually he stood, thanking her for the use of her chair. He made no mention of the new motel. She made a mental note to ask Teak about it. Brenda straightened her desk, wondering why he was being so neighborly. She couldn't help but be suspicious that he was up to something.

Later that afternoon, Ellie supplied the answer.

"Look at this picture." The little girl held out a page torn from a magazine. She tapped a black and gray spiral on the top of the page. "It seems like it's moving."

The picture was hypnotic, but what caught Brenda's attention was the title of the article: Five Psychological Tricks to Get People to Do What You Want. She took the well-worn page from Ellie and smoothed the creases.

"Wherever did you find this?"

"Over there." Ellie pointed in the direction of the car dealership. "On the ground."

Brenda read the list of tricks, her lips tightening.

•Number one. Be extremely charming, confident, and likeable.

•Number two. Mirror the person's behavior to make them feel more at ease. They'll trust you more.

•Number three. Do a favor so the person feels obligated to reciprocate.

•Number four. Ask "Yes" questions. Once you get someone saying yes, they are more apt to continue, up to and including "Yes, I'll buy it."

•Number five. Act interested in the person's life and problems.

Carl's change in attitude and demeanor suddenly was making a whole lot of sense. But if he thought it would get her to agree to sell the property, he was mistaken. She folded the article and paper-clipped it to the cardboard backing of her fresh legal pad, wanting to keep it for future reference.

Later, when she glanced out the window to check on Ellie, she saw the little girl was holding an ice cream bar and talking with Carl.

When Ellie came in, remnants of the ice cream on the bar and a smear of chocolate on one corner of her mouth, Brenda asked her, "Where'd you get that?"

"Carl," Ellie said breezily. She finished her ice cream and threw the stick in the trash.

"Check your face," Brenda told her, so Ellie went over to the mirror and wiped off the chocolate.

"What did you talk about?" Brenda continued the questioning.

"He wanted to know if I missed Prairie City at all. I don't."

How did Carl even know they had lived there? Brenda's brow

furrowed. The only thing she could think of was the application she'd filled out the day they wanted to borrow a car. Brenda winced. She had unwittingly provided Carl with a dossier of information.

Ellie wasn't finished.

"And, he was wondering why I lived with you and not my mother."

"What did you tell him?" Brenda straightened the box of keys on the table and moved the vase filled with fresh-picked daisies a fraction.

"I told him she went away when I was little. And you kept me."

Brenda's hands stilled. She smiled at the child.

"Yes, Ellie, I'm the lucky one! We've managed pretty well, you and me, haven't we?"

"Yeah. But Carl thought maybe I was missing my mother. I said no. I don't hardly remember what she looked like. Where's our pictures of her, Granda?"

Brenda resumed shifting items on the table, regretting that she had questioned the child, for now she was going to have to deal with the consequences.

A trip down memory lane would not be pleasant. Reliving the quarreling, the tension, the wondering every night if Janna would come home, and what condition she would be in if she did. Rehashing the harsh words and uncomfortable atmosphere when she was in the house, the worry when she failed to arrive. So reminiscent of how it had been in her father's house after her mother's death, and also in her marriage.

Brenda had thrown everything into caring for Ellie, tiny Ellie, who had been walking, but delayed in talking. Ellie and Brenda had become a serene twosome.

Why did Carl have to rock the boat?

"Our old photo albums are in the house, in the sewing room," she said finally. "I'll check with Mary, see when I can stop in."

"I'll come with. We can get my baby book, too. I want to look through it again."

***

Ellie and Brenda looked at the books together, sitting side by side on Ellie's bed, Ellie's knobby bare knee pressing against Brenda's wider, blue-jeaned thigh.

First the oldest album, started a quarter of a century ago, with blurry pictures of a younger Brenda, strained and unhappy; Dale, bored and superior; and a cute little blondie. Janna. The pictures grew more and more scattered until they ceased abruptly in the middle of the book. Ellie picked up her baby book and paged through it.

"Granda, there's not many of me," complained Ellie. "This was my mother, right?" There was a picture of a shell-shocked young, young girl holding a red-faced squalling infant.

"Yes, and that is you," Brenda said. "You were a little bit of a thing, just six pounds. But you had such nice strong lungs. And look! Here's your ankle bracelet." She pointed to the narrow band, held in place with yellowing tape.

There were a half-dozen more pictures of baby Ellie, a few notations in a curly writing, with hearts dotting the i's. Most of the book was empty.

"I wish I could see my mother again," Ellie said. Brenda's heart pinged at the wistfulness of her expression.

"Do you know where she is?" Ellie asked.

Over the years, Brenda had foisted love and attention on the little girl but had avoided the topic of Ellie's mom. They had been Granda-and-Ellie for so long, and the little girl had accepted the arrangement.

Until now.

Thank you, Carl Levy.

"I don't know where your mother is, sweet thing," Brenda told her. Her heart ached for her innocent granddaughter. In a desperate attempt to change the subject, she added, "And it is a shame we stopped taking photos. I had a bunch on my one camera, but I never printed them out, and they got lost when the camera broke." She closed the baby book and set it aside.

"It's a real shame," she repeated. "But, Ellie. Would you like to go to Walmart and buy a camera? You could take pictures, all the pictures you want, and we'll be sure and print them out. You can start your own photo album."

Could we, Granda?" Ellie was eager, and, to Brenda's relief, said no more about her mother. They took a trip to the store where they bought a disposable camera and a little album.

Ellie got the Fields kids to pose for her, and by the end of the day had an entire collection to print out. Brenda did not really need the extra expense but decided it was worth it to have the child distracted and happily busy. They went back to Walmart where Brenda perched on a stool in front of a photo kiosk and managed to print out the pictures, Ellie peering over her shoulder all the while.

Brenda was sitting on the step in front of Unit One making approving noises while Ellie explained the stories behind some of her photos when Teak and Hailey stopped by on Wednesday. After they, too, had admired Ellie's photos, Hailey revealed that they were taking a vacation trip, their first of the summer.

"My sister Julie took advantage of a Groupon deal in Wisconsin Dells," Teak said. "Kind of last-minute, but that's how she rolls."

"We're renting a suite together," Hailey said. Usually calm, the notion of this surprise vacation had her uncharacteristically animated. "We can go down waterslides and everything."

"Hailey doesn't get to see her cousins very often," Teak said. "And it will be fun hanging out with Julie." She asked if the Millers could possibly keep an eye on their house and cat.

"Smokey has a cat door into the garage, so you won't have to keep her here," said Teak. "Just be sure her water and food dish are filled."

"Of course we'll be glad to take care of things," Brenda said, pleased for the chance to do a little something to repay Teak and Hailey for their many kindnesses. "How long will you be gone?"

"Three nights," said Hailey. We'll leave first thing tomorrow, back Sunday."

"I will pat Smokey so she's not lonesome," inserted Ellie. Hailey offered to show Ellie where Smokey's supplies were, and the two girls disappeared through the gap in the cedar hedge. Teak settled in the spot Ellie had vacated and tapped the pad in Brenda's lap.

"New legal pad?"

Brenda blushed.

"Yeah, Jimmie sent it."

"Oh-ho," Teak sing-songed. "Are you sure there's nothing going on between you two? Besides him keeping you supplied with legal pads, I mean." Her dimple appeared briefly.

"There's nothing." Brenda kept her tone as bland as she could.

"You guys were thick as thieves."

Brenda dearly wanted to tell Teak to mind her own business, not go down this rabbit trail she did not want to explore. But Teak had become a true friend, and she would not risk marring their relationship by rebuffing her.

She took a deep breath, pressed a finger against her lips, and offered, "He did give me his phone number and said I should call him when I had a chance." Before Teak could ask any more, she added, "But I threw it away. There's no point in talking to him. He lives over a thousand miles away." Brenda stood, searched her mind for a change of subject. "Want some coffee? Tea?"

Teak stood too. "Thanks for the offer, but I better get packing. See you Monday." She paused and added, "Don't be so quick to dismiss him, Brenda."

***

The phone rang right after lunch the next day.

"Neat as a Pin Motel," Brenda said, smiling to infuse cheer into her voice. "How may I help you?"

"Mom?"

Brenda's heart clenched. A wave of dizziness swept over her. She was not prepared to hear that voice.

CHAPTER TWENTY-SEVEN

B renda's fingers tightened on her phone. "Janna?"

"Must be...unless you got other kids."

It had been years since she'd been subject to her daughter's blatant mockery. Nevertheless, Brenda's maternal heart sprang to the fore. "Honey! It's so good to hear you. Where are you? Was it hard for you to find me?"

"Not at all. A fellow in your town tracked me down. He gave me a call, said I should know how tough things are for Ellie. He said he even has to feed her sometimes because she's starving. And there's rodents in her room!"

Carl Levy. He was the only rodent that Brenda had dealings with now.

"No, Janna. It's not like that."

Janna went on talking, steamrolling over her mother's comments as she always had.

"He suggested I do some checking up on you, online. And I saw you got your little motel mentioned on U-Stay."

The review.

"It's not true—" Brenda began.

"I couldn't believe my eyes when I found out you were taking advantage of Ellie like that. I trusted you, Mom. I gave her up so she could have a better life."

Overwhelmed, Brenda sat abruptly on the bed, her hand clutching her neck.

"Janna, you know I take good care of her. I love her. Do you want to come here? See Ellie? See—me?"

There was a pause, the silence speaking volumes.

"I'm thinking more like taking Ellie. "

Brenda's heart twisted.

"Don't, Janna. She doesn't even know you. We need to explain things, have you two meet each other, see how it goes."

"My daughter, my decision."

"But she doesn't remember you at all," Brenda persisted. "You can't just pull her out of her home. It will be enough of a shock for Ellie to learn her mother is back in touch."

"You're talking to MY MOTHER?"

The opening of the door registered with Brenda a beat too late as Ellie's scream reverberated through the motel unit. The little girl snatched the phone from Brenda's hand.

"Mommy? You're my mommy?"

Brenda cradled her head in her hands as she listened to Ellie's excited side of the conversation and Janna's muffled responses.

Ellie flipped the phone shut, buzzing with enthusiasm.

"I'm going to live with my mother now. I need to pack up my stuff. She's coming tomorrow. Early, she said. Be ready, she said." Ellie gave her grandmother a quick squeeze.

"What can I use to put my clothes in?" she asked.

Brenda stared at her granddaughter. She had expected her to be bursting with questions, confusion, fear, as she herself was. She saw only excitement.

"Do you want to think it over, sweet thing? Talk about it?" she managed. Scrambling for something that might entice Ellie to not want to leave, she added, "You told the Andersons you'd watch Smokey, remember?"

Ellie shrugged.

"She'll be all right," she said, suddenly indifferent to the responsibility she had embraced. "And I don't need to think it over. I can't believe I'm going to live with my mother! I've always wanted a mother." She raced out, heading for her own quarters.

Alone, Brenda punched in the number that Janna had called from, but although there was ring after ring, no one picked up.

She had the thought to call Suzanne Waters at Child Protection Services, see if there was a way to block Janna from swooping in from nowhere to take the child. Hands shaking, Brenda flipped through the pages of her legal pad and found where she had, at Suzanne's insistence, jotted the number.

Her palms were clammy as the phone rang, made connection. After greetings were exchanged, Brenda went straight to the point.

"Ellie's mother got in contact with me and she's planning to take her tomorrow."

"Thank you for letting us know. We appreciate the information." Brenda could hear keys tapping before Suzanne added, "What is Ellie's new address?"

"No! I mean, I don't want her to go, I was hoping you could do something, um, she's used to me…" Brenda knew she was rambling, scrambled, desperate.

"Are you the legal guardian?"

"N-no, but I've always had her," said Brenda.

"In that case," Suzanne went on smoothly, while Brenda, stricken, stood woodenly, phone to her ear, "the mother has rights to her child and you cannot stand in the way. It might be for the best.

"She is not in an optimal situation with you, living in the motel. You have been careless with her safety, most recently allowing her to be afflicted with that dermatitis. We have been Very concerned."

Brenda tried to give her details, make her realize that Janna had never chosen to be a part of Ellie's life, was an unknown, but Suzanne was firm.

"As the child's mother, she has the legal rights, Brenda. You need to accept that."

***

Ellie, too excited to eat breakfast, was ready to go by seven-thirty the following morning. She had donned her newest pink t-shirt and favorite pink-and-navy capris, and brushed her brown hair until it shone. She stood by the window, on the look-out. An hour drifted by, two.

Brenda, not knowing how the reunion with her estranged daughter would go, and not wanting to mar it with any interruptions, walked to the end of the parking lot and turned the sign to NO Vacancy.

At eleven, Brenda persuaded Ellie to sit down and have a sandwich.

"You need something to go on," she told the little girl. Brenda made the sandwich as special as she could, even cutting off the crusts. Ellie ate dutifully, seemingly not noticing the extravagance. She made a quick stop in the bathroom and then manned her post beside the opened window once again, although the only activity in the parking lot was the shifting shadows.

It was almost two o'clock before a blue Nova with rusted fenders pulled up in front of Unit One. Brenda and Ellie were silent, watching, as the driver sat for a moment before opening the car door.

Tears filled Brenda's eyes as she caught her first glimpse of her only child in almost a decade. She walked to the door of the motel unit, held it open. Ellie bounced up to stand beside her.

Janna. Stick thin, with red, red lips and facial piercings. Hair still long and straight, still blonde. As she came toward the motel, walking with her familiar hippy swing, a citrusy smell preceded her. Her face, emotionless until she caught sight of Ellie, was transformed by a wide smile.

"My baby! All grown up!" she marveled, giving the little girl a hug. Ellie hugged her back, giggling nervously.

Brenda stood by, watching the reunion.

"Hello, Janna," she said, making a tentative move to embrace her daughter.

Janna ignored the overture, keeping her attention on Ellie.

"All set?" she asked briskly.

"Don't you have time to sit down and have some lunch?" Brenda asked. "I'd love to catch up with you." She kept her tone civil, even upbeat. Inwardly, she was crumbling. She had dreamed about seeing Janna again, imagining a wonderful reconciliation, never anything like this. Her daughter was a hostile stranger.

Janna shook her head once, quick, definite.

"Nope. I'm running late."

"Where do you live?" Brenda was eager for information.

"Eau Claire. In a nice house. No more motel rooms for you." She shared a private smile with Ellie. The stud in Janna's nose caught the light, sparkled.

Ellie picked up her plastic bin of clothes and toiletries.

"I'm ready," she said.

"Great! Let's get on the road."

"Bye, Granda," Ellie said, giving her stricken grandmother a little wave.

"Thank you for the roses," Brenda said to her departing daughter's back, a desperate effort to find some connection that would keep her from leaving.

Janna glanced over her shoulder and shot her mother a look that was both puzzled and sneering. "I never gave you no roses."

CHAPTER TWENTY-EIGHT

After Janna left with Ellie, Brenda wandered into Unit Two and curled up on Ellie's bed, where she was overtaken by her grief. She sobbed for Ellie, so captivated with her new parent. She sobbed for her once little girl Janna, whose brittle animation did not ring true. She sobbed for herself, the one left alone. There would be no beauty from these ashes. When she ran out of tears, she fell asleep on top of Ellie's bed. She slept the sleep of those who grieve, the deep sleep of escape.

Brenda was disoriented when she awoke the following morning with aching eyes and swollen eyelids. She staggered from the bed into the bathroom. She was crying before she hit the shower. Later, returning to Unit One, she spied Schmoe, forgotten in the excitement, and her tears returned.

She lifted the stuffed animal to her nose. The faintly musky smell that was so uniquely Ellie permeated it. Brenda closed her eyes as pain pulsed. She would keep it safe for her granddaughter, but needed, for her own sake, to put the worn plush toy out of sight.

Brenda squeezed Schmoe onto the crowded shelf above the

clothing bar. Her fingers brushed the green-and-silver tin, and she pulled it from its storage spot. She sat down on the bed and pried open the lid. A faint floral scent wafted upward. She contemplated the dried Mother's Day roses she had received over the years. Where had they come from? She had always assumed Janna had sent them, uncharacteristic but not inconceivable gestures of thanks. But yesterday Janna had made it quite clear that they were not from her. Brenda could not fathom any other person who possibly would have sent a rose one year, let alone been committed enough to follow through every Mother's Day.

She was alone and lonely. All she had now were a few dead roses from a mysterious source and a bunch of memories. A moan escaped, and she closed the tin and put it away. Every instinct screamed to curl up and wallow in her pain, but Brenda knew she had to reopen the motel. Every dime was still necessary. She took a deep, shuddering breath and ran her fingers through her hair.

But before concealing the "NO" portion of the motel's "VACANCY" sign, Brenda slipped through the cedar hedge to check in at the Andersons'. Their cat was glad to see her and accepted a little stroking and petting readily.

"Oh Smokey," Brenda sighed, sinking her hands into the cat's thick fur, "You'll miss Ellie too, won't you?" She replenished the supply of dry cat food and refilled the water dish.

Brenda returned to Unit One to await the arrival of potential guests. Determined to keep busy, she opened the legal pad Jimmie had sent her and, using an agreement she had found online as a model, drafted a Pet Policy for pet owners to sign if they wanted to have a furry friend spend the night.

"Available in Unit Ten only," she wrote firmly. Monday, she planned, she'd take it to the library and word-process a more official version.

There were three rooms taken on Saturday night, and Brenda spent an hour on Sunday cleaning and restocking the rooms. How she missed having Ellie's companionship and sweet chatter as she did so.

The rest of her Sunday was quiet. Brenda idly flipped pages in her new legal pad, crossed out completed items on the to-do lists, made a few fresh notations. She had worked hard, and the motel had come so far, but now it all seemed pointless without Ellie. Brenda could not keep the tears from spilling over. When Teak stopped by late in the afternoon, wanting to thank Ellie for caring for Smokey, Brenda kept her head averted so her friend would not see her puffy red eyes.

Teak was not fooled.

"What's wrong?"

"I'm fine." But Brenda's chest heaved.

"Brenda. You are not 'fine'." Teak was gentle but firm. "Talk to me."

Misery washed over Brenda.

"Ellie's gone." She sank into the green Adirondack chair and buried her face in her palms. Teak squatted down next to her, rubbed her shoulder, silently encouraging her to go on.

Brenda lifted her head but closed her eyes.

"I led you to believe Ellie's mother was dead. She isn't." Brenda spoke into the darkness, continuing the conversation she had avoided since their Stillwater trip, sharing her heartache. "When Ellie was a baby, Janna abandoned her, left her with me. We haven't seen her since.

"Somehow, Carl Levy tracked Janna down, and on Friday, she came and took Ellie." Brenda took a shuddering breath and added, on a hiccough, "Janna still can't stand me, wouldn't even look at me, and now Ellie's been ripped away."

Teak listened intently while Brenda spilled her fears for Ellie's wellbeing.

"I don't know if Janna has the financial capabilities of caring for her. I don't know if Janna knows how much attention and love a child needs." She opened her eyes and admitted starkly, "I'm angry and worried and sad."

"I'm going to bring you a sandwich," Teak said, rising to her feet. "When the soul is in trauma, we still must care for the body." Teak's practical nursing background was coming out. "You need to eat. You'll feel better." Brenda was glad that Teak did not offer any other platitudes, for she could not bear them.

When Teak returned with a thick ham and cheese sandwich, Brenda took a few bites, and did feel marginally better.

"Is it ok if I pray for you guys?" Teak asked.

What good would that do? Brenda thought. Still, she nodded her permission, consenting to the prayer.

***

Brenda got a call Monday mid-morning that the embroidery on the vests was finished. She had so anticipated surprising Ellie with the junior size vests she had ordered for her. She collected them now without pleasure.

Once home, Brenda checked out her vests and was disappointed to find that only her name was stitched on the black material. She called the embroidery shop.

"I thought you were going to embroider the name of my motel, "Neat as a Pin Motel," with an oversized pin beneath it," she said, striving to keep the irritation out of her tone.

The seamstress claimed to have no record of this request. "But if you return them, I certainly can do that for you," she said, "for an additional ten dollars per vest."

"Never mind." Brenda ended the call. It no longer seemed

important. It was merely one more little disappointment, appropriate for the way things were going. She slipped into the vest and surveyed herself in the mirror. The vest was crisp and snappy, but the face above looked washed out and unhappy. She needed to look the part of a successful innkeeper, even if she didn't feel it. Brenda unearthed her makeup kit. When she had makeup on, even with the shadows under her eyes, the improvement was marked. She smiled tentatively, straightened her vest and her back, and greeted the latest arrival.

***

The rhythm of the days was different with Ellie gone, and Brenda found it difficult to adjust. Patches of red began to appear in the trees, and the grasses grew golden. Although Brenda's marigolds continued to thrive, it was apparent that summer was on the wane. With the coming of September, the Fields packed up their things, forming a temporary mound on the front porch of the brown house. Mary's parents showed up in their old truck to assist with the move.

After the Fields had left, Katie came back to do a thorough house cleaning.

"I told Mary, leave it, she's got enough to do with those two live-wires, and Ollie starting 4-K on Tuesday! But this has been a real nice transition for them to live here, I'm so glad it worked out like it did."

Then she sighed, and Brenda knew she'd miss having her daughter and grandchildren in town.

"I hope you'll still stop in sometimes," she said impulsively.

"It's been great getting to know you," Katie said. She adjusted her ball cap, winked. "You haven't seen the last of me, that is for sure."

The Gordon family--Bill, Katie, the twins Josh and Kyle, and

Lizzie–surprised Brenda by reappearing on Labor Day. Brenda had started to turn the house into her home and office and was finding it to be a gigantic job. When the Gordons showed up, they cheerfully helped Brenda move everything she owned out of Unit One and into the brown house. Kyle and Josh lugged the service desk from where it had been stored in Unit Three and set in up in the hallway of the house, and Brenda polished it until it shone. She also dusted off the call bell and organized her materials in the cubbyholes.

Hailey wandered over and Brenda enlisted her to work with Lizzie in setting up the key board on the wall behind the desk. The two girls sorted out the box of keys onto the hooks, diverting Brenda with their chatter. Katie fashioned an attractive coffee station in one corner of the entryway so guests could help themselves. Bill Gordon wrestled with the OFFICE sign and returned it to its former location on the wall of the porch of the house. Soon it was lit and encouraging guests to come on over to the house to register. The tasks that might have taken her an entire day were accomplished in little over an hour.

Brenda thanked them all, and could see in their faces that they all felt sorry for her and were glad to be able to be a help.

After they left, she installed herself into the big white bedroom at the top of the stairs and closed the door of the room Ellie loved. She yearned for her little girl. But it was good to live in a house, especially after four months in a motel unit. For the first time since she was a child, she was living in a real house.

CHAPTER TWENTY-NINE

Five weeks drifted by. To Brenda's frustration, Janna seldom picked up when Brenda called to check on Ellie. Business had been brisk due to the many tourists enjoying the region's spectacular autumn leaf show, but this particular Thursday was quiet. Brenda positioned herself at the service desk anyhow, trying to will some of the passing cars to enter the parking lot. She could badly use the income from a few rooms. Three units, she reckoned, three units taken tonight and she'd fill her car up with gas and buy something special for supper. Maybe she should look into finding something to do as a sidelight. Now that the renovation was pretty much completed, there were hours available that she could do something else. Could she find a work-at-home opportunity? Something she could do and still check in guests? She would probably need Internet service, she decided. And having the Internet available to guests would be a draw. Brenda added "Find a job/ check into getting Internet...cost?" to the never-ending list in her yellow legal pad.

The ring of her phone interrupted her musings. It was Ellie!

"Mom said I better call so you don't have a spaz attack. We

stayed up all night watching movies," Ellie bubbled. "And I didn't get up until it was time for lunch! Tomorrow we are going shopping. Mom says my clothes are fuddy-duddy and she wants to buy me some new ones. It's fun having a mom that's not old."

Brenda's fingers tightened on her phone. With an effort, she tempered her voice to ask in a neutral tone, "Have you been reading?"

"We haven't gotten to it yet. But we will." Ellie's tone was breezy. "Well, I gotta go, bye."

"Bye." No I miss you, no how are you…just- "bye." Brenda closed her phone, shoved her feet into her flip-flops and wandered outside, looking for something to transfer her hurt feelings onto. Not the marigolds, they were vibrant and plentiful even in September. She could not find anything to complain about regarding the exterior of the motel, either. The hard work of the summer had resulted in a motel to be proud of.

She regarded the faded "Neat As a Pin Motel" sign and considered the need to replace it. Regretfully, she decided to wait until spring to see if she could afford to give it a face-lift then. She did not know how much business the winter would bring.

Carl called out a "hello, there" from where he stood between narrow rows of cars. Resentment toward Carl, he who had been instrumental in Ellie's departure, assailed her. Deliberately, she turned away, but he came toward her anyhow, his neon green shirt garish, his face a mask of concern.

"I wouldn't blame you if you decide to go on back to Prairie City, you won't want to stay on here by your lonesome," he said, voice filled with a sympathy that Brenda read as false. "I can understand why you are letting things go."

"Whatever do you mean, letting things go?"

Oh, just as an example… that overgrown grass on the end of

the motel." He gestured with his chin. "Well, I'm off. Try to have good night, Brenda."

Although Joe Fields had taken over mowing of the back yard and the expanse of grass behind the motel, and had mowed it the morning before he left, that strip of grass beyond the shed had not been touched since Jimmie's departure. Jimmie had used an old rotary mower to touch up that section since it was too narrow for the riding mower. Now that little section was, as Carl had said, unsightly.

If Jimmie had stayed, it would be getting done, she told herself, blaming him, even as she realized she was not being reasonable. With a heavy sigh, Brenda determined to do it herself. She was not going to give Carl grounds for dissatisfaction.

Brenda headed for Ed's shed. The rotary mower was rolled into a corner. She squeezed past the riding lawnmower and inexpertly tugged on the handle of the rotary mower when it caught on uneven flooring. It did not budge. Irritated, she wrenched the handle.

The machine, released, catapulted backward, rolling over her right foot. An empty beat, then an overwhelming jolt of pain. Crying out, she jerked her foot out from beneath the blade. Her toes were covered with blood.

Brenda groped for a support, grabbed the back of the riding lawn mower with her right hand. Reaching down with her other hand, she tried to staunch the flow. Blood oozed between her fingers. The pain was intense, white-hot. In a minute, she thought, she'd hobble out to the car, go for help...as soon as this woozy feeling passed. A groan escaped her lips.

"Are you all right?"

Through the intermittent black patches that obscured her vision, Brenda made out the figure of her former tenant in the doorway of the shed. Was this a hallucination?

No, it was a real T-shirt, smelling of body odor and motor oil that Buddy wrapped around her foot. Blood soaked through almost at once, and he said, "You think maybe you should go to the doctor?"

"Good idea." She hopped once, and the jarring motion magnified the pain to a level she had not known possible. She inhaled on a shudder, swayed.

"Here, maybe you should sit down." Buddy awkwardly put a hand on her waist and guided her to the seat of the riding lawn mower. He clenched and unclenched his fists, shuffled his feet. "I'll be right back. I'm gonna bring my truck closer."

Brenda bent her head, trying to will away waves of dizziness. She kept her hand clamped on the T-shirt covering her foot, trying to minimize the blood loss, concentrating on taking slow, deep breaths. She had never thought Buddy could look so beautiful, scraggly goatee and all.

***

Brenda lay in the dim hospital room, alone with her thoughts and her throbbing right foot. It was propped up on a wedge, wrapped in an oversized bandage. The blade of the lawn mower had cut into the top of her right foot, slicing deeply into her toes. Tomorrow, a specialist would be looking at it to see if the toes could be saved.

The hustle and bustle of the hospital, although greatly subdued, were still present, even at 2 AM. Across the room, the woman in the other bed snored intermittently. Despite these indications of life, Brenda had never felt so alone. Her whole foot was on fire, her eyes open and dry and her heart numb, battered, broken.

When a nurse came in offering relief, Brenda accepted the extra-strength painkiller.

***

"Feelin' blue, Mrs. Gonzales?"

An over-cheery voice roused her from her uneasy slumbers. Brenda opened her eyes a slit and focused on the dark shirt of a man talking with her roommate.

"Remember me? I'm Bill, the chaplain here at the hospital," he was saying. "We talked yesterday." His voice dipped as he asked with concern in his tone, "How are you doing this lovely morning?" Returning to full voice, he added, "And it is a lovely morning."

Brenda closed her eyes, tried to block out his jovial voice, so at odds with the darkness of her spirit.

"Here is a word from our good friend Jerry! That would be the prophet Jeremiah, and this word is found in chapter thirty-one. Verse thirteen. Here we go: 'I will turn their mourning into gladness; I will give them comfort and joy instead of sorrow.'"

Comfort would be enough, thought Brenda, lying motionlessly so as not to attract attention. She would not ask for joy.

CHAPTER THIRTY

Later that morning, two of Brenda's toes were amputated: her pinky toe and its next neighbor. She thought about calling Ellie and Janna to let them know about her accident, but decided not to. No need for them to worry. Or, worse, be indifferent.

Her hospital stay was two nights. Teak, who worked in the hospital, had been a faithful visitor, sticking her head in whenever she was in the vicinity. Katie Gordon, after she'd gotten wind of her accident, had offered to drive her home.

It was good to get home. Katie made up a bed on the living room couch so she didn't have to go up the stairs. Brenda melted into the couch, listlessly aware that her friend was bustling about, finding a pillow to prop up her foot, giving her an ice pack.

"Keep that foot raised as much as you can," Katie advised, "and ice it, too, off and on. That will keep the swelling down. And Teak said to tell you she'd bring over a little something for your supper."

Brenda dozed off, made her way awkwardly to the bathroom and afterwards concentrated on doing the few simple exercises the physical therapist had suggested.

True to her word, Teak stopped by with a chicken potpie, steaming and fragrant.

"I'll fix your coffee so in the morning you'll only need to push the brew button," she told Brenda.

"You are too nice to me," Brenda told her. After managing a few bites, she fell asleep, worn out from the pain and the events of the day.

The following morning Brenda had to reach deep within to muster the energy to drag herself off of the couch and into a fresh pair of sweatpants and a long-sleeved T-shirt.

"You have to do the hard things," she reminded herself wryly. After she started the coffee, she hobbled out onto the porch to wait for the pot to complete its cycle. She was enjoying the buttery, soothing sunshine, her foot propped up on a low stool, when Katie drove up in her old white truck. Brandishing a parcel-filled cardboard box, she mounted the porch steps and joined Brenda.

"Thought I'd see how you're doing this morning," Katie said. "Gathered up a few goodies for you. Lizzie made a pan of her famous brownies, and I saved some for you." She chuckled. "Somehow I managed to keep the boys from eating all of them. And there's a jar of beef and barley soup you can heat up and some beet pickles. Lots of iron in beets, you know.

"You did not need this, especially after..." She did not finish the thought. "Tomorrow's Sunday and Lizzie and Hailey plan to come over after church. You can give them orders. They can clean or do whatever you need them to do."

Katie's thoughtfulness brought tears to Brenda's eyes.

"I'm sorry," she apologized, dabbing at her eyes. "I don't know why I'm so weepy."

"Rain falls because the sky can no longer handle the heaviness, just as tears fall because the heart can no longer bear the pain. Go ahead and cry, honey." Katie gave her shoulder a quick squeeze. "Now, are you up for a bit of talking, or do you need a quiet spell?"

"I'd love to have you join me for a cup of coffee if you have time." Brenda was grateful for the company. "There's coffee in the kitchen."

"I'll take these things in"–Katie rose–"and fetch us each a cup."

"After losing Ellie, and now this, it seems too much," Brenda said after her friend had returned. "I am not sure if I can take much more." She paused and continued in a rush, "And I'm worried about my motel, too. I've been closed for a few days. I don't want people to think I'm not a reliable innkeeper."

Katie reached over and put her hand on top of Brenda's clasped hands. She squeezed.

"I know you are struggling now. But God has a plan for you, and His plans don't end in ashes."

Brenda jerked away, knocking Katie's hand off of her own.

"Now you sound like Teak," she said. "She always trots out some perky little saying." It was not in her nature to slander another, but in the middle of her pain she felt an annoyance toward the always-cheery younger woman that simply must be expressed.

Katie looked surprised.

"Perky little sayings? I don't know if that's what I'd call it... there's so much faith inside of Teak, it has to ooze out somehow."

Brenda met her gaze. She remembered that Teak was a single mother, had experienced her share of trouble.

"Do you guys really believe these things you say?" asked Brenda. "When bad things happen, do you really believe that God truly is behind all this, and He is okay with it?"

Katie's mug of coffee rested easy in her hands, and she sat silent. Brenda bit her lip. Had she been too forward? Was she going to lose Katie's friendship?

When Katie spoke, her voice was steady.

"I truly do believe what I'm saying, Brenda. I believe God is behind all of these things, but has decided not to share his reasons. It's the age-old question, isn't it, why do bad things happen to good people? Someday we may discover why, but for now He is asking us to trust. God doesn't do everything we ask him to, but He does keep his promises. And God loves you, loves you so much He sent His Son to die for you."

Brenda was silent, listening, while Katie, in a few simple words, outlined the Gospel message.

"It is such good news," Katie finished. She beamed a smile at Brenda who focused her attention on lifting her mug to her lips. Katie's words stirred something inside of her, but it felt too big, too new to discuss.

After a pause, Katie made a neutral comment about the weather, and Brenda gratefully followed her lead. After a bit her phantom toes started to throb, and Katie, noticing her discomfort was up at once, helping Brenda back to her bed on the couch, and bringing her a pain pill. After closing the blinds to dim the room, Katie was gone, leaving a sense of serenity in her wake.

The next couple of days passed in a blur of frustration as Brenda was not able to do what she felt she needed to, enduring pain as she overextended the use of her healing foot. While she was sitting on her porch mid-day, her foot elevated, trying to think through how to get her work done with minimal strain on her foot, Buddy pulled up in his rusty truck. He sat in the cab for a moment before approaching her.

"Doing all right?" he asked from the bottom of the steps.

"I think so. I'm glad you stopped by. I didn't know how to find you. I wanted to thank you. Buddy, you were a lifesaver."

He shifted from one foot to another.

"Yeah, glad I could help." He gulped, and his Adam's apple quivered. "I noticed that motorcycle guy isn't around anymore. I've been wondering if I could stay in a room like he did."

When Brenda didn't answer immediately, Buddy continued.

"Mom, she kicked me out." His tone was incredulous. "She said it was time I made it on my own. So I've been sleeping in my truck. And I got to thinking, maybe…"

It was more words than Brenda heard the entire time Buddy was a tenant in her house. She was silent, wondering what Buddy's intentions were. Memories of his sullen attitude and unkind remarks raced through her mind. Nevertheless, she did feel obligated to repay him for his assistance after her accident.

"Jimmie was working for me, that's why he stayed in a room here," Brenda told him. "He was my handyman."

"I could work for you." Buddy pressed on. "I could mow the grass, run errands. Whatever you need." His words hung awkwardly in the space between them, while Brenda weighed his request.

"We will see how it goes for one week," she finally said. Beginning to see advantages to the idea, especially now that her foot was compromised, she added, "This afternoon, in fact, I need a ride to the clinic. The doctor wants to take a look at my foot."

"Uh, how bad was it?"

"I lost two toes," she told him.

He blanched.

"What time?"

"Two-thirty….and, Buddy?"

He looked at her.

"I owe you a T-shirt. Thank you."

Brenda directed Buddy toward Unit Three, still a jumble of mismatched furniture. She limped over and sat in a scarred wooden chair, selecting items for him to pile into his rusty truck to be taken to the Thrift Store.

Once the room was not stuffed with clutter, Buddy vacuumed the carpet while Brenda sat on the bathroom floor, her foot propped on a rolled up towel, doing what she could to sanitize the room. She explained to him where the sheets were, and he, with more skill than she would have guessed, made up the queen-sized bed. There was a dorm size refrigerator in one corner, not impossibly dirty, that they both were happy to see functioned adequately.

By the end of the afternoon, Brenda was exhausted but satisfied. She learned from her visit with the doctor that her foot was healing at an acceptable rate, not showing any indication of infection. And Unit Three was cleared out enough that Buddy had an acceptable stopping place.

Buddy proved to be a godsend. He mowed the strip of lawn that had almost been her undoing, did maintenance on her lawn mowers, and took over the vacuuming of both her home and the motel units. He also stripped beds, swept the sidewalks, cleaned toilets.

But he was not Jimmie Stephens.

CHAPTER THIRTY-ONE

"What's going on with Unit Two?" Buddy asked, indicating its closed door. "Why don't you ever have anyone stay in there?"

Brenda's heart pinged. After Ellie had left on that terrible Saturday six weeks ago, Brenda had locked the door and not returned to the room. Walking into it now would be akin to pulling a scab from a slow-to-heal wound. She focused her attention on the spray bottle of Windex she was carrying. Such a pretty shade of blue it was.

Buddy was watching her.

"Ain't that the room where your girl slept?"

"Yep." She gestured toward the far end of the motel with a slightly trembling hand. "We'll start down there." Hoisting the bucket of window washing supplies, she limped purposefully past Unit Two, leaving Buddy with no recourse but to follow with the stepladder.

He washed the outside panes of the windows, using the stepladder to reach the top panes, and she managed the insides, standing on a chair when necessary. While she worked, Brenda's thoughts returned continually to Ellie's abandoned room. As they completed washing the windows in one room, and then another, drawing closer and closer to Unit Two, her unease increased.

At ten-thirty, Brenda invented an errand for Buddy. He seemed glad for a break from the tedium of washing windows and headed for his truck with a spring to his step. Brenda watched him drive off before she abandoned the cleaning supplies in Unit Four and walked down to Unit Two where she fitted the key into the keyhole.

Standing on the threshold, tears filling her eyes, Brenda acknowledged that entering this room was long overdue. What possible good could come from treating the room as a shrine? Still, foolish as it might be, Brenda did not want this room to serve as another guest room. This had been Ellie's room. "Lord, give me strength," she whispered. With a swift, sudden movement, she pushed open the door.

Traces of Ellie were scattered throughout the room: the hairbrush under the bed, the half-filled bin of toys, a pair of underpants lying askew next to her hamper.

Brenda approached Ellie's bed, the blankets flung over the top in the rumply fashion that the little girl had considered making a bed. Brenda pulled off the wrinkled pink fabric bedspread that had so pleased the child and bundled it into a ball. She stripped the bed of its blankets and sheets, working steadily, though heavy tears wetted the fabric. When she had finished, she sank down on the mattress and whispered a prayer for Ellie. How she missed the child!

The rattle of Buddy's truck announced his return. Brenda gathered up the dirty linens and carried them high to mask her tear-stained face. She had a sense of victory, despite her tears. She had bearded the lion and entered the den. It would never be as hard again.

The following morning, Brenda busied herself sorting Ellie's things, relegating some of the items to a donation bin, but others she packed up. Futile as it might prove to be, she daydreamed wistfully of the day the little girl would be back in her care, reclaiming some left-behind treasures.

Brenda found herself returning time and again to the room, first to clean and rearrange; later, simply to sit. There was something about the innocence of the pink curtains, the yellow and pink striped walls that was a balm to her soul. While still sad and lonely, she felt a measure of peace. She regarded the picture they had purchased that day in Stillwater. What had Teak said about the picture? Beauty from ashes? Was it possible that even though Carl had established contact with Janna to destroy Brenda, God could use Carl's mischief, and some good might come out of losing Ellie? She replayed the conversation she'd had with Katie on the porch.

She was so mixed up about God. Did He care? Or was He far away and unconcerned? Still, there was a tugging in her heart that could not be silenced. Even when she tried to put God out of her mind, He snuck back in. She picked up the pink devotional book Ellie had left behind.

"You will seek Me and find Me," she read, "when you seek Me with all your heart."

The next time Teak asked if she'd like a ride to church, she said yes.

The pastor, an older fellow with a shock of white hair and a kindly-lined face, reminded the congregation that they were not alone.

"God is as near as our breath," he said with a conviction that could not be ignored. "Come to me, all you that are weary and are carrying heavy burdens," he recited, his faded gray eyes glowing, "and I will give you rest."

Brenda bowed her head and prayed. Tentatively, she talked with God, telling Him she was sorry for wronging Him, praising Him for His goodness, asking for guidance.

Jimmie's cryptic comment about the peace that passed understanding came to mind. It made no sense that she would have such peace, but God's love is beyond common sense. It was not only peace, but joy as well, that flooded her soul.

She knew she'd be back.

***

Work at the motel continued. Brenda had Buddy junk the worse of the twin beds in Unit Four, and replaced it with one of the beds from Ellie's room. The other bed, Ellie's former bed, she pushed up against the wall, opening up the center of the room.

On her way to the grocery store for bread and coffee one morning, she spotted a pink chair by the end of a driveway. Ellie would love that chair, she thought, for it was a circular chair, soft and pink, with thick cushions, a matching ottoman. Steeling herself, she drove on. She would not think of Ellie or how much she would have loved that chair. Later, standing in the room, her eyes drifted to the empty side of the room, where the bed had once stood.

"Buddy!" she called. "Could you drive down to Weston Avenue? If there is a pink chair still at the end of one of the driveways there, could you get it and bring it back here? I have an idea."

Buddy, willing but not eager, trudged out to his pickup truck and returned fifteen minutes later with the chair and a doubtful expression.

"It don't seem right for a motel room, Brenda," he said. "It seems like it belongs in a spa. But it is in good shape."

It was in good shape, showing little if any sign of wear. Buddy wrestled the chair into the room while Brenda followed, lugging the ottoman. She pointed to the spot she had designated for her find. Buddy settled himself in the chair, made a move to set his feet on the ottoman, but, catching Brenda's alarmed expression, kept his dirty shoes on the floor.

"This chair is the bomb." He closed his eyes. "Good grab, Brenda."

Once the chair was in place, Brenda set the little table Ellie had decorated next to it, and painted a bookcase pink and yellow. Browsing through miscellanea at the thrift store, she unearthed a wooden cross, hung it on the wall beside the door. The peaceful room was evolving into a sanctuary of sorts.

Teak presented her with a plaque.

"Something for your prayer room," she told Brenda.

Brenda read the inscription aloud.

"'You're my place of quiet retreat; I wait for Your Word to renew me. Psalm 119:114.'" She smiled at Teak. "I love it." She had not considered Ellie's room to be a prayer room, and she liked the idea. "This room can be a chapel for the motel. It will be a place for people if they need a quiet place to come away and think."

Brenda fetched the soft Bible Jimmie had given her before he had gone. She settled herself in the "spa chair" and opened the Bible to the Psalms. Words that had seemed so confusing before dovetailed, resonated. Although she was still alone, she no longer felt so lonely.

She made a little sign for the door: Chapel of the Motel. It caught the eye of a serious young woman who had stopped at the motel, her car full to bursting.

"Can anyone go in there?" she asked. When Brenda nodded,

she smiled. "I need a place to be still," she said. "When I'm still I can hear what my heart is telling me."

"I love that," Brenda said, and felt a sense of kinship with the girl, who spent an hour in the pleasant room.

It became a common thing for guests to spend a few minutes in the Chapel of the Motel. One woman who had been quarreling with her husband stormed into the room. Later, Brenda found that the woman had jotted a few lines of appreciation and words of praise to the Lord in a legal pad Brenda had left on the little table.

After that, Brenda found other entries in the pad, words of praise to God as well as appreciation for the space, how unexpected it was, and how perfect.

Brenda herself spent time in the Chapel of the Motel every day. While there, she felt a sense that even though she could not see it, there was a reason for all the pain and misery she'd been going through, and carving out a place dedicated to considering the mightiness and holiness of God was a very good thing.

Two weeks after she had started attending services at Teak's church, the pastor and his wife stopped for a visit. Diffidently, she asked if they'd like to see her chapel.

They were both charmed. The pastor put a hand on Brenda's shoulder. "There are many that will be blessed by coming here," he said. He prayed a prayer of dedication to the space and a prayer of peace to all who entered it.

It was a glorious afternoon, the best in a long, long time.

For the rest of the day, Brenda's smile remained intact as she greeted guests, scrubbed toilets, ate a solitary dinner. Later, she ran over to Teak's and shared with her all that had happened: how the sermon had so resonated with her heart, the visit from the pastor and his wife, the dedication of the chapel room.

Teak's eyes were glistening long before Brenda finished. She squeezed Brenda's hands.

"I'm so glad!" said Teak. "Things are falling into place."

Walking back to the brown house, Brenda had to wait to cross the alley to allow a rusty maroon sedan to pass. She wasn't sure, but she thought she saw Carl's daughter Gretchen in the front seat, sitting too close to the driver.

Brenda knew too well from her own experience with Janna at that age how important it was for parents to stay abreast of relationships and friendships. She hadn't, and how it cost her. Tomorrow she'd tell Carl he might want to check into his daughter's whereabouts.

CHAPTER THIRTY-TWO

But Janna's phone call the next morning pushed thoughts of everything else to the back of her mind.

"Me and Ellie are gonna stop over on Friday, okay?"

"Of course it's okay." A smile creased Brenda's face. "I'll fix a real nice dinner."

"Oh, you don't have to feed us," Janna said. "We thought we'd just stop in and say hi. Ellie has the day off, teacher meeting or something."

Eau Claire was over a hundred and fifty miles away, quite a distance to drive to say hello. Brenda insisted on serving a meal, and Janna agreed, adding to expect them around noon. Brenda flipped her phone shut. It had been over two months since she had last seen Ellie. She couldn't wait to see that girl! As far as seeing Janna again…her stomach clenched.

Filled with uneasy anticipation, Brenda fetched the cleaning cart and freshened up all of the motel units. In Unit One, she scrubbed an already immaculate kitchenette. She sat a moment in the "spa chair" in Unit Two and tried unsuccessfully to quiet her spirit. She passed over Three, the unit Buddy was staying in, noticed the sink in Four was dripping and needed the attention of a plumber. Brenda made a call, moved on to Unit Five.

By the time she had completed her review of all ten units, she was calmer and had a menu in mind. Pot roast, she decided, with potatoes and carrots and onions. And she'd make apple crisp! Janna had loved it as a child. Brenda's mouth watered. She hadn't fixed such a meal in a long time. A family meal!

A car pulling up in front of the house interrupted her musings. She met the middle-aged couple and their dachshund in the office. They inquired about a pet-friendly room and signed the pet agreement readily. Soon after, the dog-run Jimmie had built for Punk was put into good use. He had been right about the advantage of having a pet-friendly unit.

***

It was drizzling when Janna and Ellie arrived that first Friday in October, shortly after one o'clock. Brenda, filled with anticipation, had been waiting on the porch, accompanied by the savory smell of the pot roast and onions. Ellie launched herself into her grandmother's arms and Brenda returned the hug wholeheartedly. Over Ellie's head, Brenda could see Janna observing the two of them with an odd expression on her face.

When Brenda made a motion as if to include Janna in the hug, Janna recoiled and shook her head. Brenda did not know why Janna was so resistant to opening herself to affection. Still, she told herself, she would not let it spoil this occasion. Dinner with her girls!

"Come on in," Brenda said briskly. "You can wash your hands and sit right down. I hope you're hungry!"

"I'm starved," Ellie said, leading the way into the brown house. "Granda, it's so cool you're living in the house now!"

They sat around the dining room table, carefully set for the occasion. Brenda had used Aunt Ruth's china, white with yellow roses curling about the rims of the plates. Ellie touched the edge of the matching butter dish with a pinkie. Janna chattered away steadily, talking about her job at a home improvement store, the traffic on the highway, the new outfits she had bought for Ellie. She did not make eye contact with Brenda.

When there was a pause in her discourse, Brenda turned to Ellie. "How is school going? Have you made some nice new friends?"

Ellie nodded, but offered no details. After the main course, the little girl slipped away, disappearing up the stairs.

Janna joined her mother in the kitchen, where she was dishing up re-warmed apple crisp.

Brenda took advantage of the private moment.

"How are things going?" she asked.

Janna leaned her angular frame against the counter and gazed out the window, ignoring the question. When she spoke, her voice was low.

"Would you take her back?" She pushed her hair behind her ears before continuing, "She's a good girl. She is. But I didn't realize it would be such a hassle…I don't want her after all."

Not want Ellie! Brenda scooped generous dollops of ice cream onto the top of each piece of apple crisp. How she would love having her sidekick back in her life, sharing meals, hearing confidences, creating memories! It would fill the emptiness in her house and in her heart. She loved the little girl so much…but what would be best for her?

Brenda tried to pray, but her mind was whirling. With precision, she laid a fork on each plate next to its portion of cinnamon scented dessert. By the time she had settled the third fork onto the third plate, she reached her decision. She knew what she must do. She had done hard things before, but this might be the hardest thing she'd ever done.

Brenda faced Janna.

"That would not be fair to the child." Brenda's eyes searched her daughter's face, silently pleading with her to understand what she was saying. "We can't be having Ellie tossed back and forth between us. She isn't a plaything, Janna. Unless–" Brenda was struck with a sudden thought. "Do you want to come live here, too? We had a good day today, together, didn't we?"

"Mother, I can't believe you'd suggest such a thing." Janna's chin came up. "There's no way I'd ever be able to do that." Her hands moved restlessly. "I was kidding about you taking her back anyhow. Ellie!" She raised her voice. "It's time for us to go."

They would not even stay for dessert, leaving the ice cream to melt into the abandoned apple mixture. Brenda scraped it all into the trash, her eyes swimming with tears. Already she had started to second-guess her decision.

Had she done the right thing?

CHAPTER THIRTY-THREE

Brenda still felt unsettled in her spirit as she stood in front of the kitchen sink later that afternoon scouring the roasting pan. The meal had been prepared with such hope and anticipation of a wonderful reunion with her daughter, and it had ended with more hostility than before. She was not at peace with the way she had left things with Janna.

She hoped the next decision she had to make was an easy one.

"I pray, Lord, there is something I do soon where I feel secure in knowing I absolutely made the right choice." She attacked a particularly burnt corner of the pan. A mirthless chuckle escaped. "Something bigger than choosing to do a thorough job of scrubbing."

A car pulled up in front of the house as she set the pan to dry on the rack. When she came out of the kitchen, wiping her hands on a dishtowel, a tall young man with a glint in his eye was tapping the service bell on the desk.

"Hi there. Name's Devon. Do you rent rooms by the hour?" he asked smoothly.

Rooms by the hour. That could meet only one thing, and it

was not something that Brenda wanted to promote or endorse for her motel.

Here was an easy no.

She walked past the young man and opened the door, silently giving him a negative response.

"Excuse me, but I don't think you have any right to refuse me," he protested.

"I don't rent by the hour."

Devon sighed.

"Fine, I will pay for a night." He reached for his wallet. "How much?"

Brenda continued to hold the door open, her attention fixed on the passenger of the car idling outside. The girl had her head bent down, almost as if she were hiding, but there was something familiar about that golden head. And wasn't it the same car she'd seen in the alley a few days ago?

"Is that Gretchen Levy with you?" she asked sharply.

"What if it is?" the man leered.

"Do you know she's only thirteen years old?"

He shook his head, rejecting her comment. "She told me she was seventeen."

Brenda persisted. "She's in seventh grade."

"I don't believe you." Shoving his wallet back in his pocket, the man pushed past her and down the steps. "And I don't need your crummy motel either."

Brenda was right behind him. She was not leaving a young teen alone with this man. As he opened the front door of the car, she hopped in the back seat.

"Thirteen-year-olds need a chaperone," she said.

"What are you doing in here?" hissed Gretchen, regarding Brenda with something akin to horror.

"Wait a minute," the young man barked. He did not get into the car but stuck his head in the open door and addressed Gretchen. "Tell me the truth. How old are you, anyway?"

"She's in seventh grade," Brenda insisted.

"Shut up. I'm asking her."

"I'm almost fourteen." Gretchen's voice was unsteady but defiant.

He cursed, reached past her, and jerked open the passenger door. In moments, Gretchen and Brenda were both standing outside and the car was squealing out of the parking lot.

Brenda took a deep breath and blew it out.

Gretchen's hair was tousled and her cheeks very red. "Thanks a lot," she said, venom dripping from her words.

"That boy was trouble," Brenda told her. "I couldn't let him hurt you."

"We were just kissing," Gretchen said. She glanced across the parking lot and muttered a nasty word. Brenda looked too.

Carl was striding toward them, hands on his hips.

"What's going on? What are you doing to my daughter?" he blustered as soon as he was within earshot.

Brenda sighed.

"Saving her, I hope," she said.

Carl's brow furrowed. He glared at Gretchen. "You said you were going to Kayla's."

Brenda waited while the girl stammered an explanation.

"I was! But Devon texted me and wanted to go for a ride, and so I was just riding around with him."

"He was wondering if I rented rooms by the hour," Brenda told Carl.

Carl's face reddened. Without another word, he took his daughter by the arm and marched her back to his dealership.

Brenda filled a couple of units with bona fide guests before Carl returned.

He shifted from side to side.

"I haven't always treated you the best. And you still–" He stopped, started again. "Gretchen is–" He pressed his lips together, shook his head. "She's everything to me."

"Maybe," Brenda ventured, "it's time to accept that I'm here for good."

His teeth made an appearance. "Today it was definitely good."

.

CHAPTER THIRTY-FOUR

Three long weeks limped by with no word from Janna or Ellie. Brenda's own calls went unanswered, unreturned. Despite the bright blue skies, Brenda felt off-kilter and the serenity she had enjoyed before their visit evaporated.

The unseasonably warm weather abruptly shifted near the end of October, and business was slow. Brenda sat idly at the service desk, considering how to fill the empty evening ahead. A sudden gust of wind brought a lashing of rain against the window, and she peered past the drops. The clouds, dark and lowering, suited her mood. Her cell phone rang, the screen displaying Janna's number.

She flipped it open.

"Hello?" she said breathlessly.

"Hi, Granda."

"Hello, sweet thing!" Brenda anchored the phone between her ear and shoulder and rose to her feet. "How are you? How's school?"

"Okay." Ellie's voice lacked vibrancy. Brenda, not wanting to turn the conversation into an inquisition that might discourage Ellie from calling, stemmed the threatening flow of questions. She wandered into the living room where she settled on Ruth's comfortable couch and talked brightly about the influx of guests in the motel the previous weekend, the leaves on the backyard tree that had turned a brilliant red, Hailey's new bike.

"How's Smokey?" Ellie asked.

"Oh, as cat-like as ever. I saw her stalking a robin yesterday. Of course, the robin had no problem getting away!"

Ellie giggled, and the familiar sound warmed Brenda's heart. A comfortable silence hummed between them.

Abruptly, Ellie broke it. "Mom's been sleeping a lot. Sometimes she don't get out of bed all day."

For the child's sake, Brenda tried to make light of it.

"Oh, some people need more naps than others. Maybe she's not feeling well. What did you have for supper tonight?"

"Cereal. Mom didn't want to get up, so I fixed myself some cereal. But the milk tasted funny." Ellie gave a small sigh, and Brenda's heart broke.

"Sweet thing, if you're still hungry, open a can of soup," she suggested. "Just be careful with the stove, won't you?"

"Granda, I'm not a baby. Anyway, I don't think we have any soup."

An arriving guest forced Brenda to end the conversation. After the newcomer, a tall, thin lady with a mass of curls reminiscent of a poodle, had been settled into Unit One, Brenda crossed the alley, headed for Teak and some advice.

She had barely perched herself on Teak's couch before she confided, "When Janna was here a couple of weeks ago, she seemed so energetic. And Ellie said they were staying up late at night, doing all sorts of things. Now Ellie says her mom won't get out of bed."

The younger woman was quiet. After a moment she offered

hesitantly, "Sounds like peaks and valleys. I recently took a mental health course as part of my continuing ed. I wonder if Joanna has some kind of a personality disorder? Is Ellie safe with her?"

The sense of unease Brenda had been feeling consolidated into a mass of panic.

"I can't believe I didn't realize…was that what Janna was trying to tell me when they were here?" Her head moved from side to side. "What if Janna harms her? Oh no!" She shot up, ready to bolt.

Teak put a restraining hand on her arm.

"Wait a minute," she said gently. "Let's take it to the Lord, okay?"

Brenda squeezed her hands together, bowed her head. Her heart was hammering, and she tried to focus on what Teak was saying.

"– with dear Ellie and be with Brenda as she goes forth. Give her strength and wisdom," Teak prayed. "And help her to remember that all things work together for good for those who love You. Glory to your precious name. Amen."

Teak had a Verse-A-Day calendar on her counter. She ripped off the current page. "Take this good Word with you," she said, pushing it into Brenda's hand.

"Thanks, Teak." Brenda accepted her friend's hug, and backed out of the kitchen, thrusting the calendar page into her pocket.

Despite the rain, Brenda punched in Janna's number as she hurried back to her house. Although the phone rang and rang, no one picked up. She left a short message, asking for a call back.

"As soon as you can, please," she said.

Brenda stood near the desk in the hallway, drumming her fingers on its surface, her mind racing. The weather was getting nasty: it was not a good night for travel. No matter: she would do whatever it took to rescue the child and bring her home again, where she belonged. Brenda grabbed her keys, her purse, a blanket, a bottle of water. What else?

"Strength and wisdom please, Lord," she whispered. She bit her lip, considering the motel, the curly-haired guest installed in Unit One. Seeing no other option, she threw on her raincoat and crossed the parking lot to Unit Three.

"Buddy," she said, after beating a tattoo on his door, "I need to leave. Can I tell the woman in Unit One that she can call on you if she needs anything?"

Buddy, who had opened the door with reluctance, straightened.

"Sure. And I can check in anyone else that shows up, if you like."

Brenda threw some breathless instructions at him and rushed for the car.

She was only ten minutes on her way before the rain began transitioning to sleet. The visibility was poor, the headlights doing little to break up the darkness. Brenda's hands clutched the wheel so tightly her knuckles were white. This weather, this dark and slippery road, was bringing back memories of that terrible night, thirty years ago. She slowed the car, eased onto the shoulder. Her heart was pounding. She would go back to the motel and attempt this trip in the morning.

As she prepared to make a U-turn, her headlights caught a wriggling black bundle in the ditch. Brenda delicately applied her brakes and got out of the car. She was immediately assailed by bits of needle-sharp ice and made a move to return to the car.

Whimpering howls arising from the bundle caused her to pause and instead of returning to the car, she slipped her way toward the bundle. Cautiously, she bent over to examine the mound. A head lifted, dark eyes met hers. A pup! Brenda scooped the creature into her arms and deposited it on the front seat. She used her sweatshirt to rub some warmth into the dog. A he, she discovered. Gratefully, his tongue licked the side of her hand. Brenda cranked up the heater to max, angled a vent so the warmth would blow on the shivering animal.

"Well, pup?" she said. This small but successful rescue, along with the presence of another living creature, bolstered her confidence. "We might as well go on."

Gingerly, she resumed her journey. After a few minutes, the dog was revived enough to rise shakily to his feet and, balancing there, shook himself vigorously, covering Brenda with muddy drops. He stank.

"Lay down," she ordered, nose wrinkling. Thankfully, the dog lay down once again. Her foot, sans toes, began to throb. The damp air was not its friend. Carefully she drove on through the gathering darkness.

Brenda reached the freeway and merged onto it, heading east. A mileage sign informed her that Eau Claire was still fifty miles away. She sighed, and flexed her shoulders, trying to relax. The roads were slush covered, and growing more and more slippery. She did not dare to drive as fast as she wished.

It was a long ninety minutes before Brenda and her animal companion reached the outskirts of Eau Claire. A car in front of her slid sideways, corrected. The red roof of a Woodman's Market caught her eye, and she pulled into its parking lot where she sat, trembling slightly, taking deep breaths. Beside her, the dog sat up, sensing a change in circumstances. Brenda huffed out a deep breath, and, with determination, reached for her phone. She must press on. She punched in Janna's phone number, crossed her fingers.

"Answer, Ellie," she breathed.

It went directly to voice mail. Brenda left another terse, "Call me, right away, please," message. She closed her phone, dug into her purse for her legal pad. She had written Janna's address on the cardboard backing. 813 Bollenger Street.

It had not been easy, she remembered, wresting the address from Janna.

"I don't want you coming down, checking up on me," she had told Brenda. "Why do you need it anyway?"

"I want to write to Ellie, send her a card on her birthday." She was not being unreasonable, she had thought, wanting to be able to contact them. Now she frowned. Eau Claire was a bigger place than Brenda had bargained for. How was she going to find Bollenger Street?

Beside her, the pup whined.

"Are you hungry, boy?" Brenda asked. "I suppose I could go in the store, get you something to eat." She turned on the inside car lights and took a good look at the dog. He was a smallish dog, not a puppy as she had originally thought, but a small breed dog. His matted fur was dark, but she wasn't sure what color it would be if he were washed. Although he had no collar, he was docile. Tentatively she reached over and gave him a scratch.

"Be right back."

The grocery store was clean and well-lit. Brenda's first stop was the restroom. The woman who stared back at her from the mirror looked like she had been in a war zone: dirty and tear-streaked, but determined. Brenda reached in her pocket in search of a tissue, but instead pulled out a calendar page, the calendar page Teak had given her.

"And call for help when you're in trouble," Brenda read, "I'll help you, and you'll honor me. Psalm 50:15." There in the restroom, Brenda bowed her head and prayed, calling on the Lord for help, before using a brown paper towel to wipe her face.

Returning to the main part of the store, Brenda grabbed a basket and found the pet section where she bought two pouches of dog food. She could open them wide, she reckoned, and the dog would be able to eat right out of the pouch. Thinking of Ellie, she added a couple of ready-made sandwiches, a quart of milk, a package of Oreos, a bag of carrot sticks, and a single-serve container of ranch dressing.

The windshield of the car was coated white by the time she returned with her purchases. The pup greeted her with a high-pitched yip. Before she resumed her journey, she gave Buddy a call, wanting to see how her motel was faring.

He answered on the fourth ring. "Brenda's Motel," he said, an edge of importance rimming the words.

"Buddy, that's not the name of our motel," Brenda said.

" 'Neat as a Pin' is a dumb name. What's up?"

His voice sounded different, buoyant. Was he drunk?

"Did anyone else check in?"

"A coupla guys lookin' for a place to par-tay. One of them—Devon—says 'Hey.'"

He was definitely drunk. And Devon. Wasn't that the guy who booted Gretchen out of his car?

"Buddy." Brenda felt frantic but impotent. "Don't drink any more. And watch out for Devon. He might be wanting to get back at me."

"Whatever," he said before disconnecting the call.

Brenda hit redial but Buddy did not pick up. Brenda huffed out a frustrated breath, and with determination, tried to push the situation at the motel out of her mind and concentrate on the mission at hand. Find Ellie! But how?

She had a highway map of Wisconsin in her glove compartment, she remembered. Was Eau Claire one of the cities expanded on the edge? Worth a try. She reached in front of the pup and pushed at the latch. It was stuck, so she jabbed again, harder. This time it released, and she fished inside the glove box for the map. The pup was very interested in the expanding paper as she unfolded it, and she swatted him with a corner of the map.

"Knock it off," she ordered. Eau Claire was indeed one of the cities featured on the edge of the map, but it was not detailed enough to include Bollenger Street. Strike one.

Brenda trudged back into the grocery store, clutching the map. She hesitated at the nearest counter.

"Can I help you?" The clerk was young with pink and brown hair and a bored expression.

Brenda extended the map. "Do you know where Bollenger Street is?"

"No idea."

Strike two.

As Brenda turned away, the clerk suggested, "Go check at a bar. Guys in bars always know their way around."

Brenda had not been in a bar since she'd been married to Dale, was not anxious to visit one now; but, "Where's the nearest one?" she asked.

Brenda followed the clerk's directions, "First left, then a quick right" and arrived at the Idlewild Bar. When she bustled in, the four men sitting at the bar and the two playing pool in the back looked up in unison. She slid onto a bar stool, conscious of the ice pellets decorating her hair and shoulders, conscious of their attention.

"The storm must be getting pretty bad." A solid man in soiled blue coveralls said conversationally, eying her. "Lemme buy you a drink," he added. He displayed a set of yellow, well-spaced teeth.

"No thank you," she replied. "I'm looking for Bollenger Street." She raised her voice. "Anybody know where Bollenger Street is?"

The men at the bar shook their heads, but one of the pool players chimed in, "Bollenger Street you say?" He put down his cue stick and came over. "Why don't you let me drive you over there? We could make a quick stop at my place first."

There was a guffaw from the general area of the pool table. Brenda's face grew hot. Inspiration struck, and she shook her head.

"I don't think Charley would like that."

"Charley?"

"He's in the car."

"Why didn't he come in?" the pool player challenged.

Brenda told the truth.

"Charley doesn't know how to ask for directions." There was a general laugh then, and the pool player surrendered.

"Take a right on the road out front and turn left onto Hastings Way. Stay on that a few blocks. When you get to Highway Twelve, turn right. Look for State Street. Bollenger is off of State somewheres." He gestured with his hands as he spoke.

"Thank you," she breathed fervently. "Left on Hastings. Right on Twelve. State."

Soon she was back in the car.

"Hello, Charley," she said, introducing the pup to his new name. Once she was on Hasting Way a blur of neon lights, obscured by the sleet, greeted her. Brenda took a deep breath and strained to read the signs.

CHAPTER THIRTY-FIVE

Brenda's fingers tightened on the steering wheel as she peered at the house numbers. 309...311... it had to be the next house. She pulled over to the curb, and the car that had been closely following zipped past, horn blaring.

In the gathering darkness it was difficult to discern the color of the small house, and no lights brightened the interior, but the number beside the door was clearly 313, so Brenda cut the engine and drew a long shaky breath. She had made it.

She'd grab Ellie and head straight back to Miskomin. With any luck, they'd be back at the motel long before daylight, long before any guests were ready to check out or be looking for hot coffee. She did not place much confidence in Buddy's ability to handle either task.

"Stay," she ordered, and the tired pup offered no objection. With resolve, Brenda opened the car door and stepped into a puddle of icy cold water. She yelped involuntarily before picking her way to the house, the slush on the sidewalk making the journey a precarious one. She mounted three crumbling steps and came face to face with a soiled white door. After curling her cold fingers into a fist, she rapped twice.

Silence answered her. She waited, stomped her cold feet, knocked again.

A mournful howl filled the air. Was it coming from the house? Brenda bent her head, listened with intent focus. No, she decided, straightening, the howl was coming from behind her.

Charley.

The porch light on the house next door flashed on, and a voice snarled, "Shaddup!"

Brenda lifted a hand in an apologetic wave, and picked her way back to the car, where she banged on the passenger window.

"You cut that out," she hissed.

Charley subsided, but only until Brenda had regained her position on the step. Then he resumed howling with renewed vigor. Brenda hurried back to him as fast as conditions allowed.

"Come on, then," she said, hoisting him into her arms. She could only hope he wouldn't cause problems inside. For the third time, she sloshed back to 313.

Abandoning the futility of polite knocking, Brenda pounded on the door and was rewarded by a thin voice.

"Who is it?"

"It's me." Brenda's relief at hearing Ellie's voice made her weak. She almost dropped the little pup. "It's Granda."

Ellie fumbled with the lock and flung open the door. She jumped into her grandmother's arms, crying and laughing.

"Granda, you came! You came!"

Brenda, almost strangled by the little girl's grip around her neck and rendered immobile by the legs wrapped around her waist, lost her hold on Charley. He landed on the floor with a thump and scurried into the dim house.

"Let's turn on a light and see where Charley's going," said

Brenda, untangling herself from her granddaughter and her over-powering cloud of cheap cologne.

"The lights don't work," Ellie replied in a matter of fact tone. "The electricity got shut—"

Her explanation was interrupted by a voice both strident and lackluster.

"Get this hound out of here. Ellie, what's going on? I told you to let me rest."

Janna.

"Is your mom alright?" whispered Brenda, pushing the front door shut and leaning against it. She looked for a mat on which to wipe her wet shoes, but there was none that she could see. Her eyes, adjusting to the low light, took in an untidy living room, with an equally untidy kitchen off to one side. Brenda's nostrils twitched as the rank smell of spoiled food assailed them.

Ellie ignored Brenda's question. She crossed the living room and slipped through a partially opened door. After a few moments, she reappeared, holding Charley. She shut the door firmly behind her.

"Mom says stay out of her bedroom."

Ellie was dressed in a black skirt, too short for Brenda's liking, and a skimpy top that exposed her belly. Her legs were bare. A crooked line of dark red lined her young lips. Brenda opened her mouth, searching for something to say that was not critical. Ellie, oblivious to her grandmother's discomfort, was crooning over the dog.

"Granda, I love this dog. Where did you get him? Is he ours?"

"Ellie, what's going on? Talk to me. How long have you been without power?"

Ellie shrugged.

"I think when I came home from school, maybe Tuesday?"

She petted the dog again and added in a small voice, "I'm scared because Mom just lays there. I'm glad you came."

Brenda put a hand on her shoulder.

"You wait here with Charley—"

"You named him Charley? Oh Granda!"

"—and I am going out to the car. I got you something to eat." Brenda was so glad she had taken the time to make that stop. "You can have a snack, and I'll go see what's going on with your mom."

Despite the gloom of the room, Brenda saw Ellie's eyes brighten at the mention of food. It wasn't long before the little girl was tucking into the bag of provisions, and Brenda was pushing open Janna's bedroom door.

"I said stay out. Can't you do anything right?"

"Janna, it's Mom." Brenda directed the remark to a ball of greasy blonde hair at the top of the lump in the bed. The room was stale and stuffy, with an undercurrent of urine and unwashed body.

Janna uttered a foul word.

The viciousness slapped like an ocean wave. Brenda stood motionless for thirty full seconds before she backed out of the room and closed the door as noiselessly as possible. She and Janna had never been close, but she held her palm against her chest as physical pain threaded her heart. With effort, she set her hurt aside. Janna needed help, now. Brenda tapped her bottom lip three times, thinking, before joining Ellie in the kitchen.

"Who does your mom hang out with?"

Ellie, kneeling on a wooden chair surrounded by remnants of her repast, stuffed an Oreo into her mouth and spoke around it.

"Meredith."

"Meredith?" With the Oreo in the mix, Brenda was not sure she heard correctly. "Do you know her phone number?"

"No. But it's in Mom's phone." The little girl started to rise, then sank back. "Her phone died, and we can't charge it up with the power out."

That explained why all her calls had gone straight to voice mail. Brenda pressed on.

"Do you know where Meredith lives?"

"I think so." But Ellie sounded doubtful. "You go to that one corner and turn and go to that other corner and turn. By that one store."

Brenda considered driving around in a city she did not know in deteriorating weather following Ellie's sketchy directions and decided to try a different tack. Desperately seeking inspiration, she sifted through a pile of brochures, magazines, and envelopes dumped on one end of the kitchen counter. They were almost unreadable in the unlit room. She was turning away when an oft-folded brochure with NAMI written in bold black letters caught her eye. She picked it up and held it close.

NAMI, she learned, stood for National Alliance for Mental Illness. Smaller print implored, "Don't struggle alone! Bipolar Support Group Here...We Support Each Other." Could Teak's hunch about Janna be correct? Brenda flipped over the brochure. Beneath the 1-800 number on the back there was a second phone number, this one handwritten. Brenda recognized Janna's distinctive 2's. She swallowed hard, opened her phone, and made the call.

The phone rang several times. The woman who eventually picked up sounded groggy, perhaps had been sleeping when the phone roused her. The exasperation in her voice dissolved after Brenda mentioned Janna's name.

"She had been coming to our group, but petered out the last couple months. We've been worried. I will send her buddy over right away."

"Group?" Brenda repeated dumbly. "Her buddy?" Her head buzzed, her fingers tightened on the phone.

"Granda, I think Charley has to pee." The urgency in Ellie's tone demanded action. Brenda wrapped up the call and guided Charley outside. The snow had stopped falling, but the wind was sharp and frigid. She stood shivering, encouraging the dog to finish his business. Something under the pine tree in the front yard captured Charley's interest. Brenda eventually corralled him and returned to the living room, where the little dog immediately jumped into Ellie's lap. She had finished her snack and was seated cross-legged on the couch in the living room.

Brenda lingered at the window. It wasn't long before a white Jeep pulled up behind Brenda's car and a lanky woman, her features indeterminate beneath a pulled-down bomber hat and up-turned collar, stepped out and, after a token knock on the door, entered. She removed her hat, revealing a head of thick black springy curls and complementary eyebrows.

Charley barked a greeting.

"Hey, Meredith! This is my new dog!" Ellie was exuberant.

Meredith cast an eye on the pair.

"Yeah? Keep him away. I'm allergic." She turned to Brenda. "Where is she?"

"Bedroom," Brenda said, matching her terseness.

Meredith raised her generous eyebrows and slipped into the bedroom without another word.

Brenda sank into a stained armchair in the dim living room, trying to decipher Meredith's muted words.

"Dr. Jordan," she heard, and, "Hospital." In an attempt to alleviate any worries Ellie might have, she smiled at the child.

Ellie smiled back. Then her countenance clouded.

"I don't like it here anymore. I want to go home, Granda."

243

Brenda leaned forward, hands clamped in her lap, her eyes fixed on Ellie's small face.

"Sometimes I do my homework and sometimes I don't and Mom acts like it don't matter. I remember you said you loved me too much to let me sluff off. And Mom lets me sluff off." Ellie's words came out in a flood. She blinked rapidly several times before continuing, "I love my mother, I do. But I want to go home." She set Charley aside and launched herself into her grandmother's lap, hugging her fiercely. "Please take me home, Granda."

Brenda's arms went around the little girl. She could feel her spine, her bony back, her need. "I will, sweet thing," she promised.

Charley woofed as Meredith returned to the room.

"I'm taking Janna in," she announced, shooting Charley a warning look. She pulled on her bomber hat. "You think you can help me get her to the car?"

"I want to come with you," Brenda said, rising to her feet.

Meredith shook her head.

"Stay here with Ellie. But I do need to bring her meds. Yeah. Can you find them, Ellie?"

"Middle shelf of the medicine cabinet. But I'm not allowed—"

"I'll sweep the whole shelf into a bag," Meredith interrupted. She came back in seconds holding a couple of pill bottles. "Middle shelf, are you sure?"

Ellie nodded.

Meredith shook the two bottles. Nothing rattled.

"These suckers are empty," she announced unnecessarily. "I wonder how long she's been out." She stuck the bottles into her coat pocket and returned to the bedroom, where she coaxed Janna to her feet. Brenda grabbed a sweater off of the floor and draped it over her daughter's thin shoulders.

With Meredith on one side and Brenda on the other, Janna

shuffled through the living room, head down. She was almost at the front door when she lifted deadened eyes and rested them on Ellie.

"Don't go with her."

Brenda opened her mouth in protest, but after Meredith frowned fiercely at her, closed it. Meredith urged Janna forward and Brenda, unspoken words begging for release, helped to escort her sullenly unresponsive daughter to the Jeep. Ellie stood in the open doorway, Charley in her arms.

Brenda watched the vehicle make its way slowly down the slushy, sloppy street. She fingered the calendar page in her pocket.

"Rescue me, Lord," she whispered before returning to the dark house.

"Mom won't let me go with you," Ellie said in a small voice, her hazel eyes filling with tears.

"I will work it all out in the morning," Brenda said with more confidence than she felt. She took Ellie by the shoulders and pointed her toward her bedroom.

"Let's get you to bed," she suggested briskly. Realizing full well that a dirty dog and bed sheets were not compatible, she added anyway, "Would you like to sleep with Charley?"

Ellie's smile was answer enough.

After Ellie and the pup were settled, Brenda punched Buddy's number into her phone. She listened to it ring. Five times. Six.

"Brenda's Motel." Buddy spoke as if irritated by the interruption. Brenda could hear the throb of heavy metal in the background.

So frustrated she hardly knew where to begin, she scolded, "Buddy, that's not the name of the motel. You better not be disturbing the guest with that music." She heard her shrillness and with an effort modulated her tone. "Is Devon causing any

245

trouble?"

"Not any more. He's sleeping." Buddy giggled weirdly.

Brenda felt as if she were drowning in trouble. She gritted her teeth.

"The reason I called was to tell you I won't be home until tomorrow sometime. But now I'm thinking I better drive back right away. And you will have to find someplace else to stay." It was a threat, but not an idle one. Despite the treacherous roads and Janna's demand, she would rouse the child and bring her to the motel if she was needed there.

"Ah Brenda." Buddy sounded much more congenial. He issued muffled directions and the music was silenced. "It's all good. All settled down."

Brenda wasn't convinced, but when he agreed to her weak, "Time to call it a night," she told herself it would be fine. She was desperately tired. After ending the call, she curled up on the lumpy couch beneath a musty throw blanket. The house was silent, except for an occasional gust of wind rattling the windows. Her breath hitched. Visions of police lights pulsating in front of her motel and another rotten review on the U-Stay site were interspersed with worries about her daughter and granddaughter.

She had been so sure Janna would be relieved to have her take the little girl; that it would be a simple matter to pick up Ellie, turn around, and get back to her motel. That was not the case. Janna had expressly forbidden Ellie to leave. Anyway, it would be heartless to abandon her daughter in such a fragile state. A wave of anger washed over Brenda, displacing the pity she'd been feeling. How dare Janna, so weak and broken she could barely make it out to the car, dictate what Ellie could do?

Despite the situation, Brenda felt a flicker of admiration for her strong-willed daughter. Even now, when Janna could not care for herself, let alone anyone else, she was still trying to orchestrate things. Brenda's emotions vacillated between admiration, concern, and frustration. She turned over, covered her face with one hand, and tried to quiet her mind.

A loud hammering on the front door jolted her from her almost slumber.

CHAPTER THIRTY-SIX

"Sorry to bother you," said Meredith. Her voice was flat, heavy with exhaustion. "Wanted to let you know Janna's been admitted. You can go on in and see her in the morning. Probably should drop Ellie off at school first."

"Meredith." Brenda swung the door wide, urging her into the dark house. "What's going on with Janna? Is she–bipolar?"

After a moment's hesitation, Meredith stepped inside.

"Yeah. She has a bipolar disorder. We belong to the same support group. She joined up when she came to town."

"When was that?" Brenda was hungry for information.

Meredith regarded the ceiling for a moment, calculating.

"Oh, maybe two years ago. She came to town with a guy she met in her last group....in Billings, wasn't it? Yeah. He didn't stick around, but Janna was doing good, working, pretty steady." Meredith stopped talking and adjusted the strap on her hat.

"What happened to change that?" Brenda had so many unanswered questions, she hardly knew what to ask.

"Yeah, well, after Ellie came, she got out of sync. Missed meetings, didn't call like she was supposed to. And I–maybe dropped the ball too." Meredith edged toward the door.

"You're her buddy?" Brenda prompted.

"Yeah, it's an accountability thing. But it only works if you're honest, and I think Janna…" She shifted her feet, yawned hugely. "I gotta get my sleep." After giving Brenda the name of the hospital, Meredith headed for her Jeep, turning to add grudgingly, "It's a good thing you did, coming over here. Let me give you my phone number. You maybe could call me, let me know how things go."

Brenda was soon burrowed under the thin blanket again, but sleep was slow in coming.

"So much I didn't know," she thought. Brenda had assumed her daughter had stayed in the Chicago area. But if Meredith was correct, Janna had lived out in Montana. That was news. Had she made contact with her father, with Dale, while she was out there? And Janna was—mentally ill? Brenda's thoughts raced, thinking back on Janna's teen years, hunting for signs she completely missed or misread. Eventually she fell into a fitful sleep.

***

An insistent nudging against her dangling right hand roused her. She opened her eyes a slit and regarded Charley, whose cold, damp nose was pushing into her palm. A whine escaped him, and she sat up, tossing aside her flimsy covering.

"Let's go, boy," she said and ushered him outside.

It was morning: damp, gray, and chill. "I'm glad you're housebroken," she told the pup, hugging herself. As she waited, she tried to reconstruct a successful plan of action. First and foremost, she would find out how Janna was doing. And she needed to call Buddy, find out what was going on back home. She longed for a cup of coffee.

Glancing at her watch, she saw it was 7:30, high time to get Ellie up and off to school. They'd drive through a McDonald's and pick up some sort of breakfast for Ellie and a coffee for herself. They both definitely deserved a break today.

The power was still out, but the daylight shining through the picture window brightened the living room. While Ellie readied herself for school, Brenda scanned the room, noticing details that had not been evident the previous evening. Besides the couch and chair, there was a small flat-screened TV on a plastic stand, an artificial potted plant, and hanging on the wall next to the useless light switch was a photograph of–Brenda, not believing her eyes, rose to draw closer–Janna, a grown-up, beaming Janna, standing next to her father. Dale. His arm was draped around her neck, and he was beaming, too.

"I think I'm ready, Granda," Ellie said, coming into the room with Charley in her arms. She was wearing a pair of pink leggings and a Green Bay Packer jersey. Her hair was combed and most of her lipstick had been scrubbed off.

"I figured you wouldn't like me to wear makeup," she said by way of explanation. "But do I really have to go to school? I want to go back to the motel with you. And what will we do with this good boy?"

"Ellie." Brenda interrupted the flow of questions. She cleared her throat. "Do you know who this is?"

Ellie shot the photograph a careless glance, her attention plainly focused on the dog.

"Sure. That's Mom and Grandpa."

"I didn't know Dale–Grandpa–was in touch with her at all."

Ellie shrugged.

"I guess so. Charley really likes his tummy rubbed, did you know that?"

"I can't believe it," Brenda whispered. That Janna had not made any effort to stay in contact with her mother or daughter, instead apparently establishing a relationship with the father who had abandoned her as a vulnerable twelve-year old was more than she could wrap her mind around.

"What, Granda?" Ellie peered at her, ignoring the dog for the moment. "What did you say?"

"Have you met him? Your-grandpa, I mean."

Ellie shook her head.

"No. He lives in Montana. I talked to him on the phone, though. He's nice."

When did Dale get involved in Janna's life? Maybe she should call him and find out if he knew anything about Janna's condition. Her stomach recoiled at the thought of reestablishing contact. Life was so pleasant without him in the picture.

Ellie interrupted her musing to repeat her questions, this time in a slightly raised voice.

"What are we doing with Charley while I'm at school? If I have to go. Do I have to go? Do you know where Meredith took my mom? And when are you going to tell her to let me go back to Miskomin?"

"Charley's staying in your bedroom. Put a bowl of water in there and shut the door. Tight. Yes, you are going to school." She squeezed Ellie's shoulder. "It's the best place for you while I get this all figured out, sweet thing."

Ellie was excited with the novelty of an Egg McMuffin for breakfast. After dropping the child off at school, Brenda pointed her car and her thoughts toward the psych ward of the hospital Meredith had indicated. She was concerned about Janna, but hopeful she was receiving the care she needed and would agree to allow Ellie to return to Miskomin.

"Let's make this quick," she chanted silently as she approached the reception desk in the spacious lobby of the hospital. A middle-aged woman in a forest green cardigan greeted her with a questioning smile.

"I'm here to see a patient," said Brenda, managing a thin smile in return. "Joanna Miller."

The receptionist tapped at her keyboard, the glow from her computer monitor reflecting on the lenses of her glasses. She leaned forward to read the screen, then frowned.

"I can neither confirm nor deny that Joanna is a patient here," she said.

Brenda was dumbfounded. Meredith had told her that Janna was here. But perhaps there was some privacy act blocking her. Now what? Brenda tapped her lower lip, searched the ceiling for inspiration.

Finally she asked, "Is there any way I could talk to someone who might be able to tell me?"

The receptionist was shaking her head before Brenda finished her question. Not knowing what else to do, Brenda murmured a thank you and headed back to Janna's house. She'd busy herself doing some tidying while she figured out what to do next.

As she worked, her thoughts were in a muddle. How could she get Janna to give her permission to take Ellie, when Janna wouldn't even speak to her? And what state would the motel be in when she returned? She groped to commune with God, but sensed no response.

Brenda eventually decided her only recourse was to call Meredith. Maybe she would be willing to contact Janna and get her to see reason. As she flipped open her phone, she glanced out the window and saw a slender young woman walking up the sidewalk. Brenda met the woman at the door, Charley at her heels.

"Hello." The young woman stretched out a hand. "I'm Melissa Storm, an Eau Claire County social worker. I am looking for an

Ellie Miller. I was contacted—" she did not finish her statement.

Brenda helped her out.

"I know my daughter, Janna, is a patient." She named the hospital. "I'm Ellie's grandmother. Please come in."

"I didn't know there was a grandmother in the picture." Melissa looked relieved. She followed Brenda into the house and cast an assessing eye around the dim room.

"I am willing and available to take care of Ellie," Brenda assured her, giving Charley a reassuring pat.

"That would be wonderful. This would be a temporary measure, until Joanna is better," Melissa said. "I will need to run a background check on you, of course." She pulled a laptop computer from her oversized bag. "Do you mind?"

Feeling cautiously optimistic, Brenda dutifully answered questions and offered Teak's phone number when asked for a character reference.

"I need to go to the office and process a few things," Melissa said. "I will get in touch with you as soon as I can. This will be a temporary arrangement," she reminded Brenda. "Only until Janna is able to take care of the child again."

Brenda, who earlier would not consider having Ellie pulled back and forth between two homes, recognized it as the best-case scenario for present.

"Will Janna be okay with me taking her?" she asked.

Melissa shrugged, but her compassionate smile belied the insouciant action. "She didn't mention you, so I am guessing she's not promoting the idea. Still, as the nearest relative, you would be the best placement choice. I will be going over to the school to talk with Ellie right now, and I will explain things to her."

"If at all possible," Brenda said, "I would like to bring her home with me today."

***

Late that afternoon, as they drove through the outskirts of Eau Claire, heading for Miskomin, Ellie said, "I'm glad to be going home." She was silent for a beat before asking in a tiny voice, "Are you glad, too? Or will I be a nuisance?"

"Child!" Brenda pulled the car over to the side of the road, cut the engine, and fixed her full attention on the child. "Am I glad you're back? Do you even have to ask? Of course I am glad, sweet thing." She raised her hands over her head and waved them dramatically. "Hallelujah, Ellie's home!"

The relief that shone through the little girl's giggle tore at Brenda's heart.

"We'll have to register you at school again," Brenda said into the happy space.

"Do you think Gabby and Karen and Lilly will still like me?"

"I'm sure of it. I saw Stacy Bornson at Walmart last week, and she asked me how you were doing. Those girls will be thrilled to have you back here, Ellie."

Ellie patted the little dog curled up in her lap. "Will Charley be an inside dog or an outside dog?"

They had an important discussion about Charley's new lifestyle, until Ellie fell asleep, her head against Brenda's arm.

Brenda welcomed the weight.

Ellie roused when they passed the Miskomin city limit sign and turned off of the highway.

When they arrived at the motel, they both gasped.

CHAPTER THIRTY-SEVEN

The Neat As a Pin sign was lying in the driveway, split in two pieces. The oversized pin from which it had hung was dangling from the cracked pole, the point poised dangerously downward. Beyond the ruined sign, the door to Unit Nine swung wide, revealing a mess within. Brenda steered around the sign and parked in front of the open door. Both Brenda and Ellie jumped out of the car.

A trio of odors: tobacco, alcohol, and vomit greeted them as they entered the room. A half-eaten pizza lay abandoned on the disordered bed, its orange grease soaking through the sheets, cheese congealed.

Ellie wrinkled her nose.

"Gross," she said. Clearly wanting to get away, she added, "Can I go get Charley? He probably needs to go to the bathroom."

Brenda nodded in agreement, and Ellie hurried out of the room. Almost mechanically, Brenda righted a tipped chair, picked up a beer can, frowned at a stain on the new carpet.

"Knock-knock!"

Wincing at the sound of the upbeat greeting, Brenda turned

to find Carl Levy and Officer Rollins in the doorway.

"Thought it would be the neighborly thing to inform Rollie that you had a problem here," Carl explained.

"Your sign, or what remains of it, is a safety hazard," the officer interrupted. "You need to clear it away at once." His eyes swept over the disordered room. "The condition of this unit is not acceptable either."

"I will deal with it." Brenda waited silently, hoping her minimal response would suffice. It was all she could muster. Officer Rollins hesitated, nodded once, departed.

Carl lingered.

"I suppose you're going to give me more grief about the new motel coming to town and how stable their sign will always be," she said.

"Nothing of the sort," Carl replied. "And I don't think there's going to be any new motel coming to town."

"There's not?" The shard of good news heartened Brenda. She opened her mouth to ask for details, changed her mind. "Excuse me, I need to get Ellie and our new dog settled."

Carl acted like he didn't hear her.

"Yeah, the investors determined Miskomin isn't a profitable place for a big motel. They pulled out. A shame," he went on, sucking in his gut as she inched past him, "It was a good price on the land."

"Maybe you should buy it." Brenda threw the suggestion over her shoulder as she headed toward her granddaughter, still holding a beer can. "Give you a lot of room to expand your dealership."

Ellie was positively hopping with pleasure as they entered the house together, and she clattered up the stairs, the pup at her heels.

"Hello, dear bedroom," Brenda heard her exclaim.

"I'll be right back, sweet thing," Brenda called up after her.

Needing to talk to Buddy, find out what transpired during her absence, she made her way to the unit he was staying in and rapped on the door.

A bleary-eyed Buddy finally opened the door. He shifted from one foot to the other.

"Um," he said. "I didn't hear your car. Don't, um, look in Unit Nine. I didn't get a chance to clean it. Yet."

"What on earth happened?" The beer in the can she was holding sloshed. Its wheaty smell sickened her.

"Those guys, I tried to tell them to stop, but." Buddy looked dreadfully hung-over. "Devon said he needed to even a score. I'm gonna clean up," he said again. "Just had to take a little nap first."

"And the sign?" Brenda gestured with the beer can.

"They ran into the pole. I did get their insurance information. I'll take care of it," Buddy promised. He extended two palms. "I'm sorry, Brenda."

"See that you do." She placed the beer can in his right hand and left him to it. I'll fire him, she vowed, but not until that unit is back in shape.

Returning to the house, she cobbled together a simple supper from leftover pork steak, veggies, and rice. It was wonderful to have Ellie back home. Her presence made everything different, brighter, happier. Charley, of course, added to the excitement.

Brenda encouraged Ellie to walk the dog around the yard, familiarize him with his new home. She sat at the picnic table and watched them, so tired she could barely sit upright, uneasy about the temporary nature of Ellie's placement, but content in the moment.

A car pulled into the parking lot and soon she was checking in an upbeat middle-aged couple on their way to the North Shore of Minnesota. She walked them over to their unit, playing the part of hostess to the hilt, and taking advantage of the trip to check surreptitiously on Buddy who was hard at work in Unit Nine. She also took a few minutes to strip the bed and grab the trash from Unit One, the unit that had been occupied the previous night, before rejoining Ellie and Charley in the brown house.

She settled the little girl in her bedroom before enjoying a hot shower and changing into sweats. It was good to get out of the clothes she had worn since her hasty trip to Eau Claire. Unwilling to go to bed and miss out on any potential guests, Brenda dozed in the big living room chair where she would be able to hear any cars entering the lot.

She did not wake until morning when Ellie's "Granda! What happened to your foot?" jolted her out of her slumber.

Brenda shifted her position in the chair and regarded her almost-healed foot with its remaining three toes. She wiggled them.

"I had an accident, sweet thing. Let's have a little breakfast, and I'll tell you about it. First, though, do you want to see if Charley needs to go out?"

During breakfast, Brenda related her lawn mower experience and Ellie was properly sympathetic.

After she had convinced Ellie it was not cruel to fasten Charley to the dog run while they were away from the motel, they drove over to school to get Ellie re-enrolled. As they were leaving the office, Ellie caught sight of her friend Gabby, and hurried to catch up with her. Brenda watched after the two girls for a few moments before, reassured, she left the building.

On the way home, she stopped at the library to look up Dale's phone number online and to see if she could find any books on the topic of bipolar disorder. She needed to educate herself, fast.

After scribbling his name at the top of an empty page of her legal pad, her pencil stilled. She did not relish the thought of getting in touch with him, and remembering his taunts sent ripples of unease coursing through her. Brenda tightened her lips. She was willing to face anything for Ellie's sake. And Dale always had had more influence on Janna than she had. Maybe his input would make a difference.

She located Dale's number without any difficulty. So easily, in fact, that, impulsively, she searched for one other number.

There was one James Stephens listed for Columbia, South Carolina. She felt her heart rate increase as she added his number to her contacts.

"Not that I'll ever call him," she said to herself.

After locating two books on bipolar disorder, Brenda headed home. She turned into her parking lot, noting that Buddy had removed the broken pieces of the sign and secured the dangling pin to the pole so that it no longer posed a danger.

He was waiting on the porch of the brown house, sitting on the steps, resting on his elbows.

"Come and check out Unit Nine," he said. "I think I got it squared away."

Brenda wanted to fault-find, but the unit appeared to be back in shape. There was one small stain on the carpet, but other than that, all was well. A layer of cleaning product hung in the air, so Brenda opened a window to coax in some fresh air.

"I'll need a new sign," she said, half to herself.

"I can order one for you," Buddy promised. "I know a guy who works up at SignSmiths. You won't have to think about it one bit."

Brenda was leery, but also preoccupied. She nodded her consent.

"If the insurance don't cover it all, I'll help pay for it," he promised. "I'll find me a job."

She could hardly believe her ears. Was this really Buddy speaking?

"You've been good to me. I didn't know them guys would get rowdy." He faced her squarely. "Please don't kick me out."

Brenda took a deep breath. She was weary to her bones. "Don't let it happen again."

Relief flooded Buddy's face, and he thanked her before he left to see about a new sign.

***

In the outer hallway, seated at the oversized cherry desk, realization swept over her. She reread the words…adult onset… genetic…blame-shifting….irrational. "Bi-polar disorder can be triggered by a traumatic event in susceptible individuals. It is an inherited disorder."

Brenda gasped, read on.

"This condition most typically skips a generation."

She closed the book, holding her place with a finger. Taking a deep breath, she allowed her thoughts to swirl from the present situation to distressing past experiences. She thought of her father's mood swings, his disappearances, his gambling addiction. And how everything had gotten so much worse after Mom had passed away, definitely a traumatic event.

Maybe her father's thinking and behavior were flawed because he had this disorder, too, and his insistence that she was she was responsible for the death of her mother was out of line. Wasn't that what Jimmie had tried to tell her, back on the beautiful day they had taken that motorcycle ride together?

And Janna. This could explain why she was treating Brenda the way she was. Oh my goodness, thought Brenda, maybe everything isn't my fault at all.

For a long time she sat, grappling with a host of new concepts and ideas, trying making sense of it all and realigning her part in it.

Filled with fresh resolve, she closed her eyes, sent a swift, silent prayer upward, and grabbed her phone. It was time to talk with Dale.

***

"Yeah?"

She thought she was prepared, but the rasping syllable unleashed a host of unwelcome memories. She picked up a pen, began to doodle circles in the margin of her legal pad.

"Dale? This is Brenda."

"Brenda?" He huffed out a short, unbelieving laugh. "What's up?"

"I've been to see Janna. She's not well."

Dale swore.

"Hadn't heard from her lately. Wondered what was going on."

Brenda's circles morphed into spirals.

"She's in the hospital—"

Dale interrupted.

"I knew she shouldn't of went back to the Midwest, she was doing good here."

The hallway seemed to be closing in. Rising, Brenda wandered out on to the porch and gazed in the direction of the motel. Buddy drove back into the parking lot, gave her a big thumbs up, disappeared into Unit Three.

"I heard she had been living in Billings...so you saw her sometimes?"

"Sometimes?" He snorted. "She lived in a trailer house here on our property. We saw her all the time. She came out here, oh, six-seven years ago? And was she a mess. Something was starting to break down inside. But Denise and her, they really connected.

261

Denise figured out Janna needed medication, therapy, something. She got her seein' a doctor and stuff."

Brenda, chilled and revived by the fresh air, went back into the house and stared at her doodles.

"Denise?" She pulled out one question from the many that emerged.

"Yeah, me and Denise, we've been together about twenty years now," Dale was saying.

"Twenty years ago, you and me, we were married," Brenda reminded him.

"Yeah, I guess you two overlapped a bit." Dale cleared his throat before continuing, "Denise is a real fine lady. Why, she's the one who suggested sending you them Mother's Day roses. After we heard you was raisin' Janna's baby, I mean."

Dale went on to explain that it was Denise's brother Bob, still living in Prairie City, who informed them when Brenda and Ellie had up and moved to Wisconsin.

"Brother Bob? You don't mean Denise Collins, do you?"

"Yeah, that's her all right. I think maybe you went to school with her."

So her old friend Denise had taken off with Dale.

"I didn't know you kept track of me," she whispered, whirling under the discovery that the roses she'd cherished over the years came from her former friend, who was also her ex's lady.

"Yeah, I always felt kinda bad for the way I ran out on you and Janna. But, man, I couldn't stand–" He did not finish the thought. After a pause, he went on, "I'll give Janna a call, see if there's anything I can do. What hospital is she in?"

Brenda told him.

"Okay, well, I gotta go. It was good to hear your voice and find out you're doing good and everything."

"I'm doing fine," she replied, realizing it was true. Despite everything, she was doing fine. Dale meant nothing to her now, but hearing his deep voice brought to mind another deep voice she longed to hear.

"Good bye, Dale," she said.

CHAPTER THIRTY-EIGHT

Two weeks passed, three. The days were busy. Despite the lack of signage, business in the motel was steady. Brenda was learning that Ed and Ruth had built up a large group of regular visitors to the motel prior to its demise, and they were thrilled to see it back on its feet again.

"This used to be our favorite place to stop on our way to the North Shore," one guest, a stately woman with salt-and-pepper hair, confided to Brenda. "It is so quaint."

"We're glad to see how you've revived it," added her companion.

Brenda kept the coffee hot and fresh, and began to offer raspberry muffins to the overnight guests.

Thinking it would be helpful in managing reservations and keeping records for the motel, Brenda purchased an Acer computer, solid, but not too expensive. She enlisted Buddy's aid in connecting it to the Internet, and he demonstrated an aptitude that surprised her. The system was capable of providing wireless access for her guests as well, a service that had been requested repeatedly.

She positioned her new computer at the front desk and tapped a few keys. Buddy hovered nearby.

"It's asking for a password," she called out.

"BRENDA," Buddy responded.

"What's the password?"

"It's BRENDA," he replied. "All caps."

"Shouldn't it be NAP?" she countered, thinking of the acronym for her Neat As a Pin motel.

He shrugged.

"I already set it. Sorry."

Sighing, she typed it in and was gratified to be connected without any further issues. Now she could research work-from-home options. She was going to enjoy this perk, and hopefully so would her guests. Ellie, proudly wearing the little black vest Brenda had put away for her, painstakingly created a neat little sign for the counter: Wireless Internet Available/ Password: BRENDA.

Suzanne stopped by more than once to check on Ellie, lanyard prominent, spouting words like "jurisdiction" and "compliance." She told them that Janna was out of the hospital, but undergoing intensive outpatient therapy, and a care conference involving everyone participating in Janna's care and ongoing recovery would be scheduled once she was stable.

Ellie was doing well, slipping seamlessly into life in the brown house, glad to be reunited with her friends, and attending Kids' Club with Hailey on Saturday nights. She was delighted with the transformation of her old unit into a chapel and paid it an occasional visit. And of course, there was Charley. Caring for him was an important part of her day.

Brenda was thankful for how smoothly everything was going, for the utter normalcy of it all, but she worried every day that it was not going to be permanent, and how it would affect Ellie if she were uprooted again. How it would affect Brenda, herself. It would be excruciating to have the child removed from her life again.

"Lord, help me to love her fully but hold her loosely," she whispered.

***

"Teak." Brenda greeted her friend one morning shortly before Christmas. It was a cloudy afternoon, cold, but still no snow. The natural world seemed to be in limbo, waiting for its white blanket, and it was exactly how Brenda felt. In limbo.

"It's scheduled," she said. "The care conference with Janna is set for this Thursday. At the behavioral health center in Eau Claire, where she's been getting therapy."

"I can keep Ellie for you," Teak offered at once, but Brenda shook her head.

"She needs to come along. Janna will want to see her." Brenda paused and gulped. "It's very possible Janna will be keeping her." She turned her head away, trying to conceal the emotion sweeping through her.

Brenda felt Teak's eyes on her, felt the younger women's concern.

"Let us come with you," Teak said. "Hailey and I will keep Ellie occupied during your meeting. We can go out to the Oakwood Mall. It's probably all decorated for Christmas." Her dimple flashed. "And maybe we'll run over to CherryBerry. A frozen yogurt bar is fun, even in December."

If Ellie ended up staying with Janna, the ride home would not seem as long and bitter with Teak and Hailey's presence and support. Brenda accepted the offer gratefully.

While not convinced she could trust him, Brenda left Buddy in charge, for he knew the procedures and the routine. He was surprisingly willing to monitor the front desk, as well as care for Charley. Brenda explained that she was going to discuss where Ellie would be living going forward. She emphasized that she was not going to put up with any trouble at the motel. She had enough to worry about. He nodded, seeming to sympathize, and Brenda hoped for the best.

CHAPTER THIRTY NINE

Brenda passed through the double paned glass doors into the carpeted, brightly lit Behavioral Health Center, and glanced around curiously. She had never been in such a facility before, and found it to be an unassuming, ordinary place. The reception area was flanked with a comfortable lounge on one side, a tiled snack area on the other. Straight ahead ran a short hallway lined with several closed doors.

A tall young woman with shoulder-length dark brown hair and matching brown eyes greeted her with a friendly smile.

"I'm Hanna Cole, the coordinator of the center." After Brenda introduced herself, Hanna told her, "I'll be facilitating our meeting, and you are nice and early. There's plenty of time for a cup of coffee." She gestured toward a self-serve display and slipped away.

More for something to do rather than any actual desire for caffeine, Brenda dispensed a cup of coffee and selected a bagel from the assortment of pastries displayed. Raisin spice, she thought. The cinnamon scent was warm and soothing.

She settled at a small round table in the far corner of the snack area, a bright, well-lighted corner, with a floor to ceiling window for company. The landscape outside was leafless and brown. Dreary.

Forty-five minutes to wait. The outcome of the meeting ahead of her weighed heavily. Brenda had tried to talk to Ellie about her future, but the little girl, normally so chatty, refused to discuss it.

Brenda broke off a piece of her bagel and nibbled. The movement of her hand reflected in the window, catching her eye. She studied her translucent reflection. Yesterday she had gotten a cute haircut from the barbershop across from the motel, an inverted bob, and had even sprung for highlights, hoping the updated look would provide moral support. And she did look confident and poised, she decided, but inwardly she was still a wreck.

Jimmie, she thought, considering how caring, strong, and comforting he was. How she needed to hear his voice right now! Too agitated about the meeting to fixate on ramifications of making contact with him, Brenda swallowed, reached for her phone. Scrolling through her contact list, she found his number, and with trembling fingers, punched the SEND button.

Her heart was pounding in her chest, and she deliberately kept her thoughts at bay as she waited for him to pick up.

"Stephen Brothers Construction."

It was not Jimmie; this voice was noticeably younger, deeper. Distinctly Southern.

"I'm sorry," Brenda apologized. "I was looking for, um, Jimmie Stephens, I must have the wrong--"

"Hold on, ma'am, I'll get him for you."

Brenda waited. She dug a raisin out of her bagel, checked her reflection in the window again.

"This is Jim. How can I help you, ma'am?"

Brenda cupped the phone in her hand and took a deep breath. "Ma'am?"

"Jimmie, this is Brenda."

"Brenda?"

The disbelief and joy in his voice brought tears to her eyes.

"Yeah, um, I don't want to bother you, but I had a few minutes and thought maybe I'd call and say hi."

"Good, good," he said. "Hold on a minute, Brenda." In a muffled tone, he told someone to "go on ahead, I got an important call."

"I'm sorry to bother you," she apologized when he came back on the line. "I just..."

"No bother, you're never a bother. It's good to hear your voice. How've you been? How's Ellie?"

"That's a long story," she said, still trying to wrap her mind around the salutation, the young man answering Jimmie's phone. "Do you own a business or something? Stephens Brothers?"

"Oh, just a little construction business my brother and me, and now my son, too, got going here. I'll tell you about it later if you want. But what's happenin' with you?" His voice was as firm and strong as she remembered. As dear.

"Well...I'm in Eau Claire right now," she said. She looked at the sterile table in front of her. "At a hospital here."

"Oh." The syllable, while flat, was rich with concern, even alarm.

"I'm not sick or anything," she hastened to add. "I'm here for a conference. About Janna."

"Oh?" This time, the syllable encouraged her to continue.

"It's going to be a decision meeting," she said. Closing her eyes, Brenda could picture Jimmie's kind blue eyes, his alert listening posture. There was something about the way Jimmie listened that made it easier to marshal her thoughts. She gulped.

"I'm kinda nervous. I'm gonna find out if Ellie will be coming back with me, what Janna's going to do next, everything."

Jimmie hadn't heard that Janna had entered the picture, had taken Ellie for a time. Brenda shared the bare bones of the story.

"Now that I've had her back, I cannot fathom losing her again. But I don't want to hurt Janna, or alienate her anymore. I'm in knots. I can't see how this can possibly end well." She finished the recital, and there was a silence between them.

"If any two people belong together, it's you and little Ellie," Jimmie said. 'I don't have a doubt things will swing that way. Trust the Lord, Brenda. This will work out for your good and His glory."

It was exactly what Brenda needed to hear. The butterflies in her stomach quieted.

They chatted a bit longer until Brenda reluctantly ended the call when Hanna Cole approached.

"Good-bye, Jimmie. It was good talking to you."

"I'll be in touch," he promised.

CHAPTER FORTY

"Lord, restore Ellie to me," Brenda murmured, "and give Janna peace." Remembering Jimmie's words, she added, "For our good and Your glory."

She entered the conference room that Hanna had indicated. It was empty except for a long rectangular table with a box of tissues and a telephone in the middle of it. She chose a seat near the door.

Melissa and Suzanne came in together. Melissa smiled. Suzanne did not. The three waited in silence as a low murmur of voices in the hallway grew nearer.

Janna entered without fanfare. Although pale, she looked infinitely better than the last time Brenda had seen her. Today her hair was clean, shiny, and shorter than Brenda remembered. She wore a cheery red sweater and tight jeans.

"Hello, Janna." Brenda, sensing it would not be well-received, made no move to hug her daughter, although her arms ached to do so. Janna responded with a nod before seating herself between the two men who had joined them. Brenda, having eyes only for her daughter, paid them scant attention.

Hanna entered and closed the door.

"Everyone is here," she said, smiling. "Let's start with a who's who." She nodded at the dark, intense man seated at the end of the table.

"Doctor Rick Jordan," he said. "Physician in charge."

"Janna Miller." She addressed the tabletop.

The sandy-haired man seated next to Janna raised a palm.

"Gary Maggio. I'm the counselor who has been working with Janna here at the Center."

"I'm Melissa Storm, Social Worker for the Center."

"Suzanne Waters, from Child Protective Services in Polk County."

Stormy Waters. Brenda hoped the conjunction of their names was not a portent of how the conference would proceed.

"I'm Brenda Miller, Janna's mother," she said, managing to keep her head high.

"And I'm Hanna Cole," the brown-eyed woman concluded. "Janna's father, Dale Miller, asked to be patched in. Okay?" She looked toward Dr. Jordan. At his nod, she leaned forward to punch buttons on the telephone.

After connection was established, introductions were made around the table again, this time directed toward the unseen participant.

"Hello, everyone." Dale's muffled voice echoed slightly. "Thank you for including me."

"We're glad to do it," said Dr. Jordan, assuming charge of the proceedings.

Janna and her care team provided an update on her progress. On the positive side, Janna's moods were stabilized, and her medications, at least for the time being, were effective. She was finding success in cognitive behavioral therapy, living alone, managing well. On the negative side, she had lost her job due to absences, and her rent was in arrears.

Brenda listened avidly, finding out more about her daughter during this meeting than she had learned in years. She bit her lip. How was all of this going to affect Ellie's placement?

"So now," Janna said, "I've decided to go back to Montana."

Montana? A knot was forming in Brenda's stomach.

"She has a place to stay." Dale put in. "There's a second home here on my property. It's a mobile home, not real big…"

"That's where I lived before," Janna said. "Before I took off with that jerk."

"We all have things we regret," Gary said. "It is how we handle our regrets that makes the difference."

"We've made contact with the behavioral health team in Billings," Doctor Jordan said. "It should be a seamless transfer."

"I can come to Wisconsin next week," Dale said. "Help her move, get things squared away."

The knot tightened.

"I'm looking forward to going back," Janna said. "I was happy there."

Brenda sat in silence, too shattered to speak. It sounded as though everything had been settled prior to this meeting. And what about Ellie?

Suzanne spoke.

"Is there a bedroom for Ellie?"

"Oh yes," Janna said hastily. "There is a lovely bedroom."

"I'm sure you are anxious to be reunited with your daughter," Suzanne said. Janna murmured a response.

Brenda's hands were trembling and her vision strangely obscured. It felt like a dream. No. A nightmare.

Gary set down his pen.

"It's decided then. Agreed?"

There were nods all around the table. Dale made a sound of assent.

Years of placating first her father, then Dale, and even Janna were cords that held Brenda silent, but she had grown in confidence and ability in the past months as an innkeeper. Her faith had also grown, and she felt the comforting presence of her Heavenly Father. She spoke.

"I can't agree."

Brenda felt the weight of too many eyes upon her. Nevertheless, she continued.

"This isn't what's best for Ellie, and I don't think it is what Janna really wants either."

Janna was looking at her, really looking.

"In October you asked me to take her back. Isn't that what you still want? You need to concentrate on keeping yourself well. Ellie needs so much attention and care. Her reading…" Brenda trailed off, but not before she saw a flash of relief flit across Janna's face.

Her counselor saw it, too.

"Janna?" he prompted.

Janna bit her lip.

Gary added, "It is perfectly understandable if you are fearful, Janna, but think carefully. This is your child."

"There is no reason, Janna, why you shouldn't have your daughter with you," Melissa said encouragingly. "You may think you aren't able to care for her, but with the supports in place, especially with your dad right there, you certainly will be able to."

Janna seized the collar of her sweater and twisted her fingers in the wool. Tension lay heavy on her.

"I really don't want her." The honesty behind the stark admission was undeniable.

Janna faced her mother.

"You must think I'm a loser because I ran off and left Ellie with you. Not even taking care of my own daughter. And now I'm telling you it would be a big load off if you'd raise her. But that's the truth."

"Janna." Brenda stopped her. "Don't put words in my mouth. I never thought you were a loser. I thought you were upset with me because I was taking over with Ellie."

Janna tucked her hair behind her ears.

"Mom, if you weren't there, she would have had no one."

The light in the room shifted, brightened.

"Janna, that took a lot of courage to be honest with yourself and with us," Gary said with an approving smile.

"Suzanne?" Melissa asked. "Based on your observations, can Brenda provide a suitable living situation for Ellie? It was my understanding she lives in a motel."

Brenda squirmed.

For a long moment, Suzanne said nothing, looking first at Brenda, then Janna. Finally, she spoke.

"I kept finding cracks in the situation. I mean, they were living in a motel. In separate rooms. And there was one incident after another. Insect bites. Running away. Police called because she was left alone." Suzanne ticked them off, and Brenda's heart sank.

"But now they are established in the house next to the motel. And there was always care and concern…..The two of them, I have to say, click."

A smile blossomed on Brenda's face.

Dr. Jordan addressed the unseen Dale.

"Your thoughts, Dale?"

Dale was quick to agree.

"If Brenda is willing to keep little Ellie, it might be for the best."

Brenda looked around the table and saw only smiles.

So it was decided.

Everyone agreed it was important to make this an official placement, and the social workers would see the necessary procedures were set into motion. Ellie's stability was paramount. Janna would concentrate on taking care of herself, on staying healthy. Dr. Jordan and Counselor Gary helped her to construct a plan to continue to do just that.

**

After the meeting, Brenda contacted Teak, letting her know it was time to bring Ellie over to the center. While they waited for her to arrive, Janna and Brenda sat side by side on a couch in the lounge and talked.

"Things were going pretty good, I had a job and all, so when I heard Ellie's situation was so bad I thought I'd rescue her."

Brenda opened her mouth to explain how Carl had twisted the situation, but not wanting to do anything that might hinder Janna's explanation, held her tongue.

"But I didn't consult anyone, I should have. What with the winter coming, and my seasonal affective disorder, and the stress of having Ellie around, I got off track on my meds and my meetings."

"If you would have been honest with me when you came to visit," Brenda pointed out, "I would have taken her back in a heartbeat." Inwardly, despite the seriousness of the conversation, she was jubilant. Janna was talking without hostility. They were communicating!

"I didn't want you to know I had mental problems," Janna was saying.

Brenda studied her. "Janna, I took care of you when you sprained your ankle and when you had the chicken pox. I wish you could have trusted me about your brain not being healthy."

One side of Janna's mouth lifted slightly, an expression Brenda had so often seen on Ellie's face. Her heart pinged.

"I love Ellie, big picture," Janna said. "But I didn't realize it was so hard to take care of a kid. Just listening to her is exhausting. And Ellie—"

Ellie entered the facility and Janna broke off to wave both hands, signaling the little girl. She made a beeline for her mother.

"I missed you!" she cried, hugging her. "Are you better?"

"I'm better," Janna said, hugging her back. "How's it going?"

"Good," Ellie said. Her eyes were large and apprehensive as she seized her mother's hand. "What's going to happen to me?"

"I love you, Ellie." Janna's eyes were fierce, fixed on Ellie's. Brenda watched, clutching her own hands together. "I want you to know that. But it's better if Granda raises you."

Hearing Ellie's name for her on her daughter's lips brought tears to Brenda's eyes.

"Okay, Mom." There was relief in Ellie's voice, but she did not release her mother's hand.

"I'm going back to Montana," Janna said, "but this summer, I want you to come see me. And meet Grandpa. You are important to me. I love you," she said again. Ellie let go of her hand, stepped back, and leaned her head against Brenda's side.

Outside, it was beginning to snow.

***

Before leaving Eau Claire, Teak, Hailey, Ellie, and Brenda stopped off at Janna's house and cleared out the rest of Ellie's possessions. Brenda called for a pizza to be delivered, and they shared a midday meal with Janna. Meredith joined them. As they said their goodbyes, Janna gently nudged her mother's arm.

"See ya," she said.

It was a start.

***

They were almost home before Brenda finally voiced a worry that had niggled all day, an unease that had been steadily building.

"I hope the motel is doing okay," she said. "I'm suspicious of how willing Buddy was. He was a bit too eager for me to be gone."

"I'm sure everything is fine," Teak replied, but her tone lacked conviction. She turned onto the road leading into Miskomin.

"Look!" Ellie yelled.

Beside her on the backseat, Hailey murmured a quiet, "Wow."

There was a new sign, high and clear, in the place of the old, worn Neat As a Pin sign. In the gathering darkness of a late winter afternoon, it was visible from the edge of town, glowing yellow, with bold black letters.

Brenda's
M O T E L

Teak parked the car and the four got out. They stood in the cold, in the freshly fallen snow, looking up at the sign. Buddy stepped out of Unit Three, Charley at his heels, a broad grin on his face.

"Like your new sign?" he asked.

Brenda did like it. The curly, clever "Brenda" in an artistic but readable script, the MOTEL in solid capital letters was both classic and arresting. Still...

"Buddy, that's not the name of the motel. It's the Neat as a Pin Motel."

"It's your motel," he said simply. "It needs your name." He launched into the story of the sign, how he went up to SignSmiths with an idea, and how they had made up the sign for him.

279

"Got her this morning, after you guys left. I helped install it." Buddy thrust his fingers into the rear pockets of his jeans and studied the sign like a proud parent.

"And," he finished proudly, "the owner, Sam Smith, liked my design and how I fit in with the guys. Offered me a part-time job. I can start whenever."

Brenda did not know if the insurance money would cover the cost of such an upgrade, but at the moment, she was so impressed by its appearance, she did not care. She studied the sign. Brenda's Motel. Her dream had come to fruition.

"I'm glad I didn't get the old name embroidered on our vests," she said, smiling.

"You're gonna fill all the beds with a nice sign like that," Buddy said. Seeming to notice Ellie for the first time, he added, "Hey, you're back."

"I'm back," Ellie said with a little skip, and Charley barked.

Brenda slipped away from the cluster and entered her chapel.

She sat down in the pink spa chair and looked at the beauty from ashes poster. A small smile played on her lips. She reached for the Book of Psalms, paged through it until she found what she was looking for.

"He has done great things," she read aloud. "Glory to His name."

Brenda bowed her head and prayed.

EPILOGUE

After a long but serene winter it was springtime again. The trees were budding, and the birds began returning from warmer climes. Brenda and Ellie pulled up in front of Miskomin's post office. Ellie reached in the back seat for the box that contained a carefully wrapped present for Janna. Her birthday was coming up, and they were sending her a package filled with some of her favorite things: Swedish Fish. Colorful headbands. A scented candle. Earbuds. A sweater. A gift card for Applebees restaurant. A fun travel mug.

And a special note from Ellie.

Brenda tucked in a New Testament and a bag of black licorice for Dale.

They went in together, confident, as they anticipated Janna's pleasure at the gift.

There was a line at the window. People waited as the clerk helped a customer at the counter set up a new post office box.

"Are you moving here to Miskomin?" the plump clerk asked.

"Sure am," a strangely familiar voice concurred. "I've got some business here that I reckon will take a lifetime to finish."

Brenda's legs began to tremble. She swallowed, ran a hand down her hair.

The man finishing up at the counter turned, met her eyes.

"Brenda!" cried Jimmie Stephens.

The End

ACKNOWLEDGMENTS

Many, many thanks to the following for their help and support:

Rachael Anderson
Jeremy Appel
Christine DeSmet
Heather Erickson
Rachel Hall
Jeremy Hall
Amanda Martin
Jessica Mathson
Karen Mickelson
Debbie Milligan
Randi Shaw
Gordon Trombley
Write, Right Now writer's group of Professor Emeritus,
   Carolyn Wedin

Beta readers Pat Schmidt, Vicki Engel, Robin Maercklein, Irene Bugge, Lindsey Koskie, Michelle Carlisle, and Cathy Miles

and, of course, Meghan Muchow.

Soli Deo gloria.

Made in the USA
Monee, IL
29 January 2021